OOPS I ATE A VENGEANCE DEMON

FOILS AND FURY BOOK ONE

LAURETTA HIGNETT

FOREWORD

This series follows Sandy Becker, a young, overworked hairdresser mom. Sandy first appeared as a side character in book two of the Imogen Gray series, but something about her demanded more attention, and before I knew it, I'd drafted a whole new series with her in the starring role.

You don't have to read the Imogen Gray series before you dive into this one — all of the characters are brand-new, and Sandy's story arc begins here. But just as a reference, I've included Sandy's introduction, the first scene from Immortal Games (in Imogen's POV) as a prologue.

If you've already read Immortal Games, feel free to skip the prologue and dive right into chapter one.

PROLOGUE

Imogen Gray - Immortal Badass/Pest Control Expert

I COULD HEAR the screams from down the block.

Unholy shrieking, gutwrenching tortured screams and terrified, frantic shouting. Whatever was in Terry and Sandy Becker's house, it was making a hellish racket, that's for sure. It sounded like the audio reel from *Night of the Living Dead* was being blasted down the street.

Father Benson called me ten minutes ago, begging me to come. I didn't want to. I'd tried so many times to wiggle out of helping him with his Evil Spirit Exorcism and Pest Removal side-gig business, but I was worried he'd get hurt if he took on too much.

And there was a *lot* to take on. Since the otherworld portal had widened over Emerald Valley, we'd seen all manner of beasts accidently falling through to wreak havoc on this little town.

Benson felt vindicated. He set up his side-gig years ago,

because his parishioners had often reported strange noises and odd occurrences. Galvanized by memories of his predecessor – the vicious, sanctimonious witch-hunter Father Sampson – Benson decided he needed to investigate the hauntings, banish any stray ghosts, and exorcize rogue demons.

Most of them turned out to be confused racoons. Not anymore, though. Now that the Dip had widened and the flow of energy reversed, it was accidentally sucking in mythical creatures and cryptids that weren't paying attention to where they were going in their own dimensions. Consequently, Father Benson had a lot of callouts for his business.

So far, I'd managed to bag them all and explain patiently to him that they were normal, average animals. However, it was getting harder and harder to explain away the unnatural phenomena.

I wasn't even sure I had to anymore. I had been vaguely worried that Father Benson would have a heart attack and die if I told him the truth. But not only did he seem to take everything in his stride, he always seemed quite disappointed when I inevitably explained the otherworldly beast we'd been called out to catch was actually just an unusually big lizard or a very, very loud toad.

Last week, I had to catch a cu sith – a beautiful green fae dog – who bounded happily around Susan Keene's back yard trying to avoid me, like it was a game. He dropped slurries of drool that instantly bloomed into huge bushes of perfect Irish littlebell roses.

I caught the big dopey thing eventually. I led him to the town square and caber-tossed him straight back through the portal. I scurried back to Susan Keene's house, trying to come up with a story to explain the roses and the vivid greenness of the cu sith. When I got there, Father Benson was teaching Susan how to deadhead the roses before the spring.

Nevertheless, I was worried about him. He was very old and decrepit. I didn't want him to die of shock. Despite being annoying, he made me laugh.

I didn't think I could get him to stop the fight anyway. He was quite dedicated to fighting the Forces of Darkness and wouldn't be talked into having a rest. He called me to help him often, though, and because I was trying to get to know the townsfolk so I could find my father, I always answered.

Walking up the sidewalk towards the little townhouse, I spotted Benson sitting outside on the porch, mopping his brow.

I gave him a wave. "What've you got for me today, Father?"

His hand trembled as he put his handkerchief away. I couldn't tell if it was excitement or fear that made his hands shake. "It's not a swarm of murder hornets this time, Imogen-me-good-lass. This is Terry and Sandy Becker's house," he said, pausing as an anguished shout shook the windowpanes. "Terry called me a couple of hours ago, says he's got a vengeful ghost stalking him. I show up, and the man's being chased around his house by a giant long-haired hippy woman in a white dress and long nails that would look fabulous if there was a bit of polish on them, y'know, but they're black as night and look like claws. She's in there trying to rip his heart out," he said, jerking his thumb behind him.

He gave a big sigh, sounding disappointed. "It's not a ghost; we got a *human* problem, a hospital escapee, or something like that. I called the police station, but Gary says he's out investigating something important, and if Terry Becker can't handle a crazy little woman by himself, then he wasn't much of a man to start with."

"Hmmm." I didn't know Gary, but I already hated him. And judging by Terry's screams of terror, I didn't think there was a *just* a crazy woman in there.

I cocked my head. A baby's cry floated to my ears, sounding like a distant echo. "Is Sandy Becker at home?"

"Nooo, she'd be at work. She's a hairdresser at Curl Up And Dye, the salon down on Main Street."

"Do they have a baby?"

"They got a little 'un, a boy, he's at the daycare."

I sniffed the air. The faint smell of frangipani hung in the air; underneath that, the heavy, sickening odor of decaying flesh. It *could* be an air freshener covering up the smell of a dead racoon under the house, but I was never that lucky.

I leaned sideways, peeking through the front window of Terry and Sandy Becker's house. The living room was a mess; a cereal bowl lay upturned on the carpet, the TV was smashed on the floor, a game console's control cords tangled up and wrapped into a ball. Claw marks ripped through the wallpaper. A little blood-splatter, too, trailing into the kitchen. The only spot in the living room that hadn't been completely wrecked was in the corner. There, I could see a kid's play area – a little desk with nicely-organized craft supplies, a cute toddler stool and some toys neatly stacked onto shelves.

I mentally ticked off all the evidence, grimacing. Pale woman, long black hair and fingernails, trying to kill the man inside. Faint baby cry, smell of frangipani. I was pretty sure I knew what it was.

"Father," I said to Benson. "I might need your help with this one after all. Have a seat for a minute, while I go check it out."

He sat back down in a huff. "I'm not calling Gary again. That man's an ass."

I tried the front door; it was unlocked. I tiptoed into the

living room, picking my feet over the scattered debris, and moved slowly towards the kitchen, where sounds of fighting had escalated. I stuck my head around the corner, taking in the scene.

Terry Becker was on the kitchen table - crying in terror, pinned down, spreadeagled, and writhing underneath the most terrifying woman I'd ever seen.

Just as I thought. A pontianak.

Long, black hair covered her face completely, obscuring any other features. Her white gown was loose and billowy, flowing over her thin chest and her unnaturally bulging belly, the pale white gown contrasting the black of her hair and claws. She had Terry pinned with one hand, his t-shirt pushed up around his neck, and she was using the claws on the other hand to delicately mark out the shape of his liver on his pale, trembling belly. Tiny gashes slid open when she struck his skin with her claws. Her body trembled with anticipation, ready to plunge her hand in and rip out his liver.

He spotted me in the doorway behind the monster, his eyes wide with terror. "Help. Me." His shaking voice was barely a whisper.

The pontianak pulled back her hand, ready to plunge it into his flesh.

"Nope," I said firmly. I stepped forward and grabbed her by her hair. "No, that's not polite." I yanked her back.

She gave a howl of rage and fell off the table. "You can't go around feasting on the flesh of men," I told her sternly. "Nuh-uh."

Immediately whirling around, she swiped her long claws through the air, hissing at me. The long black hair swished back and forth as she whipped at me, cutting at my head, then my torso. I caught a glimpse of her eyes through the curtain of hair, glowing red. She was fast; I kept my eyes on her flashing claws as they whipped this way and that, trying to cut me so she could feast on my internal organs. Behind her, Terry clambered off the table and huddled into a ball near the refrigerator, sobbing.

This bitch was *so* fast; the bulge in her belly didn't slow her down at all. She came at me in an intense, furious rage. She nicked me on the shoulder with her black claws; it burned where they struck me.

I stepped back and glared at her. She moved, arms outstretched lightly in front of her, hissing like a snake, ready to strike. Her hair-covered face snapped in the direction of Terry, crying on the floor.

"You want to eat him, huh?" Her head whipped back between me and Terry, her bloodthirsty instincts warring between going for him, and defending herself from me. "You'll have to go through me first." I squared up and pulled out my knife.

Wailing like a banshee, she whirled her claws around and came at me again. I blocked her strikes with my knife; the claws flashed with sparks where they hit the metal. I pushed her back, testing her strength, but she rallied and lashed out again. She was light but strong, and filled with such an indescribable, overwhelming rage, it gave her a power that could very well be inexhaustible.

While I fended off her razor-sharp claws, I tried to decide what the hell I was going to do with her. She wasn't a cryptid or a mythical beast; she was a spirit creature. I didn't even know if I could do any damage to her. As it was, my knife-strikes were missing her by millimeters, and she was easily dodging my kicks. I needed to regroup; to think for a moment. She could fight, she could kill, she could eat, but I doubted she was thinking very clearly. I just had to trap her for a few moments, so I could figure out a plan.

Terry sobbed next to the refrigerator. Glancing over, I spotted a child safety lock on the refrigerator door.

Regrouping, my knife flashing, I started an advance, slashing and thrusting, driving her into the corner. Terry wailed again, and scrabbled into the wall as I backed the creature towards him. His terrified flailing distracted her for a moment, drawing her attention.

As soon as her head was facing away from me, I whipped open the fridge, grabbed a hank of her long black hair and shoved it inside the fridge. I slapped the door shut and flicked on the child-proof lock.

The pontianak thrust forward towards Terry, and gave a strangled yell as she stopped short, trapped. She yanked again, then turned, and scrabbled with the refrigerator door, trying to get her hair loose.

Benson was right; her long nails would probably look pretty with a slap of polish on them, but they were no good for delicate picky jobs like flicking open a child-safe lock. Her nails made the *clack clickety clack* noise as she struggled to get herself free.

Terry wailed in the corner, trapped.

Whoops. I probably should have gotten him out first. The pontianak slashed at him with her claws, missing by miles, in between trying to get herself free. As she struggled, her snow-white dress billowed out around her, stained with little spots of Terry's blood, and an embroidered logo on the left-hand side of her chest.

Wait. *What?*

Pontianaks didn't have embroidered logos on their death-shrouds. They were astral spirits; bloodthirsty, carnivorous, vengeful ghosts appearing in the form of a pregnant woman who will never give birth. They sometimes manifested as beautiful women to lure their prey, and then turned into terrifying creatures with black hair and red eyes, and used their razor-sharp claws to feast on the internal organs of your typical fuckboys.

This spirit was a classic pontianak, and they didn't come with any sort of company logo.

I frowned, looking at her closer. Edging forward, I watched carefully as she alternated between slashing at a crying, moaning Terry, and trying to get her hair free.

I peered at her dress. The logo was a pair of little scissors. The words below it: Curl Up And Dye.

Aha. This was interesting.

I put my finger on my chin, and turned to the pontianak. "Wait here. I'll be back in a flash." Leaving the sobbing Terry on the floor with the trapped spirit slashing at him with her claws, I stepped out of the kitchen and went back outside.

Benson sat out on the porch, fingering his rosary. I plonked myself down next to him. "Is Sandy Becker pregnant?"

"Why, yes she is. Only a few weeks, she tells me. She's confessed she was feeling a wee bit overwhelmed with it all."

I'd never been pregnant before, or had kids. I couldn't imagine how hard it would be to stand on my feet all day cutting hair, while growing a tiny human inside me for two-hundred and eighty days, getting heavier and more uncomfortable as the days went by, with another tiny human waiting for me to serve it when I got home. It would be like being a slave, an incubator and a hairdresser all in one. "Tell me more."

Benson frowned. "I would never break the sacred seal of the confessional, lass."

"I understand."

"But yes," he went on cheerfully, "Sandy's been having a terrible time. Almost twelve weeks pregnant and sick as a dog, you know? Morning sickness has her puking up every ten minutes. It's taking her twice as long to get through her haircuts in the salon, has to keep running to the bog."

"Poor woman. And she has another kid?"

Benson's face crumbled up. "A hellraiser, but a sweet boy. She loves him dearly."

"What about her husband?"

He frowned. "Marriage is on the fritz, that's what she's been in the confessional for. She's working full time, pregnant, looking after the toddler when he needs her at the night-time too, because Terry's a forklift driver and needs to sleep properly or else he might cause an accident."

"Does he?" I frowned, thinking for a moment. "Come on, Father. I'm going to need your help."

"Is it a ghost?" Benson's face lit up like a beacon. I'd never seen much of his eyes underneath his mass of wrinkles in his scrunched-up face, but they were now bright blue and shining with delight. "An actual, real-life ghost?"

"Sort of. You'll see. I know how to get rid of it, but I'll need your help." I led him back into the kitchen, watching him carefully in case he had a heart attack.

I didn't need to worry. Benson's mouth dropped open when he saw what was in there.

His big gummy grin was an odd reaction to the sight of the horrifying, vengeful spirit trying to slash her otherworldly black claws through one of his local parishioners. Luckily, the pontianak hadn't managed to get herself free; her long, stringy black hair was still stuck in the refrigerator. Terry had his face pressed into the wall, covering his head with his hands.

While Benson was gaping, I casually rummaged around the kitchen, finding a big salt shaker in the pantry and a fruit bowl on the counter. I plucked out a banana and an apple. I took a leisurely bite out of the apple and marked out a circle of salt around the pontianak, keeping well clear of her slashing claws.

Just in time, too. She'd worked out how to use her goth nails to click open the child-safe lock on the refrigerator. She lunged at Terry, but the salt circle brought her up short.

I grabbed Terry by the back of his shirt and dragged him out of the corner. He curled himself up into a ball on the floor.

The pontianak seethed, pacing around the small salt circle, her movements jerky. She hissed at us. The sound cut through the air with an eerie preternatural timbre.

"Benson," I said. "Have you got your exorcism stuff with you?"

"Sure do," he rummaged in his pockets. "Bell, rosary, book, holy water. I'm ready to go."

"Go ahead, do your thing."

He flicked open the pages of his book and began to chant, periodically splattering the pontianak with holy water. His voice grew in volume and confidence. The pontianak screeched and writhed in the circle. Finally, with a teeth-rattling shriek, a real, warm human body fell out of the pontianak and fainted on the floor.

I caught her just in time. She was small and curvy, with pink streaks in her blonde hair.

Benson's eyes boggled. "Sandy?"

Her eyelids flickered and popped open. "What–" She swallowed. "What happened? Who are you? What's going on?"

Trapped in the salt circle, the pontianak let out a guttural snarl. Sandy blinked, and focused over my shoulder at it. Her mouth dropped open. "What... is... *that?*"

"Oh," I said, still holding her. "That's a pontianak. She was in *you*. Or, more accurately, you were in her." I pulled her up into a sitting position. "Now, I think we all need to have a chat."

Terry sat up and backed away until his head hit the kitchen wall behind him. "What the hell! What the *hell* is that?" He looked at me. "Who are you?" He shook his head, bewildered. "Sandy, what's going on?"

I waved. "I'm Imogen. I work with Father Benson here to get rid of evil spirits, and mostly trapped racoons. That there," I pointed at the evil spirit, jerkily darting and hissing in the circle. "Is a pontianak. It's a ghost, of sorts. It got here, to our town, by accident, but I don't think it randomly chose your house. Or your wife."

"What's it got to do with Sandy? Sandy, doll, why aren't you at work?"

I sat her up, handling her gently. "I don't know," she whispered. "I dropped off Dexter at daycare, and I went to work… I think I *was* at work. Maybe I had to puke again, so I ducked home…"

"Oh, I don't think it was *her* who summoned the pontianak, Terry. Tell me, what were you doing today?" I asked him cheerfully. "What's your schedule?"

"I don't work today," Terry shook his head, confused. "I was sleeping in. I do four days at the distribution center."

"Why is Dexter at daycare, then?"

He looked at me blankly. "What?"

I repeated myself patiently. "Why is Dexter at daycare?"

His eyes blinked slowly. "Dexter is at daycare when Sandy is at work."

"Why?"

"Because…" He looked at me with an *isn't it obvious?* expression. "Sandy's at work."

"Why don't you look after him?"

"Hey," he said, obviously offended. "I babysit him some

days. When I work, I do long hours, at least nine hours a day. It's a tough job, real physical. I need the downtime."

"Nine hours, huh? That's rough," I said sarcastically. "How many days does Sandy work?"

His face turned cautiously blank. "Six. Her mom watches Dex when she works on the Saturday."

"What do you do on Saturdays?"

"I've got my fishing club." His eyes narrowed at me. "What's with the questions? What's this got to do with that… that *thing* in the corner?"

"So you never look after your own kid?"

He glared at me. "Hey, I'm a *good* dad. We all hang out on Sundays, we do family stuff together, I play with him in the evenings, when Sandy's getting dinner ready. I'm a *great* dad," he repeated defensively.

"She cooks *every night?"*

Terry didn't reply. I made a show of looking into the living room, where the gaming console and tv were smashed to pieces, and the cereal bowl on the floor.

"And now she's pregnant?" I paced back and forth across the kitchen floor, eerily aware that I was matching the pontianak's back-and-forth behind me. "She's pretty sick, yeah? Have you been getting up in the night and looking after Dexter when he needs someone?"

"He never wants me; he only wants her. Besides," he added sullenly. "She's always awake, she's up puking in the toilet anyway. There's no point in me getting up too. There's no point in *both* of us being tired."

Benson knelt down, his knees creaking, and patted Sandy's arm. I looked down at Terry hard, for a full minute. He sat on the floor, his expression sulky.

Finally, he shifted uncomfortably. "Okay, it sounds bad when I put it like that, but I'm with my kid a lot, you know.

I'm a *good* dad. I help around the house a lot, I fold my own laundry, I take the garbage out and mow the lawn."

"Once a week," Sandy mumbled. A pale blush appeared under her pallor.

"What was that, my child?" Benson patted her cheek.

"Once a week," I said loudly. "Terry does one fifteen-minute job, once a week."

"I can't cook," he said sulkily. "She knows it. I'm no good at doing the cleaning. She's good at it, so she does it. Besides, I never do it the way she wants."

Her voice was feeble beside me. "He won't learn."

Ugh. I could never get my head around mortal relationships. Men and women were ridiculous, what they did to each other, and what they put up with.

It wasn't that long ago that society had drawn strict lines between what a man would do and what a woman would do domestically. The man would have a job, a simple nine-to-five, and the woman would keep house and make babies.

Those lines had shifted and blurred. At first glance, you'd think it was because of the women's suffrage movement, but that wasn't it. This society was moving into late-stage capitalism. In the past, one man's wage would feed and clothe an entire family of six, and buy a house, with money left over for holidays and trips to the movies once and a while.

As the cost of living went skyrocketing, and wages limped lethargically behind it, men weren't bringing home enough money for the family to survive anymore. So, the wives went out to work as well. But the reorganization of domestic labor didn't go with it.

Women were told that they could have it all — a career, a family, a fulfilling life. It just meant they were *doing* it all, while a lot of men were reveling in their weaponized incompetence, just like Terry, here.

I looked down at him in disgust. He thought he was a good dad. The bar was on the floor.

"That's it." I straightened up and moved over to the salt circle. "I'm letting the pontianak out." I put my toe in the circle, as if I was going to scrape out the side of the salt. "I think you deserve to have Sandy eat your internal organs."

"No!" He screamed, scrabbling to his feet. "Don't do it!"

"It came here for a reason, Terry, and that reason is not just vengeance. It's justice. I can't believe you can look me in the eye and tell me you think you do enough around here?" I knelt down and grabbed him by the chin. "She's growing another human inside herself. She's a literal *goddess,* and you can't be bothered to get up to take your toddler to the toilet at nighttime? You're a worthless sack of shit," I spat out. "Sandy's wrecking her back at work almost every single day, and you think you do a hard job because you sit on your ass and drive a *forklift?*"

Terry's eyes wildly swung between the pontianak, and me. "I have to lift boxes, sometimes! It's hard, physical labor!"

"So is being a hairdresser." This asshole just wasn't getting it. "Let's try something," I said. "Hold your arms up like this." I brought my hands up and out, to around chin height. Terry looked at me sullenly, but copied me once I raised my eyebrow and made a reaching gesture towards the salt circle. "Good man. Hold it there. Now, let's do some math." I squatted down and brought up the calculator on my phone. "You're at work four days a week, nine hours a day. I'll make it ten, just to give you some leeway. That's forty hours a week. Sandy, how many hours a day do you work?"

"The salon is open from nine-to-five and nine-to-one on Saturdays. I open three days a week."

"Okay, you need another half hour to open…" I tapped on my phone. Terry's arms were falling. I smacked the floor and he jumped. "Arms up. Okay… so that's forty-five point five hours. So she's already doing far more hours than you."

"My job is much more physical…"

"Arms *up*," I snapped at him. He lifted them back up to chin level. "Now, let's do domestic labor hours."

Terry looked at me sullenly. "That's not fair. Mowing the lawn takes ages. I fix little things that get broken around here, too."

I made a show of looking at the broken lamp on the counter. "How long has that been sitting there?"

"Three weeks," Sandy whispered.

I tapped at my calculator. "I'm going to give you half an hour for the lawn, another hour a week to fix stuff around the house. What else do you do?"

"I fold my own laundry and put it away."

"I stopped doing it for him," Sandy's voice was getting louder.

I ignored her. "Who does the laundry, though? Who does Dexter's laundry?"

He didn't answer. I tapped on my phone. "I'm going to go with six loads a week, just to be conservative. Washing, hanging out to dry, bringing it in, ironing, it all takes about half an hour to an hour, more if you have to hang it out to dry. Now, the cooking."

"I take care of it on a Friday."

Sandy sat upright. "He picks up a pizza."

I glared at him.

"Okay!" He slammed his arms down on the floor. "I get it. I could probably do a bit more around the house."

"Arms *up*," I snapped.

"I can't! My arms are tired."

"Now you know how Sandy feels every single day. She holds her arms like that for at least half an hour at a time, probably over eight times a day. Am I right, Sandy?" She nodded. "If you can't do it for ten minutes, then her job is far more physical than yours."

"It's *her* fault," Terry whined. "She never liked how I cooked, or how I did the laundry."

"Oh, I can imagine," I said. "I bet you never checked all the pockets before you washed anything, so the whole load was covered with tissue paper. You would have been washing pants with your jocks still stuck inside them, or with socks still rolled into balls. I bet you even hung clothes out without giving them a shake first."

"I asked *so* many times," Sandy muttered. "He never did it properly."

"Yeah. Now you know. It was on *purpose*."

Terry shook his head frantically. "It wasn't!"

"Yes, it *was*. You deliberately do things badly, so you won't have to do it again. You're a sack of shit, Terry," I said, getting to my feet. "I'm letting the pontianak out."

"No!" Terry screamed and scrambled up to his feet. "I'll do better, I promise! Sandy… Sandy, stop her!"

"No, please," Sandy grabbed my arm. "Don't do it."

I glared down at her. "You want to be married to that sack of shit for your whole life?"

She cocked her head. "Oh, no, it's not that," she said. "I've thought about divorcing him *so* many times. I was always just too busy to follow through with it, and my faith has always told me I should try and stick it out. No, I just don't want to be blamed for murdering him if that thing possesses me again."

I paused. "Ah. Righto. You don't have to worry; I can help cover it up. I know at least eighty ways of disposing of a body. No one will ever find him."

Benson chuckled. "Well, I'm not sure if I can idly stand by and watch a murder." He patted Sandy on the cheek. "But, my child, I think Jesus himself would give you a high-five if you left Terry in the gutter."

"Sandy..." Terry crawled forward and took her hands. "No. Don't do this. I'll cook every night. I'll... I'll... take lessons, or something, I'll follow recipes."

I put my hands on my hips. "And if you screw it up, you'll start again from scratch, and keep going until you do it right."

He swallowed, and nodded. "I will. And I'll do all the laundry. I'll do it right, I promise. I'll even separate the colors."

There was a moment of silence, as Sandy thought about it. Finally, she pursed her lips. "Okay. This is your last chance, though, Terry," she said. "The only thing holding me back from taking Dex and going to live with Mom was my marriage vows."

Terry's eyes flashed; a calculating look came over them before it disappeared abruptly, replaced by pleading, puppy-dog eyes. "You can't break your vows, baby. You know you can't. It's you and me, forever."

Benson kicked him in the ribs. "You've some thick bollocks, Terry. You've broken your vows every single day since you wed. You promised to honor her, and you've proved yourself a dishonorable fecker, you have. You broke your vows, so she's released from hers."

Sandy gazed up to him with round eyes. "Is that how it works, Father?"

"If I say it does, it does."

"Well," she said. "I'll give it one more chance. One more chance," she glared at Terry. "You hear me?"

I flipped the banana in my hand. "If that's your final decision... And it's a stupid decision, mind you," I added, pointing the banana at him. "If you hang on a minute, Sandy,

I'll give you an insurance policy." I stood up. "Do you have any Tupperware containers?

Sandy automatically started to open her mouth, but she stopped herself. She looked at Terry and raised an eyebrow.

He went red, and mouthed like a goldfish. "I… I don't know," he said finally.

"Learn," I snapped. I turned to Sandy.

"Third drawer down."

I opened the drawer and rummaged around a neat assortment of Tupperware containers. She even had the matching lids attached to each one. I pulled out a small, rectangular container, and dumped the remaining salt inside it.

I turned, and faced the pontianak. It was still pacing in the circle, hissing. I aimed and tossed the banana at her. It hit her in the chest. Instantly, she disappeared in a blinding white flash.

The banana thumped to the floor.

I grinned. That was good. I was sincerely hoping that would work, otherwise I had no idea how I was going to get rid of her. According to legend, pontianaks usually slept in banana trees during the day. It was daytime now, so I hoped she'd be nice and cozy there.

I placed the salt-filled Tupperware container inside the circle, gently lifted the banana and nestled it inside the salt, making sure it was covered completely. That should keep her trapped, and hopefully asleep. I clipped the lid closed, and lifted it into my hands.

"I'm going to keep a hold of her," I said, cradling the container to my chest. "I'm going to keep an eye on *you*, Terry. Sandy might have given you another chance, but I haven't. If I find out that you're not pulling your weight in this relationship, I'm going to let her out, you hear me? And I'll help Sandy get rid of your body."

Sandy stood up and pulled me into a hug. It was awkward and uncomfortable, but I bore it with good grace.

"Thank you," she whispered, her voice trembling. "I was at the end of my rope." She let me go, and turned to Benson. "Thank you too, Father. You really are the best exorcist of your time."

Benson glowed with happiness. "That's not all I'm good for, my child! I'm going to stick around and give you two some marriage counseling. It is sorely needed. Terry, pop a Band-Aid on those scratches and make some coffee. This is going to take a while."

I chuckled. Terry looked miserable. "This is where I say my goodbyes," I said. "Sandy, keep me posted."

"I will." She smiled at me warmly.

I turned and walked out of the kitchen, and out of Terry and Sandy Becker's house, cradling the Tupperware container to my chest.

If only all my problems could be solved by murderous, vengeful ghosts.

CHAPTER 1

andy Becker

MY PHONE BUZZED as I was finishing off my client; I couldn't help but glance down at it, sitting on my equipment trolley. We weren't supposed to have our phones on at work. Not since Kerry's boyfriend dumped her by text mid-shift and she cried all over her client's foils, ruining her highlights.

I couldn't help but look, though.

My best friend Chloe had messaged me again. *Someone's hacked my phone! Sandy, I'm being blackmailed!*

Oh, good grief. That sounded bad. I'd have to call her back. I couldn't answer her right now, I had enough on my plate. I was juggling three clients in the salon, another one was about to arrive, and unless I ate a cracker within the next five minutes I was going to puke again.

Taking a deep breath, I composed myself. I was going to be fine. Everything was going to be okay.

I raked my fingers through the old lady's curls, ruffling

them up, patting them gently into place, and grinned at her in the mirror. "So, Mrs Poppell," I said cheerfully, tucking a curl behind her ear and whipping a hand mirror out to show her the back of her head. "What do you think?"

She pursed her lips, looking at herself. "You cut it too short."

My smile fell. She was going to be difficult. I knew it the second she walked in the door. Sometimes, you can just tell when someone is planning on being an asshole.

To be fair, Mrs Poppell complained every single time I did her hair. She was one of those people who were never happy no matter what I did. I couldn't really blame her, either. The mirror wasn't exactly kind to her. She wasn't an 'aging gracefully' type of old lady, or even a 'sweet, twinkling-eyed gray-haired grandma' type. She was more like an 'Aileen Wurnos determined to use an expired coupon' kind of woman.

It was exhausting, but it was part of my job. I had to do my best with what I had in front of me.

"I just gave it a little trim," I said perkily, forcing the smile back on my face. "It looks a little shorter because I did a tighter curl this time. You asked me to, remember?"

Her eyes narrowed. "Are you saying this is *my* fault?"

"No, no, of course not. It's just that you asked for a tighter set, so I used smaller rollers. So..." I added lamely. "The curl is tighter. So your hair looks shorter."

"You cut it shorter."

"Well..." I tried to keep my voice sounding reasonable. "I did cut it, yes. No more than usual, though. You *did* ask for a trim. I trimmed it, the same as always."

She scowled. "It looks shorter."

I took a deep breath, trying not to sigh it out. "Yes, it looks shorter because..."

There was no point trying to explain. A huge part of hair-dressing was managing your client's expectations, and I'd clearly dropped the ball with this one.

Sometimes, my job was pure performance art. I can't tell you how many times I've had a client who asked for a big change – something really different – but she didn't want to lose any length off her hair or change her color. *At all.*

The only solution is to do exactly the same thing as usual and spend two hours gassing her up. Every single time, she'll leave the salon absolutely delighted with her 'new look.'

I should have known better than to change Mrs Poppell's routine, but I wasn't thinking clearly. She caught me on a bad day. Probably the worst day I'd had in three weeks, in fact. I was stressed with a capital S.

I was newly pregnant, sick as a dog with morning sickness, and absolutely exhausted from dealing with Dexter, my overactive toddler. Jenny – the salon owner here at Curl Up and Dye – had overbooked me again, and I was running late.

Jenny insisted I could handle it. I was young and strong, she said, and built like a milk-maid: Big boobs, tight core, sturdy, childbearing hips, strong arms, honey-blonde hair, and a rosy complexion that made me look younger than my twenty-five years.

Except today, I wasn't handling it at all. The last time I'd had a bad day like this, I'd woken up on the floor of my kitchen in the arms of a strange woman, with Terry, my husband, bleeding and crying in the corner, and my local priest standing over me flicking me with holy water.

I didn't want to think about that day. *That* day had opened up a whole can of worms that I was desperately trying to seal back shut.

I plastered the smile back on my face. "Well, we can fix this." It was going to take me another forty-five minutes and put me further behind in my schedule, but if Mrs Poppell left with a smile on her face, it would be worth it. "I'll give it another wash and reset it like normal, and you'll be good as new."

My assistant Kerry sidled up to me, flicking her head back so she could see me through the thick curtain of bangs on her face. "Sandy, the client at the basin is ready for you to check the toner," she said, in her usual miserable monotone.

I held back another sigh. "Thanks, Kerry. Can you please take Mrs Poppell back through to the basin and give her another wash?"

Kerry looked at me stonily, then stared at Mrs Poppell. "Why?"

"We're going to redo the set," I said cheerfully, trying not to grit my teeth. Kerry had the tact of a rhino. I met her eye – through the thick curtain of her black bangs – and gave her a Look.

Anyone in the service industry knows how to speak Look. It was a whole language of its own. Within a split second of meaningful eye contact, you can convey a whole sentence to your coworker, using only a slight raise of eyebrow, a purse of lips, a widening of eyes.

I've seen staff at Big Chic glance at each other and say *That's not the shirt that customer was wearing when she came in here but we don't get paid enough, so girl, let's mind our own business.*

I've watched the girls at the coffee shop shoot each other with *Oh my God, extremely hot guy at two o'clock, when you get his name for the coffee, ask for his number to go with it.*

I can glance over at the receptionist, and with a tiny movement of my facial muscles, I can say *Please bring my client another glass of wine; I forgot I didn't have a clipper guard on and now his trim is a skin-fade. Oops!*

My assistant Kerry was young, and only learning to speak Look, so I put a little sauce into it. *You're happy, I'm happy, everything is fine. Everything is going to be fine. Don't push back, because if you do, this bitch is going to cause some drama and leave a hell of a Yelp review.*

Kerry's eyes widened immediately. "Oh yes," she said, forcing her overlined lips upwards in a smile. It sat oddly on her face, as if she'd never tried to smile before. She turned the toothy grin on Mrs Poppell. "Let's get you washed and set."

I hustled over to the basins, trying not to run. Now I had four clients in the salon at once, and another men's cut about to walk in the door. Jenny, my boss, looked up at me from the podium as I power-walked past. She narrowed her eyes at me slightly. *You're running very late. What's going on with you?*

I hurried past, keeping my eyes down.

I haven't told her I'm pregnant again.

She was going to flip out. I'd only just started working here when I was pregnant with Dexter. I didn't hide it; she knew I was pregnant when she hired me. It didn't stop her from being furious about it – despite the fact that I worked nine-hour days every day up until the second I went into labor, and was back at work six weeks after I'd given birth.

There were really no other options for work in Emerald Valley – no other salons, and I didn't have the money to open up my own place. Jenny was my only hope.

I wasn't looking forward to telling her about this new pregnancy. She was already suspicious of me at the moment, considering I'd been behaving a little... weird lately. Out of character, at the very least. I'm the most conscientious and customer-focused person you'll find, but three weeks ago, I disappeared halfway through putting a root tint on my first client of the day and didn't come back to work until after lunch.

And I didn't tell her why.

I couldn't. There wasn't really any rational way you could

tell your boss – *I'm sorry, I got possessed by a demon and tried to kill my husband. Oops!*

I wrenched my attention back to the present and checked my client's hair at the basin. Sophie's hair had come up nicely, thank goodness.

"Looking good, Soph," I smiled down at her, surreptitiously checking my watch. I had two other clients with color in their hair. Both would be ready in about ten minutes. I'd have to push one out a bit, not Susan's, because she had foil highlights that might overprocess and her hair was delicate enough as it is. Holly's color would be fine for a little bit longer, although she did say she was in a hurry today...

My head whirled for a second; nausea lurched in my stomach. I turned away, breathing deeply, clutching my chest. My heart was pounding.

This was too much. I was supposed to be taking it easy. I promised Father Benson. I promised my doctor. I promised Imogen, the girl who rescued Terry from the demon seconds before it ate his liver.

Before *I* ate his liver. That thought still gave me a weird frisson, halfway between terror and excitement.

Imogen – who turned out to be Father Benson's go-to girl on supernatural creatures – trapped the demon in a banana and took custody of it, and threatened to let the demon loose if Terry didn't treat me better.

The whole thing had been an enormous shock, in more ways than one. Putting aside the whole getting-possessed-by-a-demon thing, the *biggest* shock was finding out that my relationship was not normal.

Terry was not pulling his weight in this marriage – not by a long shot. While Terry took the trash out occasionally and worked four days at a distribution center, I was doing almost one-hundred percent of the housework at home, working fifty hours a week at the salon, and almost exclusively juggling Dexter and all his needs. Imogen even did the calculations to prove it.

I already knew I was doing too much. I already knew Terry wasn't doing enough. A lifetime of indoctrination about a woman's place kept me from saying anything, though. My mother had me convinced that this was normal. *Terry* had me convinced it was normal.

This new pregnancy was the straw that broke the camel's back. It was what had drawn the demon to me. A pontianak – a vengeful ghost, the spirit of a pregnant woman – took control of my body. Maybe she'd heard me silently screaming into the void and taken possession of me.

If I was being truthful, I'd admit that I was glad it had happened. Terry always had a way of getting out of helping with chores, a knack of wiggling out of looking after our son. My mom was no help, either. She was a fundamentalist born-again Christian who had drilled into me the importance of looking after your husband and children.

Which is fine, I guess. But we couldn't pay our rent unless I worked, too. So, I worked, and looked after the housework, and our kid. I did it all.

Until the demon possessed me and tried to eat Terry's internal organs.

Terry promised he was going to be a better husband and help me more. So far, it has been a complete disaster. He'd cooked dinner twice; both times it was inedible – the mash so runny it dribbled off my plate, and lamb chops so charred they fell to ash in my mouth. He'd acted hurt when I didn't eat it.

Dexter didn't eat it either. He threw the mash at the wall, and it stayed there. I left it, hoping Terry would clean it up, but he didn't. With burning shame, I wiped up the mess after two days. Terry hadn't cooked since then.

I tried leaving some chores for him, but the house was

still a mess. Terry didn't even seem to see what needed to be done until I pointed it out to him, and explaining what to do was a whole job all on its own.

Dexter woke up four times last night. Terry snored and refused to get up, even when I prodded him in the back.

I was exhausted – again. Sick, overworked, stretched too thin, just like three weeks ago. The difference was, three weeks ago I had no idea that demons were real. The pontianak was still trapped in the banana, as far as I knew, and it wasn't getting out.

I almost wished it could.

Imogen told me to call her if Terry wasn't pulling his weight, but I was too scared to do it. Father Benson also told me to call him if Terry was being a terrible husband. Again, I was too scared to admit it to him. My mother had drummed into me how important the sanctity of marriage was. Till death. You break those vows, you go to Hell.

I forced my attention back to Sophie's wet, blonde hair in the basin, and quickly mixed up her toner. "So anyways," Sophie said. "As I was saying before. Some strange shit has been going on around here lately, huh? Did you hear what happened to the statue of Sir Humphrey in the town square?"

"No," I said, trying to sound intrigued. "What's been going on?" I'd been too busy trying to deal with my own weird stuff.

"It got blown up," Sophie whispered theatrically. "Smashed to bits. People are saying that a strange monster did it. Gabby Green says she saw a giant polarbear-whale-elephant thing when she was coming out of the bar on Main Street."

"Well, she was coming out of the bar, so there's your first clue," I chuckled lightly, avoiding her eyes.

Since I'd been possessed by the vengeful spirit, I'd been seeing strange things every day, and it scared the absolute poop out of me. A tiny pixie with tennis racket-shaped wings, fluttering past the drug store; a bright green dog with floppy ears bounding through the backyard, jumping over fences like a cricket. A beautiful, otherworldly-looking man with pearly skin and eyes too big for his face had whistled at me in the street, and asked me if my flesh tasted as delicious as it looked.

I tried telling myself he was probably just European. I knew, though. I *knew*.

At first I thought I'd gone crazy, but Father Benson told me that the things were real. We only see what we know, he explained. Because I'd been possessed by the pontianak, I *knew*. So now, I *saw*. The veil had been lifted.

Sophie giggled. "Gabby Green is dramatic, but she's insisting on this one."

My assistant Kerry waved at me, trying to get my attention. Devin, my men's cut, was here already. Kerry gave me a Look. *Do you want me to wash him and get him ready for you?*

I grimaced. *No,* my Look replied. *I don't want to do him at all. He's a creep and a perve and will say suggestive things, and act offended and say he was only joking if I call him out on it. Tell him to go away.*

My stomach lurched. Oh, God, I was going to puke. "Hang on, Soph," I said.

I hurried back out to the chairs, power-walking past both of my clients still sitting at the color table, trying to keep my head down so they wouldn't stop me.

It didn't work. Holly waved at me. "Sandy, wait. Am I going to be done soon? I've got to head to the post office."

I gritted my teeth, and smiled. "Yes. Kerry will be over to rinse you off soon. I'll give you a quick trim and you can be on your way." I put my head down and ran.

I barely made it to the bathroom in time. Only water came up; I'd lost my breakfast an hour ago already. Heart pounding, I rinsed out my mouth, jammed a cracker in there, and quickly checked my phone.

My best friend Chloe had messaged me five more times. *Someone's got my nudes off my phone! They say they're going to send them to my whole contact list!*

Oh, poor Chloe.

My brain whirled. I'd have to call her later. I couldn't do much about it from here. Chloe, my best friend from hair-dressing school, was in D.C, more than two hour's drive away. She'd opened up a salon in Foggy Bottom with my other best friend, Prue, the best nail tech in town. They were living the big city life, while I had moved back to Emerald Valley to enjoy the simple, small-town life with my little family.

I grimaced, jamming another cracker into my mouth. Simple life. Sure.

The door banged. "Sandy, are you in there? You better hustle, girl. You're on track to miss your lunch break again." Jenny sounded more spiteful than usual.

I groaned. It was a rare day I got a lunch break anyway. Jenny's footsteps echoed away.

Taking a deep breath, I plastered a smile on my face and power-walked back into the salon. *I've got this. I've got this.*

First, get the toner on Sophie. "Sit up for me, hon, and I'll get this root tap on you." She shuffled forward, sitting up, and I dabbed the color on her head as fast as I could. "How are things going with Tommy?" I asked.

She sighed. "Not great. Remember how I told you about December twenty-second?"

"Sure!" I didn't remember at all.

"Well, it's coming up, and he's starting to get… weird."

"What do you mean, weird?"

"Well… he's stopped mentioning it when he gets a little

tipsy. He used to say it all the time, whenever he'd had a couple of beers, but he ...stopped."

"Stopped mentioning what?"

She paused. "That he will propose to me on December twenty-second..."

"Oh, yeah, of course, of course," I said hastily. I remembered now. It was a huge deal. Tommy and Sophie had been dating for years. December twenty-second had a special meaning for him, I'd forgotten what it was. And every time he got a little drunk, he'd tell Sophie that he was going to propose to her on December twenty-second of this year. The first time he'd told her, she picked out her dress and started to look at wedding venues.

I quickly regrouped. "I meant to say, why do you think he's stopped mentioning it?"

She sighed. "I don't know. I wonder if he just wants it to be a surprise."

"Yeah!" I put too much optimism in my voice. "I'm sure that's it."

"You really think so?"

My gut lurched. "Of course. He's been saying it for years, hasn't he? He's probably only just realized that the proposal should be a surprise."

"I hope so," she sighed. "You would say that, though, Sandy. You always think the best of everyone."

I chuckled. "It's a nice way of saying that I'm naive."

"No, you're an optimist. You're always cheerful and happy. You're a glass-half-full kinda girl," she said. "I thought I was, too, but I gotta admit, Tommy has got me a little rattled..."

"It's going to be fine, Soph."

Her shoulders suddenly slumped. "It *has* to be. We've been dating for five years. I can't start again. I'm almost thirty-two, Sandy. I want a family. My eggs are drying up. I'm running out of time."

I felt bad for her. I also wanted to shake some sense into her because I had a husband and a kid, and I was in hell.

"Could you… maybe… I don't know… propose to him?" I shrugged. "That would be a surprise, at least."

"I thought about it. He'd get mad, though. He's a traditional kind of guy, so he wants to be the one that does the proposing." She sighed heavily. "I'm stuck between a rock and a hard place."

"It's going to be fine," I said. "He'll propose in December, like he always said he would…."

Kerry plucked at my dress. "Devin is ready for you, Sandy."

I turned to her. "Oh, thanks. Can you please rinse off Holly and pop a treatment on her." I gave her a Look, silently adding *Leave her at the basin with a hot towel for fifteen minutes while I get rid of two clients, then maybe I'll be able to breathe.* "And while she's having the treatment, rinse off Susan's color and start blow waving her for me."

"I'm about to head off for lunch," Kerry said, looking at her watch.

I suppressed a scream. "Okay, just rinse off Holly and put the treatment on. I'll do the rest."

Damn it damn it damn it…

I hurried over to Devin, my next haircut. "Devin!" I plastered a smile on my face. "How are you today?"

"I'm doing good, sweetcheeks," he said.

I mock-glared at him and wagged my finger. "Now, don't sass me, Devin."

What I really wanted to do was turn on my heel and walk away from him, but I couldn't do that. Jenny was watching me. I should be able to handle this. It was part of my job.

"I meant the cheeks on your face, sweetheart," Devin

chuckled. "Not your ass." He lowered his voice until it was barely audible. "Although the cheeks on your ass are fine as hell too..."

A surge of nausea rocked through me, and I swallowed it down. Out of the corner of my eye I could see Kerry at the basin, stomping away, leaving my client Holly twitching uncomfortably with a hot towel on her head.

I grimaced. Holly was going to get up in a second. I could tell.

I smiled brightly at Devin, and combed his hair down. "So, same as usual?"

A clatter at the salon door wrenched my attention away. I glanced over. Something hit my kneecaps and squeezed. "Mama!"

"Dexter?" I bent down. "What are you doing here, buddy?"

He held up his hand. "Look at my truck!"

"Yes," I said, nodding. "I see you have your truck. That's great. What's going on, little man? Why are you here?"

"My truck goes vroooommmmm.... And CRASH!"

"Yes, it does," I said, watching my toddler ram his toy truck into the salon chair. Devin looked down at him, a deep frown crumpling up his face. My son's appearance clearly derailed whatever creepy thoughts he'd been having about me.

My husband Terry suddenly appeared beside me, smiling sheepishly, with a 'I'm such a charming mess but you can't help loving me' expression on his face. "Sorry, Sandy," he said, kissing me on the temple. "I'm just going to duck out for an hour. Your mom can't take him, she's at a church fundraiser."

I straightened up and turned to look at him. "What? Terry, what are you doing?"

"I just have to head out for an hour. It's important."

"You want to leave Dexter *here? Now?*"

"He'll be fine. I know you got a box of kids toys here somewhere, just dump him in the playpen. Just for an hour, okay?"

"Terry..." My head spun. I could see Jenny standing by the podium, glaring at me. My client at the basin, Holly, had pushed the hot towel off her head, and was sitting up, looking around and glaring.

I turned back to Terry. "What's going on?"

He gave me a conspiratorial smile. "Gary called. The bass are biting, Sandy! I gotta get down there!"

My mouth dropped open. "You're going *fishing?*"

"Just down to the lake. I won't be long." He turned around and practically ran out the door before I could stop him.

Dexter rammed his truck into my foot. "Crash!"

Breathe. Sandy, breathe.

I unzipped my case and pulled out my shears. My hands shook. Devin glared at me in the mirror. "A little busy today, huh?"

"Something like that." Why did my voice sound like it was coming from very far away? My heart felt like it was beating out of my chest.

"Sandy, I have to leave." Holly stood in front of me, wet hair dripping down her back. She looked furious. "I'll fix up my bill another time."

"Holly, wait. No..."

She turned around and stalked out. I'd just lost a client.

"Crash!" Dexter's truck smashed into my kneecap.

"Are we going to get this haircut started anytime soon?" Devin said bitchily.

Jenny minced behind me, looking down her nose at Dexter. "You can't have him here, Sandy," she said. "Come and speak to me when you have a minute."

Oh, God. She was going to scream at me for this. For

losing a client. For having Dexter dumped here. I swallowed a lump in my throat, and mouthed helplessly. Jenny arched her eyebrow at me as she walked past. "And Sophie's toner is turning purple," she added bitchily. She stalked away.

"Crash!" The truck hit my foot.

My vision blurred.

"This is ridiculous! I've been sitting here for almost an hour!"

I blinked. Darkness claimed me for a moment.

I was asleep and having a nightmare. Mrs Poppell's voice – screaming at the top of her lungs – was so awful, it must be a nightmare.

Pain stabbed me in the belly. I groaned. Oh, this nightmare hurt, it stabbed at me, ripping my guts out.

"Crash!"

I blinked. Light punched my eyeballs. Reality came rushing back.

Oh God, this wasn't a nightmare, it was *real.* I was at the salon. Jenny was going to fire me. I had two clients overprocessed, one glaring at me, Terry had dumped Dexter on me, and I had forgotten about Mrs Poppell.

"CRASH!"

I fell.

CHAPTER 2

I awoke to a soft, persistent beeping sound.

That was weird. Was the timer on the overhead dryer going off? I didn't think I had anyone underneath it. Panic flared in my chest. I had clients with color on; I had cuts waiting, oh, and Dexter, where was he? I'd forgotten someone, oh God, I better check...

My eyes flickered, blinking open.

I wasn't in the salon. I was in bed. Not mine, though. Was this a nightmare?

A pinch in my left arm caught my attention. There was a needle stuck in my hand. Confusion overwhelmed me for a second.

I was in the hospital.

Suddenly, I remembered. I collapsed at the salon. The pressure got too much, and I fainted.

I looked around. The room was tiny, stuffed with an industrial bed, beeping monitors, a hard vinyl visitor's chair, an IV bag on a pole and some shelves next to the bed. The butter-yellow walls should have been bright, except it was dark right now.

The darkness outside confused me. It had only been lunchtime when I fainted.

The room was empty. "Hello?" I croaked. My voice felt rough. "Hello?"

Nothing happened. No one was here.

I felt so alone.

I swallowed roughly. My throat hurt. "Hello?" Panic rose up from the emptiness inside me.

A middle-aged woman wearing green scrubs walked in, shuffling her feet. "Oh, you're awake." She bustled around my bed, looking at the monitor then down at me, her eyes glassy with bags underneath them. She was very, very tired. I recognized all the signs. She looked away from me, checking a clipboard at the foot of my bed. "How are you feeling?"

I stared back at her.

How was I feeling? I wasn't feeling anything. I was nothing. Endless blackness. A void. I was nothing, and I had no words. There *were* no words.

Her glassy eyes blinked; a light of understanding came on. Her expression softened. "Do you know what happened?"

I opened my mouth. My lips felt dry. "I…" I licked my lips. "I was at work. I fainted."

"Yes," the woman said. "You lost consciousness." She shone a little pen flashlight into my eyes, one after the other.

It was dark outside, I must have been out for hours. "Do you know where my husband is? And my son? I have a little boy… he was there when I fainted…"

"Your mama has your boy; she showed up at your salon and took him home," the nurse said. She pursed her lips. "I haven't seen your husband yet. The doctor called him and told him that we'd keep you overnight, so he said he'd check back tomorrow."

"He… he hasn't come in?"

She shook her head. The look of pity on her face almost cracked me in two.

Terry hadn't even come to see me in the hospital. And he'd given Dexter to my mom to look after.

I could almost see him now, playing Xbox at home and eating Cheerios out of the box. I knew what he'd say when he saw me, too. *I was so worried, Sandy, I couldn't think straight. Dexter was so worried, too, he was being so crazy, you know what he's like! I couldn't handle him. Your mom wanted to help.*

"How long have I been out for?"

The nurse looked at me. "In here, eight hours." A flare of anger flashed in her eyes. "You didn't faint; you had a seizure and fell into a coma. It took your boss a whole hour to call the ambulance. She was under the impression that you were faking it to avoid some drama at work."

I cocked my head. "...What?"

The nurse looked down at my chart again and ground her jaw. "Honey, look, your life is none of my business. But if I were you, I'd get myself another job, quick-smart. Your boss didn't call the ambulance until she noticed you'd started bleeding."

Her words felt like they were coming from far, far away, and I couldn't process what she was saying. They echoed over me as if I were sitting at the bottom of a well; they bounced around within the emptiness surrounding me. The words finally reached me, crossing the immense void between my physical body and my spirit, which had crumpled up into a ball, and lay flat and lifeless.

"I... I was... bleeding?"

The nurse took a deep breath. Her mouth flattened into a hard line. "Darlin', I'm sorry. I understand you were pregnant."

"I *was?*"

She sucked her bottom lip through her teeth. “You’ve lost the baby. I’m so sorry.”

The emptiness condensed on me. I closed my eyes, and drowned.

CHAPTER 3

When I opened my eyes again, it was still dark. The butter-yellow walls looked sickly, and much closer than they were before; almost suffocating. Blinking, I focused on the little monitor to my left. In the lower corner I could see the time. It was ten o'clock at night. Only a couple of hours had passed.

I shifted, suddenly aware that someone was in the room with me.

I had a visitor.

Terry? My heart throbbed, threatening to erupt in pain. This loss wasn't just mine; it was his too. We had to share this.

We *had* to share it. I couldn't shoulder this loss all on my own. It would kill me. I blinked harder at the chair, willing my eyes to focus.

It wasn't Terry. No. It was a woman.

She sat up straighter in the visitor's chair. "Oh, hey. You're awake."

My brain finally delivered the right information to me. "Imogen?" It was the strange, extraordinarily badass girl who had shown up at my house with Father Benson and pulled the demon out of me three weeks ago.

Her appearance in this tiny hospital room was utterly bizarre. Terry wasn't here. Neither was my mom, or my boss. But this kick-ass girl had somehow heard I was in hospital, and had come to visit me.

"What are you doing here?" I croaked. "Is it… visiting hours?"

She chuckled awkwardly. "Not exactly. I didn't come through the front door. The nurses don't know I'm here. Only partners allowed, apparently." She raised her eyebrows. "But… I notice your partner is *not* here…"

I swallowed. The hard lump in my throat didn't budge. "No."

"I thought you were going to call me if Terry didn't step up."

I stared at her. I couldn't think of anything to say.

After a moment, she nodded in understanding and sighed. "I should have known. Tigers don't change their spots."

"Leopards." My lips felt numb. My whole body felt numb, in fact.

"Whatever. Men like Terry don't change. You know it, and I know it. What I didn't factor in is that *you* won't change either. You'll keep shouldering every single burden in your life and keep working yourself into the ground because you think it's the only way." She curled her lip. "He treats you like shit because he wants to. And you let him treat you like shit because you don't see any other option."

A tiny spark of anger flared in my chest. "I don't *want* him to treat me like shit."

"No. You *let* him. Because you know he won't change."

I pressed my lips together. She was right. Terry wasn't going to change. Not for me.

Imogen sighed. "The alternative is leaving him. You don't want to do that, because you've got that weird religious shame thing going on. And you know that if you *do* leave him, the second you walk out the door, Terry is going to join some bullshit men's group and start to whine about how you took all his money and won't give him access to your kid."

I almost laughed. We didn't have any money. We lived paycheck to paycheck, like most families did. I made more money than Terry, but that was because I worked far more hours.

And I would definitely give him access to Dexter. My beautiful little kid loved his dad.

The only problem was this: Whenever I daydreamed about leaving him, and seriously thought about my options, I quickly realized that Terry wouldn't *want* to have Dexter. He'd take him for a couple of days a fortnight, maybe. Not overnight. He wouldn't cope. I couldn't count on him. If I left him, I knew I'd have to look after Dexter all on my own.

And I had nowhere to go. I couldn't afford our rent by myself. My mom wouldn't take us in – her house was too small, and my stepdad John wouldn't have us.

I was raised as a strict Catholic, but John was an evangelical fundamentalist, and would be horrified at the idea that a woman would ever dare leave her husband. He'd call me a whore and bar me from their house forever. He barely tolerated me as it was, because I didn't convert to his church.

I was sixteen when my dad died of a heart attack. I can't say I was affected too much – I barely ever saw him. He was from the 'children are to be seen and not heard' school of parenting. My dad went to work at an insurance brokerage, came home, and drank scotch in the living room in front of the T.V. He had no interest in me or my little brother Antonio, and he never tried to pretend otherwise.

It didn't bother me. I didn't know any different.

When he died, my mother married John – also recently widowed – and converted to his evangelical church. To be honest, the fire-and-brimstone evangelicalism suited her aesthetic better. Despite John's daily bullying, I stuck with my local Catholic church.

I liked the quiet. And I much preferred Father Benson's gentle spiritual guidance to John's constant threats of damnation. Luckily, I only had to put up with him for a year or two before I left to go to hairdressing school in D.C.

My little brother was less lucky. For some unfathomable reason, John seemed to absolutely despise Antonio. I sheltered him from most of the abuse, but he ended up running away from home when I left for D.C.

We kept in touch, but Antonio was so secretive. He avoided direct questions with the flair of a matador whirling a red cape around a bull. I didn't really know what he was up to these days.

Living in D.C. had been the best time in my life. I stayed with my great-aunt Marcheline, a wacky old spinster, in her big red-brick apartment in Foggy Bottom while I got my diploma. I had great dreams of staying in the city and opening up my own salon. Then, on a visit back home, I met Terry and we started dating. He was great; ruggedly handsome, good fun, my own big goofy cowboy. He came to visit me in D.C. a couple of times and despite being on birth control, I somehow fell pregnant.

Terry begged me to marry him. My mom and John organized the wedding before I'd even said yes.

My mother said I was lucky. I should count my blessings. Terry was very handsome, and had a good, stable job with benefits and insurance. He joined their church, and sometimes, he even went to services. My mother thought Terry was wonderful.

It didn't matter to her that he did nothing around the

house. Men weren't supposed to. Women looked after the home and children, and did a little paid work on the side if they had to. That was how it was supposed to be.

"You're right," I finally said out loud. My upbringing, religious shame, all this baggage I'd taken on because of my mom, and I was stuck. "I stayed because I had to."

There was a long, long moment of silence.

Imogen took a deep breath. "I'm sorry about the baby."

Oh God. A throb of grief shook my whole body. I clamped my arms over my chest, trying to hold myself together.

I'd wanted this baby. In my head I still had a picture of how I wanted my life to be. Three gorgeous children, Terry doing the dishes and helping pack the schoolbags, me piling the kids into the minivan and dropping them off at school before heading off to do a couple of hours work at the salon.

How did it come to this?

I was lying in a hospital bed miscarrying my baby after my bitch of a boss overbooked me, my morning sickness crippled me, and my husband dumped my toddler on me while I was working so he could go *fishing*.

I covered my face with my hands. Heaving sobs shook my body.

How did I let everyone do this to me? *Why did I let this happen?*

It was all my fault.

Grief tore me in two, and I cried and cried, lost in a heaving ocean of misery.

After a long, long time, a gentle pat on my shoulder forced me to resurface. Imogen was still there beside me.

"I would say it's going to be okay, but I'd be lying," she said, patting me awkwardly. "Your life sucks."

I choked out a laugh through my tears. Somehow, it was the right thing for her to say. My life sucked. I tried to reply, but grief swallowed me again, and my words were lost to the endless tears.

Imogen waited patiently for me to stop crying. It took a long time. I expected she would leave once she got bored, but she didn't. At one point, she melted into the corner and hid behind the curtain just before the night nurse came to check on me.

The nurse gave me a quick nod, and left. She was clearly not surprised to see me crying.

Finally, the numbness claimed me again, and my tears dried out. I felt desiccated, wrung dry and empty again.

Imogen edged closer. "I get why you didn't want me to know that things weren't any better. I guess you thought that I'd force some sort of decision on you, something you weren't ready for." She looked me in the eye, her expression frank. "I think you're ready now, though."

I stared at her, feeling the cold tears dry on my cheeks. I didn't know what to say.

She cleared her throat. "I know I can be... blunt, when it comes to this sort of thing. Without going into specifics, Sandy, well, I'm older than I look. I've been around the block a few times. I can be cynical and hard sometimes. I know what humans are like." She shrugged. "But I'm trying to do a new thing where I give people a chance."

My brow furrowed. A chance?

"Not Terry." She understood my confusion. "I mean *you*." She leaned forward, fixing me with her beautiful dark eyes. "You're worth so much more than this, Sandy. I don't think you understand the power you have inside you. I want this to be your decision. Here." She rustled around in a grocery bag and pulled something out.

Gently, she placed a Tupperware container on my lap. "Take this." She fixed me with a meaningful stare. "Do whatever you want."

I looked at the container. I knew what was inside.

Imogen stood and balled up the empty grocery bag. She grinned down at me. "I'm sorry, I've got to run. I've got a kid of my own now. I mean, he's a teenager, but still, I feel like I've gotta be home to look after him. You never know what kind of trouble they'll get into. Plus, y'know," she added absentmindedly, "there's a bunch of werewolves trying to kill all the kids at the Outdoor Education Center, and an evil vampire army in town, they're probably going to wipe us all out tomorrow." She smiled down at me brightly. "It's a Tuesday in Emerald Valley, so you never know what will happen."

I nodded dumbly.

Imogen hesitated for a second, and put her hand on my arm. "Again, I'm so sorry." She turned and walked towards the window, slid it open effortlessly, and leapt out, disappearing into the darkness.

CHAPTER 4

The night felt neverending. Sleep didn't claim me again. I sat in the darkness, listening to the beep of the monitor next to me, staring at the Tupperware container on my lap.

Emptiness surrounded me. I didn't even have any thoughts running through my head. I was an endless desert of nothingness. Floating in space, cold, with no one and nothing around me.

Slowly, I picked up one edge of the lid, and peeled it back.

Inside the container, the banana sat on a thick bed of rock salt. I pulled off the lid completely and dropped it down on the floor where it bounced underneath the bed, and I stared at the banana. Nothing happened.

My hand moved, independently of any commands from my brain. It reached into the container and pulled out the banana.

Sparkly crystals of salt clung to the skin; I brushed them off gently. The banana was still bright yellow and fresh as it had been three weeks ago. No black bruise marred the silky skin. The fruit inside was firm, the scent sweet and luscious.

I cradled the banana in my hands. Nothing happened.

Without thinking, I gripped the stem between two fingers, and pulled. The bright-yellow skin cracked, giving way. I peeled one strip down, then another, then a final strip, until the pale, soft flesh of the banana was revealed.

It smelled beautiful. Tropical and wild, like a place that I'd only ever visited in my dreams. I brought the banana closer and inhaled deeply, savoring the sweet scent.

There was no demon here. No violent, vengeful flesh-eating monster. Just freedom, and humid, dark nights filled with passion and power and intrigue.

Before I knew what I was doing, I placed the banana between my lips. The soft flesh gave way beneath my teeth. I bit, and I chewed.

I swallowed.

Another bite. Then, another, until all I had left was the empty bright-yellow skin.

Still nothing.

I put the empty banana skin back in the Tupperware container and slid it onto the table next to me.

Nothing happened.

I closed my eyes, and slept.

CHAPTER 5

"You okay there, honey?"

I blinked. Bright light streamed into the room through the window, turning the butter-yellow walls almost fluorescent. Morning had come, and I hadn't expected it to. I felt like it should stay dark forever.

The nurse from last night was back, her round face peering straight into mine.

I swallowed, clearing my throat. "You look better."

She laughed. "That's my line." She bustled around me, checking the chart, running her expert eyes over my face and body. "You look much better. Your vitals are good." She tapped the monitor. "The doctors are going to send you to have some tests, but it looks like whatever seizure or stroke you had didn't do any long-term damage." She glanced up, grinning. "I got almost five hours of sleep last night," she confided. "It's the most I've had in a week. I feel amazing!"

I wrinkled my nose. "I've got a three-year-old. I know exactly what you mean."

I hadn't had more than three hours of sleep in a row for a long time. Did being in a coma count as sleeping? My eight hours of unconsciousness yesterday was the longest time I'd been out since before I was pregnant with Dexter.

My gut clenched, reminding me that I'd lost the baby.

I lost the baby. I bit my lip.

The nurse looked down at me. "You've got someone to talk to, darlin'? I know it's hard, losing a baby. Even when you're only a few weeks along."

"Twelve weeks." My voice wobbled.

"Did you have your ultrasound?"

I shook my head. "I was supposed to go on Friday."

"Well." She patted my arm. "I'm sorry, hon. Miscarriages are so hard. I've had three myself. You don't get used to it."

My mouth dropped open. "Three?"

She huffed out a bitter chuckle. "It's something we don't talk about enough until we're commiserating with each other, huh? The fact is, we should talk about it more, so it's not so much of a shock when it happens." She peered at me, raising her eyebrows. "Did you know that almost a quarter of women miscarry their first baby? It's so common that doctors call it a test-run pregnancy. But every single time, the woman is so shocked and upset it happened, and they always blame themselves. It's heartbreaking. We should talk about it more. It happens a lot."

I nodded dumbly. My chest ached.

"Especially with shifter women," she added idly, wrapping my arm in a blood pressure cuff. "Wolves have the worst time."

"Excuse me?"

"Hmmm?" She looked up.

"Did you say–"

"You heard me. You know." She winked. "I *know* you know. I'm one-sixteenth fae. You've had the veil removed from your eyes, I can tell."

Just for a moment, I was shocked out of my misery.

She leaned closer. "And you should never blame yourself," she said fiercely. "It's not your fault. We don't get looked after properly." Curling her lip, she added under her breath. "Especially not you."

I couldn't think of what to say. Stubbornly, I decided to stick to practical matters. "Is my husband coming in?"

"He called to say he'd be in. With any luck, I can get you discharged this afternoon." She smiled at me, and handed me my phone. "Here. I didn't want to give it to you until you were feeling better. It looks like you are." She tilted her head. "Do you want some breakfast? You must be hungry."

A chill ran through me. *The banana.*

I'd eaten the banana with the demon inside.

What the hell had I been thinking?

Nothing, apparently. I didn't remember having any thoughts at all while I was biting and chewing and swallowing the vessel that held the angry evil spirit.

Aware the nurse was waiting for a response, I gave her a tiny smile. "Yes please. I'd love some breakfast."

She grinned back at me. "Cold toast and watery tea, coming right up." She bustled out of the room.

I took a deep breath and shuffled up into a sitting position, taking stock of my body. There was no sign I'd been possessed by the demon again. The needle was still stuck in my arm, the cord running to the drip above me. I hadn't left the room. And Terry was still alive.

I looked over to where the empty banana skin sat in the pile of salt crystals. It must have been a dud. The demon must have escaped somehow, and disappeared to wherever evil spirits go when they're not out tormenting and murdering people. I let out a breath, trying to feel relieved.

I felt... disappointed.

Immediately, I mentally slapped myself in the face. Disappointed? *Disappointed?* How could I be *disappointed* I didn't get to eat my own husband?

A weird feeling rolled over me, like I'd been hit with a bucket of ice-cold water. Cold, hard reality set in. I'd purposefully tried to let an evil spirit out of its cage so it could possess me, knowing I would attack and kill my own husband if I set it loose.

Who *does* that?

I didn't have to live like this. And Terry didn't have to die like that. This was insane. *I* was insane.

Just then, as if I'd willed him into existence, my husband walked through the door. His hair was disheveled, eyebrows pinched together, his big mouth drooping down into an almost comical frown. He looked haggard, as if he'd not slept in a million years. It was his 'I've been working so hard and I'm so tired' face – the one he pulled when I asked him to watch Dexter for me while I cooked dinner for us all. After working ten hours. Without a break. On my feet all day. *Pregnant*.

He saw me looking at him and he opened his arms expansively, lumbering towards me like a grief-stricken mourner. "Sandy," he crooned mournfully. "Oh, Sandy…"

I looked at him blankly, trying to find the words I wanted to say to him.

They finally came to me.

"Fuck off, Terry."

He reared back, shocked. I never swore.

It felt … good. I should swear more often.

I never talked to Terry like this, either. I gently cajoled him, I often diplomatically remonstrated, and I occasionally sassed him a little. But I never swore at him.

A flash of pure outrage sparked in his eyes. He was too shocked to try and mask it, but I'd seen it before, hidden deep down in the depths of his shambling, good-time cowboy persona.

I recognized it from behind my father's uncaring, granite-faced expression. I saw it everyday in my stepfather's eyes. Rage. Entitlement.

I knew it was there, in Terry. I'd always been too scared to do anything to bring it to the surface.

Until now.

I took a deep breath. Deep within me, I found more words I wanted to say.

"Terry, I want a divorce."

He turned on his heel and stalked out of the room.

CHAPTER 6

The first thing I did when I was alone was call my mom to check on Dexter. The poor kid was confused, but mostly annoyed that he couldn't come and hang out with me in the hospital, but I promised I'd be there later on to pick him up. Next, I called Chloe to check to see what was going on with her, and why the hell anyone would want to blackmail her.

Her text messages had gotten increasingly hysterical. She didn't answer her phone – she was probably working, so I left a message for her and got busy on the internet, looking up divorce lawyers.

A steely determination drove me forward. I was going to divorce Terry. I didn't care what my mother would say.

Well, I did care. It just wasn't going to stop me. Even if I had to live in a tent with Dexter and eat ramen noodles, I'd be happier than having to pick up Terry's skidmarked briefs from the bedroom floor every day.

My phone buzzed. "Hi, Chloe."

"Sandy! Oh, Sandy..." Chloe dissolved into tears immediately.

"Honey..." My heart ached for her. "What's going on, honey? What happened?"

"I...I... I..." She heaved out a series of wet sniffs. I waited patiently. "I..."

"It's okay, love. Take your time."

It might take a while. Chloe was a big softie. She cried in sad movies. She cried at life insurance commercials.

She took a big breath and cleared her throat. "Someone's blackmailing me, Sandy!"

"Who?"

"I don't know!" She made a noise that sounded a little like a cow heaving up soiled hay from the depths of its fourth stomach. "I don't know who it is!"

"Okay, hang on," I switched the phone to my other ear, then switched it back again. My ear was sore. I must have landed on it when I fainted. "Tell me what happened. Start from the beginning."

"I started getting..." Big sob. "Messages." Sniff. "On my phone." Sniff, and big, wet swallow.

"Yes," I said. "Who from?"

"They didn't say. It was an anonymous number."

"Okay. What did the messages say?"

"They started out by sending me a nude photo. Of me, Sandy! Of *meeeeee!*"

"Okay..." I bit my lip. I'd have to be delicate about this. "Is it a photo that you've sent someone recently?"

"I'm not an idiot, Sandy," she said, suddenly drying up. "I haven't sent anyone any of my nudes. These are photos I took of myself, for fun. Because I'm hot, and I want to document it for when I'm old and ugly."

"Oh. Of course, honey. I understand."

Chloe cleared her throat. "If a boy asks me for a pic, I've got a whole folder of random tits from the internet to send them. I've even got a few enormous dick pics I send to men who annoy me with their own tiny flaccid pee-pees."

"Okay." I nodded to myself. "It's not a photo that you sent anyone. So, your phone has been hacked."

"*Yeaahhhhhh...*" She started sobbing again. "They sent me one of my own photos, a really bad one that I probably should have deleted. My hair was a mess, and the lighting was all wrong."

"Okay..." Oh God, poor Chloe. "Was there a message?"

"No. No message at all. Just the picture, from an anonymous number."

"Did you call the number?"

"Of course! I tried a million times. It was switched off."

"So they sent you a nude photo of yourself from a burner phone, then switched it off?"

She broke down in sobs again. "Mom is going to kill me. Daddy is going to literally *killlll meeeeee*."

This was bad. Chloe's father was rich. I mean *rich* rich, intensely powerful old-world oil money rich, the founder of some conservative superpac. He spent most of his time in D.C, lobbying the government so he could get richer.

Chloe's mom had been his mistress for a couple of years while she stripped her way through nursing school. She was now one of the most outspoken nurses' union representatives, a passionate spokesperson for fair working conditions and women's health. She had a high profile, and was often in the news. She was a fabulous woman and I loved her a lot.

By contrast, objectively speaking, her father was a terrible person, but he seemed quite fond of Chloe. He paid for her education and gave her the money to open her salon, and he seemed quite proud that his illegitimate daughter was so sweet and unspoiled.

Although, that wouldn't be hard considering that his three legitimate children were evil incarnate. One had founded an outrage-porn news channel that peddled conspiracy theories, another was in France hiding from a statutory rape charge, and another was constantly in the press for manufacturing body insecurities so she could peddle her laxative lollipops.

Chloe, on the other hand, was an absolute sweetheart. As well as having a soft heart, she was a beauty – tall and leggy, with thick honey-colored hair and big blinky green eyes. Despite not being what you would call 'book smart', she was a very talented hairstylist. Chloe sometimes got confused and put aluminum foil in the microwave, but she could calculate the perfect angle for curtain bangs and mix up the precise color formula to counteract a sickly green tinge in your highlights.

I'd met Chloe and Prue, the nail tech wiz, at my first year of beauty school in D.C. and we'd quickly become best friends. Where Chloe was a soft-hearted, slightly ditzy blonde, Prue was raven-haired and dark-eyed, skinny as a rake, razor-sharp, witty, and as hard as the acrylic nails she bedazzled. Like Chloe, Prue was a local girl who was as passionate as me about protecting her friends.

I wondered what Prue was doing about this nude photo saga. Knowing her, she'd be threatening suspects with murder.

I cleared my throat. "Did you get any other messages?"

"Yeah," she sniffed wetly. "They sent another photo a couple of days later."

"Chloe," I gasped. "How long has this been going on for?"

"A couple of weeks," she said in a little voice. "I've been too scared to say anything to anyone."

"So what changed?"

"They sent me a message this morning," she said. "Another nude photo, and my contact list!" She wailed again for a long moment. "My whole contact list. The message said 'play nice, and I won't send these photos to this list."

Oh, God. This was awful.

"No other messages?"

"None!"

I took a deep breath. "Chloe, will you take this to the police?"

"I did!" She howled mournfully. "There's nothing they can do just yet. The photos haven't been sent anywhere else. It's a burner phone, and the communications unit at the police station is too overwhelmed to investigate it. The threat was carefully worded, and it didn't demand anything. Just that I 'play nice'," she said bitterly.

"Okay, well." I rubbed my chin. "It's okay, Chloe. It's going to be okay."

"I don't see how it is! My dad will kill me! Literally! I heard him talking to his assistant last week about hiring a contractor to do some wet work. I thought he meant he was getting his pool re-tiled, but I googled it." Her voice dropped to a whisper. "He meant *assassinated*, Sandy!"

"He's not going to kill you, honey."

"Maybe not me," she sniffed. "But he'd kill someone. If he couldn't find the hacker, it would be someone in my orbit, I just know it."

"Babe, his other daughter literally leaked her own sex tape."

"It's different when you're legitimate."

I wanted to disagree, but she was right. This would hurt Chloe's dad more. He thought she was a sweet, innocent girl. He'd be horrified.

"And it's not just him. My mom is doing a big media campaign right now; she's all over the news."

"Chloe, your mom would understand. If anyone would understand, it would be her."

"Of course she would. That's the problem! She'd probably work it into one of her speeches. I'd be a case study in her new mission to reform revenge porn laws, or something like that." She paused, and took a deep breath. "I love my mom, Sandy, but I don't want to be her case study. She'd want me to be strong, and not ashamed or embarrassed." She chuckled bitterly. "Hell, if I even told her about this she'd probably make me leak all my nudes to my contact list myself to get ahead of the blackmailer."

I bit my lip. She was probably right. She was caught between two diametrically opposed ideologies. Poor Chloe.

"Okay..." I thought for a moment. "We need to figure out what the hacker wants. They said they wanted you to play nice, is that right? That's your first clue. It's someone that you're playing with now. Who are you seeing at the moment, Chloe?"

"There is someone," she said, her voice wobbling. "It's really new, though."

"Who?"

"I've seen a guy from one of Daddy's firms a couple of times. His name's Gregory. He does something with gardening and finance..."

That sounded weird. "Gardening *and* finance?"

"Yeah. Hedge funds, I think he said. Is that a thing?"

"Uh... yeah."

"It's not him, though."

"How do you know?"

"I told him all about it," she said in a little voice. "I was with him when I got sent one of my nude pictures. I was so scared and frightened, and I burst into tears, and I had to tell someone. He managed to coax it out of me." She took a deep breath. "He was amazing. He was kind and gentle, and said that if my nudes did come out, he wouldn't care. He's nice, Sandy, a really nice guy. It's not him."

"Okay. Is there anyone else?"

"I'm talking to a couple of other guys. We haven't met yet, though. Gregory is the only one I've kinda been seeing, but it's not serious."

"Okay. Well, is there anyone else that would like to be seeing you, but you've rejected?"

"Uh… yeah, I guess. There's a guy at Scarlett's who keeps hitting on me, but I've managed to put him off. The new bartender at The Dog and Bone keeps asking me out, too." Scarlett's was an upmarket wine bar across the road from Chloe and Prue's salon. The Dog and Bone was an old-school English pub next door. They were the only two main places we ever went out.

"None of them were angry that you rejected them?"

"None of them were angry at *me*. They were a little mad at Prue, though."

Prue had no problem telling men to fuck off. She was a rottweiler. That is, if a rottweiler could throw drinks in people's faces and key their cars.

She sighed heavily. "I don't think it's any of them."

"What about enemies of your dad or mom? Anyone that would want to blackmail you to lean on them to do something?"

"Oh yeah," Chloe said breathlessly. "I didn't think of that. Yeah, probably a couple of people. My mom's assistant wants her to run for office; she'd love to have this kind of thing blow up. It would galvanize my mom into action, and it would be free publicity. It could be her."

"Maybe. We'll put her on the suspect list and check her out."

"And my daddy's getting courted by a new young lobbyist. I met him the other day; he was skeezy." I heard her shudder over the phone. "If anyone would do something like this, it would be him. I'd put him number-one on my list."

"Okay. So, we've got the guy from Scarlett's, the bartender at the Dog and Bone, your mom's assistant, and the new lobbyist. We've got a suspect list, so it's a start. All we can do now is wait to see what they ask for, and then we can narrow it down."

Chloe sighed. "This is a *nightmare*."

"I know, honey. You'll get through it, though. Once the hacker demands something, we'll be able to figure out who to focus on."

She took a deep breath. "Thanks, Sandy. You always know how to get my head straight." She sighed out her breath. "How are you, anyway? Still puking your guts up?"

My heart froze in my chest. For a few moments, I'd forgotten about my own shitty life. "Uh…" I stammered. I bit my lip, and tried again. I couldn't force any words out.

"Sandy?"

I swallowed. "I… uh…"

There was a long moment of silence.

Chloe's voice lowered. "Sandy, what's going on?"

I took a tiny breath. "I lost the baby."

"What? Oh, God! Sandy…. Oh, honey. What happened?"

Quickly, I outlined what had happened to me over the last twenty-four hours. I left out a few key things, like the fact that a strange, apparently immortal woman had visited me in hospital and given me the spirit of a vengeance demon that possessed me a few weeks ago, trapped in a banana, and I'd *eaten it...*

Chloe didn't need to know about that.

"... and I woke up in hospital," I finished. "I told him I wanted a divorce," I added in a little voice. "I'm scared, though."

There was dead air on the phone. I could hear rustling, and a slight echo.

Did Chloe put me on speaker? "Hello?"

Chloe coughed. "Sorry. Just to clarify... Terry dumped Dexter on you at the salon so he could go *fishing?"*

I hated when I was forced to tell people the shitty things that Terry did to me. It made me feel like a pathetic doormat. It was true, though. I had been a doormat. But not anymore.

"Uh, yeah," I said.

There was a long moment of silence.

Another voice snarled on the phone. "Mother *fucker*."

"Prue?"

There was a clatter, and the sound of footsteps stomping away.

"Sorry, Sandy..."

"Did Prue hear all that?"

"Yeah. She's gone now, though."

Oh, God. It was easy to share my problems with Chloe; she was a little meek scaredy-cat sometimes, like me. We often talked about how instead of all these songs about how great it was to be a strong, kick-ass woman, there needed to be more songs about how it was okay to be meek and gentle, and that people just needed to be a lot fucking nicer to soft-hearted women.

Prue had been raging at me to leave Terry since I married him. Instead of listening to her, I stopped telling her all the shitty things he did to me.

Chloe cleared her throat. "We're a right pair of nincompoops, aren't we?"

I laughed sadly. "Yeah. I guess we are."

"It's going to be okay, Sandy."

"I know, babe."

* * *

I HUNG up when the doctor came in to check on me. They wheeled me away for a couple more tests, and returned me to stare at the ceiling, thinking about my next steps. I tried to make an appointment with a divorce lawyer, but the fee they quoted was beyond anything I could imagine.

We had practically no savings, so there was no money to split. We'd only been renting our house, and it was in Terry's name.

I'd have to move out. I called my mom, and, with my heart in my mouth, told her I was planning on leaving Terry.

As predicted, she refused to believe me. "You'll work it out, honey," she said dismissively. "You can't divorce him, it's against God's word, and it's against God's plan for you. You need to surrender to your role. Surrender, and you'll be happy."

I hung up, feeling sick but still determined. Not this time. I was *not* going to surrender this time.

I picked up my phone again and had a look at rental apartments in Emerald Valley. There were none. Next, I looked at apartments in Cedar Hills, the next town over. Again, none. The cheapest rental was a disgusting run-down one-bedroom shack at double my budget.

With a sick, churning feeling in my stomach, I looked up homeless shelters. The closest one was in Richmond.

I threw my phone on my lap and gritted my teeth. Not this time. I would *not* surrender.

Just then, Terry walked into the room, his face curiously blank.

Three men followed him in. Two cops, and a thin, middle-aged man with glasses and a beard, wearing corduroy pants, a brown knitted jumper, and a lanyard around his neck.

The cops both paused in the doorway. Terry moved to the side of the door, staying well away from the bed. The bearded man stepped closer and smiled at me, showing extra gum. "Hello, Alessandra!"

I frowned. "It's Sandy."

The man grinned wider. "Of course. Sandy. How are you feeling today?"

I cocked my head, confused. Who was this guy? And why were there cops here?

"I guess… I'm feeling as well as I can be, having just woken up from a coma," I said lightly. "I don't mean to be rude, but who are you?"

"My name is Eric," the man said, a gentle expression on his face. "I'm just here to have a chat."

"A chat about what, exactly?"

Next to the doorway, Terry shifted on his feet. "Just answer his questions, Sandy. Everything is going to be okay."

I frowned. This was weird.

Just then, a strange feeling erupted in my chest, a sudden swell of intense outrage – so powerful and dark I almost blacked out.

It took me by surprise. I blinked, took a breath, and steadied myself. "Answer what questions?" I asked. My eyes flicked to the two police officers in the doorway. Why were there cops here?

The man – Eric – slid his butt up onto my hospital bed, perching near my knees. It was too close for my liking. He pulled out a little notebook and smiled, revealing two inches of gum. "Nothing to worry about," he said mildly. "I'm just interested in hearing about how you're feeling, that's all."

I stared at him. "I'm feeling confused."

"That's understandable," Eric nodded. "I expect everything is quite confusing for you right now."

The dark, intense outrage swelled again, ballooning so powerfully within me that my shoulders lifted from the pillow. A strange voice echoed inside me, low and growling. *He thinks you are crazy.*

"What?"

Where did that voice come from? It wasn't me.

Eric tilted his head. "I said, I expect everything is confusing for you. You've gone through a lot, Alessandra."

"It's Sandy," I repeated.

"Sandy. Can you tell me where you are?"

"I'm in hospital."

"And you know what day it is?"

"Tuesday." I narrowed my eyes. "What's going on?" I looked over at Terry, standing stiffly by the wall. He was acting weird. Normally, he'd be leaning against the wall, having a good chat with anyone who was close enough. But now, he was looking at me as if he was scared. "Terry, what's happening?"

He lifted his head. "Please just talk to Eric, Sandy." His voice shook. The cops behind him shifted, watching me carefully.

The outrage swelled in me again. *He is not scared,* the voice growled. *He is pretending.*

"Just stay calm, Sandy," Eric murmured. "Everything is okay. We're just trying to understand how you are feeling about everything that has happened."

He is attempting to get you placed in an insane asylum. He intends to get you certified as insane, then have you brainwashed into thinking he is the victim, so he may bring you back home to be his slave forever.

My mouth dropped open. "Is that true?"

Eric's brow furrowed. "Is... is what true?"

Oh, shit. They couldn't hear that voice. Maybe I *was* crazy.

Well, fuck it. I guess this is who I was now. I might be crazy, but I was never going to be Terry's slave again. Never.

I shuffled up into a sitting position, noticing that both cops put their hands on their guns when I moved. It was almost funny.

I looked up, and met Eric's eye frankly. "I mean, is it true that you're here to understand how I'm feeling? Or is it more accurate to say that my husband has fed you some bullshit about how I've gone crazy?"

Eric shifted awkwardly. "Well, I understand that Terry has some concerns for his safety…"

I let out a bark of laughter. I couldn't help it.

Terry wasn't wrong, after all. He *should* be scared. And I should have realized he might do something like this. He was amazing at rewriting history to suit himself.

When the demon attacked him, at first he had no idea I was even in there. From his perspective, an evil monster had tried to eat his liver. It was only after Imogen and Father Benson pulled the demon out of me that he even knew I was in the room.

I had no control, and no memory of it happening, but I'd seen the demon with my own two eyes, just like Terry did. And now, I saw *so* much more.

Terry didn't. He never mentioned the pontianak ever again. Instead, he made the cold, deliberate decision to ignore the fact a proper demon had manifested in his kitchen. He changed the narrative in his head to believe that I'd snapped, and attacked him.

Oh, he knows, the voice inside me whispered darkly.

"Why would Terry be concerned for his safety?" I asked, raising an eyebrow.

Eric shifted uncomfortably.

"You attacked me, Sandy," Terry said sulkily from the corner. "Three weeks ago. You know what happened."

I raised both brows, eyeing him steadily. "What happened?"

There was a long moment of silence. A flash of anger sparked in his eyes. Terry did *not* like this new version of his wife. Not at all.

Eric raised his hands, palms up. "Sandy, Terry has shared with us that he had quite a frightening experience, where you may have had some very big feelings–"

"He was frightened? Of *me?*" I huffed out a chuckle, and sat up straighter, fixing Eric with a steady stare. "Why would he be frightened of me? He's got a foot of height on me, and he's more than double my weight. His reach is far further than mine, too."

"Well, I think that–"

"I don't even have a gun," I added. "I sure as shit don't have a license. He's got one, though. A gun, I mean. He doesn't have a license." I smiled sweetly at Terry. He ground his jaw.

One of the cops glanced at him, narrowing his eyes. They'd be having a conversation later.

"No," I added. "There's no reason for Terry to be scared of *me*. There's every reason for me to be scared of Terry, though. He's bigger and stronger, and he's got weapons. He refuses to do any work around the house, he forces me to work fifty hours a week, while in the same breath telling me he can't do more than four days at his own job because he's *tired*." Oops, it was all coming out of me like a faucet had been turned on. "He controls all our money; I have to beg him for grocery money. He never lets me watch anything I want to watch on TV, and he throws a tantrum if I try and stand my ground on *anything*." I stared at Eric. "Did he tell you he dumped our own son on me at work, in a hair-dressing salon, on the day he was supposed to be looking after him, so he could go *fishing?*"

Eric's expression was getting more and more horrified. I steamrolled on.

"The truth is, I was so stressed out and overwhelmed, I miscarried our baby." My voice broke.

Eric gasped. Literally *gasped*, and clutched his heart.

"It woke me right up. Four hours ago, I told Terry I wanted a divorce. And he's run off to you to try and get me committed. Then he'll have a bit of time on his hands to try and brainwash me into believing I am insane, and I need to stay with him and be his slave forever." I lifted my chin. "Isn't that right, Terry?"

He mouthed uncontrollably. His face quivered with rage. "You… fucking… *bitch*."

There was a long moment of silence. One of the cops coughed, and jerked his head at the other one. "I don't think we're needed here." He nodded to the social worker sitting on my bed. "Eric, you need to vet these cases more carefully."

Eric slid his butt off my bed, his gummy smile long gone. "Indeed," he said fussily. Suddenly, he paused and looked down at me. "You're not concerned for your safety, are you?"

I held Terry's furious gaze. "No. Terry's weapon of choice is emotional manipulation."

Actually… Terry *might* get violent. Judging by the look in his eyes, he could easily strangle me to death right now. I was strangely indifferent to that fact.

Eric patted himself down and pulled out a card. "Sandy, I am sorry to bother you. I wish you well in your endeavors. Call me if you ever need anyone committed." He walked out, shepherding the police in front of him, leaving me alone in the room with my husband.

There was another long moment of silence. I held his stare.

Terry tilted his head back, glaring at me. "If you leave, you'll never see Dexter again. I'll make sure of it."

He turned and stomped out. A cold chill clutched my heart.

CHAPTER 7

We only had one car. Terry had it, and I wasn't planning on calling him ever again. So when the doctors told me they were discharging me, I was forced to call my mom and get her to come pick me up. She arrived, tight-lipped, eyes guarded. She refused to engage with me.

On the bright side, she still had Dexter. My little man was overjoyed to see me, smothering my face with slobbery open-mouth kisses. It was adorable and disgusting at the same time.

"Hello, little guy," I said, gently disengaging his mouth from my nose. "It's great to see you too."

"Mama is okay?" He asked me, driving his truck carefully over my chest.

"Mama is fine now," I squeezed him. "Now that I've got you."

My mother drove me home. She pursed her lips, frowning in silence for five whole blocks. I knew it wouldn't last. "Now, Alessandra," she said primly. "You need to stop all this garbage about divorcing Terry."

I sighed. "I'm doing it, Mom. I can't live like this. I've

already lost one baby. I don't want to lose my mind as well." My sanity had already taken a good shake, but I wasn't going to elaborate on that for my mom. "If I stay with Terry, that's exactly what's going to happen."

"Now, now. I know it's tough. But it's our lot in life. A woman's burden is troublesome, but the Lord lightens the load."

"No, he doesn't," I muttered under my breath.

She glanced at me sharply. "What was that?"

"Nothing." My voice was meek. The sound of it disgusted me. How long had I been such a pathetic doormat?

We drove down Main Street, turning off on Third, headed towards our little home. "You need to accept your role as a wife, Alessandra. You must."

I bit back my retort. There was some kind of commotion going on in our street. Up ahead, through the trees, I could see a cop standing with his very muscular arms crossed over his chest, and what looked like an EMT standing next to him. They were facing my front yard, away from me, so I couldn't see their faces, but I was sure I didn't recognize either of them.

My mother slowed right down. "The Bible is clear on this, Alessandra. We must serve our husbands and be submissive to them. They must be the leaders of our families, dear. You need to accept this."

I barely even heard my mom. I wasn't listening. As we moved forward, the view in front of my house opened up. The cop and the EMT were talking to Terry, who stood stiffly in the front yard, facing them. The expression on Terry's face was defensive; his jaw was clenched hard and he was biting out his words.

"I'm sure the Lord will forgive you of your sins, darling, and Terry will forgive you, too," my mom went on.

Standing in between the two burly men, shouting at Terry, was a skeleton.

An *animated* skeleton.

What the fuck?

I froze.

I could see every bone move as it raised its bone arms and jabbed a bone finger towards my husband. It's jawbone opened and closed rapidly, clacking furiously. It was *talking* to Terry. Shouting, in fact. I could see the cop and the EMT on either side of the skeleton, looking like they were listening intently to what it was saying.

"And he will accept you into the bosom of the Lo–"

I slapped my hand on her arm and squeezed. "Stop here!"

Mom's head swiveled towards me. "What?"

I gave her a huge, bright smile, well aware that I looked crazy. "Just, uh, just stop here, Mom. This is fine. I see Terry up ahead, I hope you don't mind, but I want to talk to him in private."

Mom frowned, and pulled over. The big cedars in the sidewalk blocked some of the view of my house.

She peered out the windscreen. "It looks like you have company anyway. There's a whole mess of people on your street, Alessandra." My mother seemed entirely unperturbed that there was an animated skeleton standing on the sidewalk, right outside my house, yelling at my husband.

She couldn't see it.

"Oh, I'm sure Terry's just shooting the breeze, like he always does," I unbuckled my seatbelt, turned, and unstrapped Dexter from his seat. "Let's go, little buddy. Say goodbye to grandma."

"Gamma!" Dexter head-butted my mom, leaving a strip of spit in her hair.

"Bye, darling." She patted him fondly. "Be good."

I slammed the car door and walked up to my front yard,

heart hammering wildly in my chest. I hitched Dex on my hip, rapidly approaching the backs of the cop, the EMT, and the animated bone monster standing in between them.

Terry saw me approach. He glared at me over the heads of the strangers. "You're not leaving, Sandy. I won't have it." Apparently he was so worried about me leaving him he could entirely ignore the nightmarish skeleton in front of him.

The skeleton screeched, jabbing an index finger bone at him roughly. "Oh, she's leaving, you fuck-knuckle. She's coming with *me.*"

My mouth dropped open. Oh, it happened. I *had* gone crazy. I was about to get abducted by a monster. Although, strangely, I think I'd take the monster over having to stay with Terry. At least the monster brought back-up. I couldn't think for the life of me what a police officer and an emergency medical technician were doing with an animated skeleton.

Maybe the skeleton wasn't so bad. It wasn't attacking anyone. It wasn't doing spells or curses. Unless you counted calling Terry a 'fuck-knuckle.'

I edged forward, terrified, but determined for once to be brave. I needed to get through this. The cop and the EMT moved back, out of my line of sight, leaving me standing next to the skeleton.

Terry ground his jaw. "She's not coming with you. She's staying here in Emerald Valley with me, where she belongs."

"She doesn't belong here," the skeleton hissed, clacking its teeth. "She belongs with us."

With us? With other horrifying animated skeletons? In purgatory, perhaps? Or did she mean with the cop and EMT? Both of them seemed to have melted away behind me, staying well out of this. Perhaps they were just hired muscle. The skeleton had no muscles, after all. Or skin. Or anything else, apart from a bunch of off-white osseous tissue.

"This place has been Hell for her," the bony nightmare went on. "And it's *your* fault. You schemed and manipulated to get her right where you wanted, so you could keep her as your slave." The skeleton stomped its bone feet and waved its bone arms around frantically.

Terry's eyes narrowed. "I did not. I never forced her to do anything."

"You took advantage of her. You took advantage of her sweet nature and her pathological unselfishness, and the fact that she's been so warped by her damned mother's religious insanity she'd always put you first. I bet you even got her pregnant on purpose, so she'd be forced to marry you."

Terry flinched. It was only a small motion, but I saw it. The skeleton had hit a bullseye. My mouth dropped open.

There was a long pause. I felt like I was going to be sick. "Terry..."

The skeleton threw its head back and let out a hideous, bitter cackle. "What'd you do, swap her birth control for breath mints? Oh, no, I got it." It put its bony hands on its hip bones. "I bet you whipped off the condom halfway through, didn't you?"

Oh, good grief. My head spun.

I remembered it.

There was one time when he'd been visiting me in D.C. He swore the condom had just fallen off. He'd been so playful and charming and dismissive of the risks, I let our burgeoning love wash over me and drown any concerns that I had about it.

I turned away, trying to catch my breath, holding Dexter to me tightly. It was the strangest thing, having reality ripped away from me, leaving me in a new world that was too bright and too spiky and too bizarre to process. It was an awful fact that I'd always suspected, but never let myself entertain because the truth was just too terrible to face. Terry got me pregnant on *purpose*, against my wishes, knowing I'd see no other choice than getting married and moving back to Emerald Valley.

And there was a skeleton in my yard yelling at him for it.

I took a breath; it was far too shallow. I realized I'd started to pant. I looked away, trying to deepen my breath, forcing myself to calm down.

It was working. My eyelids fluttered. The cop stood next to me a few feet away, biceps popping out wildly as he crossed his arms over his huge chest. Despite the bulging hard muscles, he looked soft and friendly; like a burly teddy bear in a police uniform. He was a comfort to look at. His eyes didn't have the hardness, the blankness that I'd seen on most cops. I got the most bizarre feeling that he was here because he cared about me. I didn't know him, though. I'd never seen him before.

I looked back.

"She can't leave," Terry said obstinately.

"Oh, she's leaving. Forever," the skeleton cackled. "She's never coming back to this shithole! Never!"

Terry punched a hand into his fist. "I'll never let Dexter go."

I clutched my kid to my chest. I'd stay in Hell forever, rather than leave Dex behind.

The skeleton wobbled its head, laughing. "Oh yeah? What are you going to do, you moron? Petition for full custody? Look after him *yourself?*" It cackled wildly, its teeth chattering together. "We all know you can't do that. You're the most incompetent father to walk the planet. Oh, yeah, we know you *love* your kid," the skeleton sneered at him. "But you know you're not capable of it."

"I look after Dexter all the time!"

"How many times, Sandy?" The skeleton turned to me. My ears popped, and for the first time, I realized that the skeleton sounded... familiar. "How often does Terry have Dexter by himself?" It peered at me. "A couple of hours a week, at most?"

I mouthed at the skeleton helplessly. "Do... do I..."

It turned back to shout at my husband. "How many accidents has Dexter had around you, Terry? How many near-misses? How many times have you not been watching your own kid, and he's done something incredibly dangerous? How many times has he been *hurt?*"

There was a pause. Terry went very still.

"How long before something serious happens, and you get arrested for child neglect, Terry?"

He crossed his arms mulishly, grinding his jaw.

"She's leaving," the skeleton spat out. "Both her and Dex are coming home with me, and you'll never see her again."

Terry looked at me. The obstinate expression melted, morphing into his pleading face. "Sandy...*please.*" He held out his hands. "Please. Don't leave me. I love you, Sandy. I need you."

There was a long moment of silence, as I stared at my husband. The veil, indeed, had been lifted. I didn't just see pixies and fae dogs and, apparently, skeleton monsters that knew all my secrets. I also saw the truth.

I bit my lip. "Why didn't you pick me up from the hospital, Terry?"

He cocked his head. "What?"

"Why didn't you visit me?"

"I–"

The skeleton smacked me with a bone hand. "He didn't even come to see you at the hospital?" The creature's screeches reached ear-splitting levels. "Terry, she was in a *coma! Because of you!*"

I barely heard it. The illusion around him had been ripped away. I saw him for who he was. I thought I married a fun, handsome, charming, sometimes shambolic, forgetful man who loved me and loved our family.

It was all a lie.

I shook my head slowly. "You're a selfish asshole, Terry. I've known that for a while. What I didn't quite realize was how manipulative you were. You played dumb. And you were playing with me the whole time." My voice dropped to a whisper. "Don't you understand what you've done to me? What I've *lost?*"

The image in my head — my dream — appeared in my mind's eye one more time. Terry, packing lunches and piling all the kids into our minivan before heading off to work. Me at the salon, happily trimming bangs and bleaching roots, and picking up the kids after school. Soccer, piano, family dinners. Me cooking, Terry cleaning up.

The image splintered, shattered, and fell to tiny bits, lying in tatters at the bottom of my psyche along with the rest of my sanity.

I turned away and stared into the empty black eye sockets of the bony nightmare beside me. "I'm coming with you." I was dimly aware of Terry behind me, snarling with rage and storming back into the house, no doubt to burn all my things before I could take them. I didn't care.

The skeleton patted me on the shoulder. "Of course you're coming with me, babe. This time, I'm not giving you a choice in the matter."

I nodded dumbly. Off to the Underworld I go…

Hang on.

I *knew* that voice. I knew it. "What do you mean, 'this time?'"

The skeleton chuckled. "Don't you remember how I tried to abduct you a couple of years ago? When you'd just had Dexter, and Terry was putting pressure on you to have sex again, even though your vagina was still completely mangled?" The creature snorted through its nose-hole. "You didn't want to hear how fucked-up his behavior was, though." It pointed at the cop and the paramedic. "That's why I brought back-up this time."

I squinted, tilting my head, peering at the skeleton. It stepped forward and tickled Dexter under the chin. He giggled and squirmed into me.

The bony nightmare laughed. "God, I hate kids. You're okay though, buddy. I think we're going to get along fine."

My mouth dropped open. "PRUE???"

CHAPTER 8

"Yeah?" The skeleton tilted its head. If it had skin, and muscles beneath it, I'm guessing the expression on its face would have been very confused. "Of course. Sandy… Are you okay?'

I let out all my breath in a whoosh. "It is you." I gaped at her. "It *is* you!"

It was her voice, anyway. Prue's voice. My best friend's voice, coming out of an animated pile of bones. I blinked, trying to clear my vision.

"Uh… Sandy…" The skeleton leaned closer. For the first time, she sounded a little apprehensive. "Can you… See me?" I even heard her put a capital S on the word *see*.

"Uh. Yeah."

The skeleton reared back. "Hoo boy. This has taken a turn. Sandy, what happened to you?"

Dexter writhed in my arms. "Down!"

Dumbly, I placed him on the ground. The cop took his hand. "Come on, little man," the EMT murmured to him. "Let's go get your stuff. We're going on a road trip!" They tottered off into the house.

I had too many questions buzzing through my brain; for a second, I was frozen. I stared at the skeleton. Prue. My best friend's voice. In a skeleton.

"I… don't… understand."

It tilted its skull on the side. Its eye sockets were completely empty. "Tell me, babe," her voice hitched. "What do you see when you look at me?"

"A… skeleton?"

"Huh." The skull looked away.

"I'm kind of freaking out here," I admitted.

It looked back. "The veil has gone from your eyes." Her voice sounded sad. "Sandy, what happened to you?"

"Me? What happened to *you?*"

The skeleton sighed heavily. "Okay. Listen. Just… close your eyes."

Relieved that someone was telling me what to do, I snapped them shut immediately.

The darkness helped. It was easier to think with my eyes shut. I took a breath, feeling a tiny bit of relief, like I'd been snatched back from the jaws of madness.

"Now," Prue's voice said to me, sounding exactly like Prue now that I couldn't see the skeleton standing in front of me. "I want you to think of me. Think of what I look like."

In my mind's eye, I brought up an image of my best friend. Her inky-black, poker-straight hair, pale skin, flinty almond-shaped eyes.

"Okay, take a peek."

I peeled one of my eyelids up. The skeleton grinned back at me.

"Still a skeleton."

She huffed out a breath. "Okay, close 'em. Let's do it again. Picture me in your head," she ordered. "Remember me doing something, maybe. The last time you were in D.C, remember how we went to that fetish club in Adams Morgan? And I fell off the table?"

She'd been wearing the most insane outfit made up of thin, strategically placed black straps. A guy wearing a spike collar had walked past and gotten tangled up in her straps, and they'd both tumbled to the floor in a heap.

Apprehensively, I blinked. The skeleton was still there.

"Still there," I said. "And now I know why that guy's spike collar didn't poke holes in your skin. Because you don't *have* any skin."

"Okay. Unfocus your eyes," she ordered. "Look into the distance behind me."

I did as she said. The skeleton drifted out of focus.

"Now, remember me, what I look like, standing in front of you.

Slowly, shimmering like a mirage, the skeleton morphed. I kept my eyes focused in the distance, not letting the illusion waver until it thickened out, taking on a human shape. A woman's shape.

I blinked, thinking of my best friend. Sassy, bitchy, beautiful, with the heart of a lion. The image sharpened.

There she was. Pearly skin, a curtain of ink-black hair, flashing dark eyes.

My chin wobbled. "Prue…"

"Babe."

I catapulted forward, enveloping her in a hug. I squeezed her, feeling her soft skin and the hard muscles and bones, thankfully underneath the skin. Breathing in deeply, I sniffed the expensive conditioner on her hair. She felt warm and clean and soft. *So* human. She was still as skinny as I remembered, but not as skinny as she was thirty seconds ago. I squeezed her again.

She chuckled. "Did you not know it was me?"

"Ha." I sniffed back a tear. "Nope. I had no idea."

"Did you think you were being abducted by a skeleton?"

"Uh-huh."

"Oh, shit, Sandy." She squeezed me back. "Things really have been bad."

"They have." I sniffed, and pulled back. "I don't understand. Why did I see a skeleton when I looked at you before?"

She shrugged. "That's what I really am. It's what I really look like. I've always been just a skeleton, Sandy. This," she said, brushing her hand over her gorgeous body "–is an illusion. A projection."

I gaped at her. "What?"

"It's a long story," she said wearily, tossing her hair back.

"Give me the CliffsNotes version."

Her mouth flattened into a thin line. "My mom was a witch," she said bluntly. "I got in an accident when I was a baby, about the same age as Dex is now, actually. I drowned in the bath."

"What?" I reared back, horrified.

"Yeah. Don't leave a two-year-old alone in the bath, that's the lesson here. Anyway, I died. To cut a long, painful, and very emotional story short, my mom went crazy with guilt and anguish and dived her dumb ass right into the most sinister blood magic. She bound my spirit back to my body, reanimating me."

My eyes bugged out. "Whoa."

"I know, right?" she said wryly. "I lived, but my body died. My spirit is tethered to my bones now. Funnily enough, they've grown to full-size while everything else slowly rotted away. My mom was forced to live with me, as a toddler, a hideous, slowly rotting carcass." She snorted out a laugh. "Can you imagine?"

"No." I shook my head. "I can*not* imagine."

"Anyways, she got some help. I had a permanent illusion put on me; it fools all humans and most supes. Some of them can see me, though." She tilted her head, peering at me. "So what happened to you? How come you can see me now?"

"Well…" I chuckled awkwardly. "To cut a long story short, I got possessed by a vengeance demon. A pontianak, to be exact."

"Indonesian vampire? Spirit of a pregnant woman who hunts evil men and eats their internal organs?"

"Uh-huh."

She frowned. "Makes sense. Terry would have been like a red flag to a bull. She'd be dying to eat him."

"Oh, she was. But she possessed me to do it. My local priest dragged her out of me, but… it opened my eyes, I guess. It ripped off the veil. I've been seeing things since."

"Seeing things *clearly*." Prue nodded, smiling. "I'm glad. I thought you were going to put up more of a fight about coming with us."

"Yeah… about that. Who is 'us', exactly?"

"Well." She laughed. "That's another story you might not be ready for."

My front door opened; Dexter came running out wheeling his overnight bag behind him. "Mama! Road trip! We go roooooaaaaad trip!"

The burly cop followed, carrying four huge bags in his arms. He smiled at me. "I've got all your clothes and everything from the bathroom cabinets, and your pillow."

"Oh, thanks." I stared at him, puzzled. "How did you know what…"

The EMT followed him out. For the first time, I got a proper look at his face.

He grinned at me. "I've got everything else."

For maybe the hundredth time today, my mouth fell open.

"Antonio?"

It was my brother.

CHAPTER 9

Emerald Valley to Foggy Bottom was only a one-hour and forty-five minute drive; I think I spent the whole first hour in stunned silence. My brother's reappearance was truly shocking to me.

He looked so different. The skinny, lanky kid with a wild mop of hair who had run away five years ago was now a handsome, well-built man with perfectly manicured stubble and a razor-sharp haircut. He still kept his cheeky smile and knowing eyes, but he was changed. Different.

I sat in the back seat next to him. I couldn't stop staring.

"Oh, relax, Sandy," he swatted me on the arm. "It's not that big of a deal."

"Five years, Antonio. I haven't seen you for *five years*."

"I've kept in touch." He shrugged.

"You barely tell me anything! And now I know why! You're mixed up in some supernatural stuff too, aren't you? That's why you ran away, right?" I narrowed my eyes at him. "So what are you? Vampire? Werewolf?"

"No." He sniffed haughtily.

"Witch? Warlock? Wizard?"

He sighed. "No."

"What are you then?"

"I'm gay."

There was a beat of silence. I cleared my throat. "I'm sorry. What?"

"I'm gay, Sandy. That's why I ran away."

There was a long silence. I blinked. It was as if another veil had slid away from my eyes, leaving me to see a lot more clearly. "You're… gay?"

"To be honest, I'm surprised I even had to tell you," he muttered dryly. "You were always yelling at me for stealing your clothes. I did your make up for the eighth-grade dance, Sandy."

There was another long moment of silence, while I mentally slotted the information into my memory banks. It fit a lot of holes, like the perfect Tetris cube.

"Huh."

Antonio peered at me. "You're mad?"

I looked up. "Of course I am," I huffed. "Of *course* I am! I'm furious!"

He turned away, sighing deeply. "I knew it. I knew it! I knew that mom had brainwashed you."

I frowned. "What?"

Antonio's head whipped back; he glared at me. "John wanted to send me to conversion therapy. He suspected I was gay and raided my room, looking for evidence, and he found it." He clenched his jaw, furious. "He destroyed my entire collection of classic Rupaul's Drag Race and Queer Eye DVD's. And it was a waste of time, anyway! All he had to do was check my phone and he'd see all my Grindr notifications."

"Conversion therapy?"

He pursed his lips. "Yeah. He smacked me around a little, and told me he was shipping me off to a camp. I looked up the camp, thinking it might be okay, y'know? I might get a little action. I mean, seriously, you put a load of gay repressed teenagers in the woods together, what do you think is going to happen? But then I found a news article that suggested the camp had…" He trailed off, and frowned. "How do I put this… contributed to the suicide of at least four young men."

My mouth dropped open. "The camp killed them?"

"Well, not directly. There were insinuations of beatings and the odd bit of torture. I think that over the years, they hounded some of those kids to suicide. Anyway, I didn't want to go, so I didn't." He shrugged. "I took off. Ran away."

I eyed him sadly. He looked so different, so grown up. The cheeky kid I knew was long gone. "Antonio… I'm *so* friggin mad at you. I'm so furious I could kill you myself."

He exhaled heavily. "I knew it…"

"No, you idiot," I smacked him on the shoulder. "I'm not mad that you're gay. I'm happy for you," I said. "I love that you love being queer. Good for you, whoop-de-do," I said bluntly. "I'm a *hairstylist,* Antonio. You think I've never met a gay man before?"

"Oh."

I punched him in the shoulder again. "I'm furious that you didn't tell me! You've left me in the dark for five years! I've been *so* worried about you!"

"Sorry." He pouted, looking a little more like the kid I knew. "But to be fair, when you left, you were showing all the signs of being sucked into John's fundamentalist cult, so I assumed you'd hate me if I came out as gay. I wasn't sure if I could handle my own sister hating me. And," he added, jabbing a finger at me. "You're an absolute fucking idiot, hooking up with Terry and being his doormat. I assumed that you'd taken after Mom, and you were a lost cause. She's John's doormat. There's no talking any sense into her."

I stared at him, aghast. "You really think that badly of me?"

"Well." He shrugged. "I don't think that *now*."

My lip wobbled. "You're being unfair. Terry got me pregnant, Antonio. Pregnancy hormones do crazy things to you."

"Yeah. I get it. I'm sorry." He patted my head and sighed. "I was mad at you that you weren't around to save me from John when he found out I was gay. Then, after I got back from working on a cruise ship, I headed to D.C. to stay with you and Great-Aunt Marche and start my EMT diploma, but you'd already gone. Back to Emerald Valley, pregnant and married. I felt like we'd missed each other by days."

He slung an arm around me and hugged me. I sniffed, and wiped away a few tears. "So tell me more," I said, leaning back. "You're a paramedic? Working in D.C?" Another idea hit me like a truck. "You know about Prue," I gasped, wide eyed. He'd been exposed to the supernatural. "How do you know about her?"

"I've been Seeing for a couple of years now." He grimaced. "I may have made a *slight* error of judgment on a date."

I eyed him carefully, waiting.

"Fine. I was… how do I put this delicately? I was walking in the park–"

"At night?

"... Yeah."

"You were cruising?"

"Sandy!"

"I'm a *hairdresser*, Ant."

"Okay, fine. I was cruising in the park one night, and I made a bad choice. The guy – who was murderously hot, by the way, you would have agreed to almost anything – he wanted a little more than fondling up against a tree. He was a vampire. A bagger, as it turns out, and he lost control and ended up almost draining me dry."

I gasped. "Oh, my *God!*"

"Indeed," he said dryly. "They're not supposed to do that, you know."

"Antonio! A *vampire?* What do you mean, they're not supposed to do that? What the hell is a bagger?"

"Calm down. Vampires are mostly fine, you know. Nice people. Great style, sometimes a little old-fashioned, and their sense of humor could use a little work too, I guess."

"Antonio, this is not funny. A *vampire?*"

Prue waved at me. "Vampires are generally fine, Sandy. They behave themselves. They mix into modern society quite well, for the most part, you wouldn't even know they're vampires unless you know what to look for."

"Excessive use of sunscreen, for starters," Antonio cut in. "They've got a king who keeps them under control. Staying under the radar is the number one priority for all supes, you know, so the balance can be maintained. Yes, they drink human blood, but most of them either have dedicated human blood pets, or they only take a little from their victims and compel them into forgetting all about it afterwards."

"Oh. They're not... evil?"

"No more than you are for eating bacon," he shrugged.

I made a face. "I'm a vegetarian."

"Well, vampires have to drink human blood. So their options are as follows: They could be an Owner, and keep a couple of human pets to feed from, an arrangement I find pretty diabolical. Or–" He ticked the options off his hands. "They could be a Little Sipper, and feed from random humans, and compel them to forget afterwards. The worst two options are Bagger and Ripper. Rippers are the ones that go mad and decide not to play by the rules anymore. It's usually an old, crazy vampire who just snaps. Those vampires absolutely destroy their victims, leaving their bodies as desiccated, mangled husks. Rippers are usually hunted and destroyed by the Vampire King's army quickly or else they would risk exposing the whole supernatural world."

"And the last one? A Bagger, did you say?"

He nodded. "They only drink donated blood. From a bag, hence the nickname. They think of themselves as vegan, as do-gooder humanitarian types. But therein lies the problem."

"The hunt sweetens the blood," Prue cut in. "And the pulse is the thing that fulfills their hunger properly. You can't get that kind of satisfaction from a blood bag. For most Baggers, it's only a matter of time before they relapse and tear some poor bastard's throat out."

Antonio chuckled. "Anyway, yes, I accidentally hooked up with a Bagger, and he almost killed me."

I gaped at him. "How did you survive it? What happened to the vampire?"

"He got staked by a cop."

I swung my eyes to the front seat where the burly officer sat. He'd been completely silent so far.

"No, not that one." Antonio's voice softened. "That one saved me later on, though."

"Huh?"

The cop turned, and grinned. "I'm Ben," he said, shaking my hand. "I'm Ant's boyfriend."

"Oh." I shook his hand, stunned. "Hi."

"Ben is my soulmate," Antonio declared. "My endless love. My everything. He's the Bert to my Ernie. I'm the Noddy to his Big Ears. He's the Starsky to my Hutch."

"Nice to meet you," I said, wondering why the hell I'd never guessed that my brother was gay before.

"No, Ben wasn't there that night," Antonio went on. "His boss was." He shivered dramatically. "*The* boss."

Ben shifted uncomfortably in his seat and sighed heavily. "Babe, come on."

"I can't help it. You're my hero. But he's the *dream*."

Prue, who was driving, took her hand off the wheel and held a finger in the air. "I second that. He's possibly the most sexy man I've ever seen in my life. And the most dangerous, too."

"Who are you talking about?"

"Detective Conrad Sinclair," Antonio said, shivering in delight again. "He's Ben's boss's boss's boss."

"Okay," I said, nodding. "So, what is he?"

"He's a cop," my brother said patiently. "Officially, he's the lead detective on homicide. Unofficially, he's the Enforcer; he hunts bad supes, and wins every Sexy Badass Thug award in town."

"Babe. I'm right *here*."

"I can't help it! Honestly, Sandy, you should have seen him. He ripped the vamp off me by the hair and punched a stake right through his chest in the matter of seconds. It was incredible. Since then, I've seen him busting supe heads all over town." Antonio sighed. "Detective Conrad Sinclair is old-school; shoot first, ask questions later."

"So what is he? Vampire? Werewolf?"

"He's a cop. Just human. Plain old delicious rough, tough, tortured and well-muscled human."

Ben's voice growled from the front seat. "He's too old for you."

"I have daddy issues. What can I say?"

"Human?" I squinted. "Oh. I thought, because he killed your vamp..."

"Nope. Sinclair is human, like you and me, and Ben. I have my suspicions though; he always seems to be in the right place at the right time. And he has no fear; none at all. He's ex-special forces, and he's as hard as a rock."

"He makes you as hard as a rock," Prue sniggered from the front seat.

Ben sighed. Antonio leaned forward and poked him with

a finger. "You can't talk, Benny. You've got a crush on him too."

"Everyone has a crush on Sinclair," Ben muttered. "The whole city is either terrified of him, or has a hard-on for him."

"Or both." Antonio grinned. "Anyways, going back to my story. After Sinclair turned my vamp one-night-stand into ash, he handed me over to Ben to look after."

"My mom's a vampire," Ben said simply. "Turned after I was born. I've always been able to See. Sinclair doesn't exactly know, but I guess he must have had some idea, because he asked me to look after Antonio. I helped him adjust to the Sight."

"Scarlett," Prue added from the front.

My head was whirling so much I didn't understand her. "I'm sorry?"

"Scarlett," Prue repeated.

"What about Scarlett?" There were too many characters in this story; I couldn't keep track. I wracked my brain, trying to put the pieces together. The only Scarlett I knew owned the wine bar across the road from Prue and Chloe's salon in Foggy Bottom. She was an achingly beautiful, ridiculously chic young Frenchwoman. I definitely wasn't gay, but if I was gay for anyone, it would be her.

"Ben's mom," Antonio answered me.

"Huh?"

"Scarlett is Ben's mom," Prue said patiently.

I took a deep breath. "Okay, everyone. Just stop a minute."

The car settled into comfortable silence, while I processed the fact that Scarlett, a gorgeous, witty and shrewd young bar owner, was actually a vampire, and the mother of the police officer in the front seat; the mother of my brother's boyfriend. Ben looked at least ten years older than her.

I took some deep breaths. Beside me, Dexter slept peacefully, oblivious to the earth-shattering information that was being dumped on me.

"Ben... Scarlett is your mom?"

He looked back to face me, and nodded. "She brought me to the U.S.A. when I was a baby. Don't worry, she's not a predator or anything. She doesn't have a pet. She's a Little Sipper."

I couldn't judge, I guess. I had sat in a hospital bed and ate a demon-infested banana, with the hope that said demon would take control of my body again, and *eat my husband.*

I moaned, and leaned forward, putting my head in my hands. What the hell had I been thinking? Thank God it didn't work. The banana was a dud. The pontianak was probably long gone.

Although I remembered the dark swell of outrage that had flared in my chest when Terry brought the social worker and cops into that hospital room, trying to commit me. It was a feeling I'd never felt before. It felt... foreign. Not like me. And it seemed to whisper things to me that I couldn't see myself.

Maybe I'd gotten a piece of the pontianak after all.

After a long while, Antonio patted my head. "You okay, Sandy?"

I sighed. "Yeah. I've got some adjustments to make, I guess."

"They will all come in time. For now, I'm going to get you back to Aunt Marche. She's desperate to have you and Dex."

I wrinkled my nose. "She is?"

"Of course she is."

My strange maiden Great-Aunt didn't have much to do with me when I'd been living with her last time. She mostly kept to herself, tottering around her massive living room, covered in cats and surrounded by a fog of incense smoke.

...Wait.

I put my head in my hands again. "Oh, good grief. Aunt Marche is a witch, isn't she?"

Antonio laughed. "She's not *a* witch."

"Oh," I breathed out a sigh of relief.

"She's *the* witch," he declared. "She's the high priestess of all the covens on the east coast."

I clenched my teeth. "Motherfucker."

Prue raised her hand again. "She was the one who created my body illusion for me. She's the one who saved my mom from being lost to the Dark Arts."

"What?"

"She's literally the most powerful woman in a thousand-mile radius, Sandy."

"The most popular one, too," Antonio added. "She's got five million followers on TikTok."

"This is insane! How is it possible that I didn't know any of this!"

Prue shot me a look in the rear vision mirror. "You couldn't See, Sandy. Don't get me wrong, Aunt Marche tried to help you when you got pregnant. Remember?"

I bit my lip, thinking. Aunt Marche had hated Terry on sight, which I found weird, considering she seemed to love every single other person she came across. He knew it too – he made sure he didn't come near her, so I dismissed it. I remembered when I told her I was pregnant with his child, too. She said she'd help me. There were options.

I assumed she meant abortion. I had thought about it, seriously, too. My life in D.C. was amazing; I'd never had so much fun. Aunt Marche, although odd, had loved me to bits, and her enormous three-story apartment complex had a ton of people staying. It was like living in a wacky co-ed sorority house.

But Terry literally stole me away. Just after I found out I was pregnant, he told me he was taking me for a romantic weekend, had me pack all my clothes, he'd love-bombed me, then told my mother the 'happy news' and drove me straight back to Emerald Valley.

Oh, Jesus. How did I not see how he was manipulating me?

I looked out the window, feeling faint. "Can we stop for a bit? I need a drink. I need to get something sugary. This is too much for me to process."

Prue indicated towards a gas station up ahead. "Sure, hon."

We drove in and parked. "I'll just be a minute."

CHAPTER 10

The door jangled when I walked into the gas station; the blank-faced cashier gave me a nod from behind bulletproof glass at the counter. Tinny music played through hidden speakers. I wandered in, heading down the aisles of snacks, not seeing anything in particular. I headed towards the refrigerators at the back, looking for icy cold sugary liquid. Running my fingers down the condensation, I let my brain wander.

The door jangled again. I ignored it, focusing on the range of sodas in front of me. Nothing too bubbly, something sweet… maybe something with a little texture…

Korean bubble tea. Perfect. That would do it.

Footsteps grew closer. A burly man walked up beside me, wearing low-slung blue work pants and a stained, ratty t-shirt. He moved too close to me at the refrigerators, coming into my personal space, letting me feel his presence. *Look at me,* his posture shouted. *I'm big and tough and I can occupy whatever space I want. Especially yours.*

My heart thudded. Automatically my body tried to move aside, but I forced myself to stay still.

Not this time. Not ever again. I didn't bend to the will of entitled men anymore. I planted my feet, and forced my attention back to the fridge.

Bubble tea. Which flavor? Cherry key-lime pie? Or satsuma candy floss?

The man swung his shoulders around, chest thrust out. He opened the fridge next to me and took out a can of soda. He popped it and took a long swig, smacking his lips and sighing loudly in satisfaction. "Ahhhh."

Surreptitiously, I leaned away. He stank. Of stale sweat, cigarettes, and something else I couldn't put my finger on. He smelled disgusting.

Suddenly, my vision went blank. A horrifying, murderous black rage swelled up in my chest. A voice in my head snarled roughly, as loud as a rockslide, and with the force of an atomic bomb. *Murderer. Slaver.*

I blinked; my vision flooded back, it was too bright. I gasped for breath. What the hell..?

"You okay there, darlin'?" The man smiled down at me, flicking the brim of his trucker cap up.

I shook. "I.... I..."

The man grinned. His front teeth were brown. I could smell his putrid breath from here. "You need some help? I can help you, if you like." He leaned down, leering at me. Looming right over me.

The darkness overwhelmed me again. *Torturer. Rapist. I will rip out your lungs and wear them as a waistcoat.*

My chin shook. "I'm okay." My voice was tiny, barely a whisper. I took a step back. Then another one. Then another one.

"You sure?" He chuckled; the sound sent a chill down my spine. "I got some time on my hands. I'm running ahead of schedule. I can help you with whatever you need."

I will grind your liver into paste to satiate my hunger. Your intestines will slurp like noodles down my throat. I will chew on your ligaments like gum and anoint my parched throat with your dying tears.

Shuffling back, I turned around, so I couldn't see him anymore.

No! What are you doing? Go back! I must feast on his flesh. He must not suffer to live! Murderer. Slaver.

Stiffly, I walked back to the counter. Breathe, Sandy. You're not going crazy. Just breathe.

I placed the bubble tea on the counter. "Just this, thanks," I whispered.

Turn around! Use your fingers to claw out his eyes so I might pop them between my teeth like that ridiculous bubble tea you are purchasing. The aqueous humor is far more refreshing than milky tea with sugary tapioca flour, I promise you. We will both *be satiated!*

The cashier looked at me blankly. He'd said something. I didn't catch it. "I'm sorry," I stammered. "What?"

"One ninety-nine," he said, bored.

I pulled out a note from my pocket, and suddenly stiffened. The man was behind me, standing far too close. The voice inside me raged, the anger pulled at my chest, about to explode.

He is the scourge of women; the most evil. He must not be permitted to breathe again.

I threw the note on the counter and ran out the door.

CHAPTER 11

I leaned against the wall of the gas station, panting, trying to get enough oxygen into my brain to slow it down. Clutching my chest, I slid down to my butt, gulping for air. Luckily, Prue was parked on the other side of the store and couldn't see me.

Get a grip, Sandy. Get a grip. You're just imagining things.

Go back in, you idiot! We must destroy him. I must feast!

Okay, this was really happening. I wasn't imagining it.

I took a shallow breath. "Who... who are you?" I whispered.

Oh, Hekate spare me. I sensed a roll of eyes, an indignant throwing up of arms. The anger ebbed away, frustration surged.

"Are you..." I swallowed a lump in my throat. "Are you the pontianak?"

Well, who else would I be, child? Her voice sounded bitchy. *Have you consumed any other demon-bound vessels lately? Do you make a daily habit of eating vengeful spirits? A little imp in your empanadas, perhaps? Some Satan in your morning smoothie?*

"Oh, God." I panted, resting my head on my knees. "Are you… inside me?"

I am *you.*

I moaned.

Would you please make haste with your mental breakdown. We have masculine flesh to consume.

"Can we… can we not? I mean, can we not do that?"

Within me, the pontianak made a face. I could almost see it in my mind's eye. Gleaming red eyes. Pursed black lips. Proud brow deeply furrowed.

We must. I am vengeance. I am the nightmare that stalks evil men. I must feast!

My hands were shaking and covered with sweat. "But… but how do you know that he is… you know..?"

How do I know that he is evil? For starters, he is a man. Most of them are evil.

"That's not…"

I can hear *him.* Her voice hissed at me. *I can sense evil intentions, child. I can hear it out loud, as clear as he had spoken. I can read abuse of power as simply as you read The Hungry Caterpillar to your born son.*

A thrill of fear electrified me. The man had been intensely creepy. Was the pontianak psychic?

"Was he going to hurt me?" I asked out loud. I wiped my sweaty, shaking hands on my jeans. "What was he going to do?"

It's what he has already done, she growled. Suddenly, I felt the need to turn my head. *Look.*

My eyes focused on a small truck parked outside the gas station, the kind you'd haul refrigerated goods in.

The door next to me slammed open; I jumped. The man walked out, whistling, holding a key attached to a large wrench in his hand.

For a moment fear overwhelmed me. He turned away,

though, headed towards the bathroom on the other side of the gas station.

Look at the truck, she whispered to me. *There are women inside there. Chained women.*

A surge of nausea rose up within me.

"No," I whispered.

Yes. They are bound in chains, some are heavily drugged. He is transporting them like cattle. They are to be sold to the highest bidder once he gets to this nation's capital.

It couldn't be true. I had to check. Shaking, I got to my feet. On trembling legs, I stepped forward, one foot after the other, headed towards the small truck.

I reached it, and put my ear to the side. My stomach lurched. Within the truck, I heard murmurs. Faint whispers. A low, heart wrenching, desperate sobbing.

See? He is trafficking women, headed to the city. He trades in female flesh.

"Oh my God. Oh my God." I swiveled around. "I have to tell Ben. He's a cop. He can help."

The trafficker is armed. He has four guns on him right now, in fact. Ben will get shot. Your brother will be killed. Your skeleton friend will get... chipped.

I clutched at my chest. "No. No no no no. I can't let that happen. No..."

He is alone now, child. Let us go to him.

I shook my head. "I can't. I can't..."

She shuddered within me, shaking me like a dog flings a toy in its teeth. *Pull yourself together. Just go and check. Check to see if he is still in the bathroom.*

"No..."

Her voice softened. *You need to urinate, don't you, child? You're about to wet yourself. Go to the bathroom, relieve yourself. You will be able to think clearer. Then, you will know what to do.*

It was true; I was so scared I was in danger of peeing my

pants. I wasn't thinking clearly. Going to the bathroom seemed like a good idea. Dumbly, shaking, I stepped forward towards the side of the gas station.

I pulled the door open. The sinks stood in front of me. To the left, a door led to the men's bathroom. The women's stood to the right. Shakily, I went to open the women's bathroom door.

The men's door banged; I jumped at the noise. The burly man stepped out, sniffing deeply and wiping his nose, his movements were jerky and animated. He scratched his chin and grinned at me, showing his rotten teeth.

"Why, hey there, girl." He chuckled lightly and nodded his head. "I knew it. I knew you were interested. You're one of those self-hating types, ain't ya?"

I clenched my teeth, trying to keep them from chattering, and looked away from him. "I'm just here to pee," I whispered. My voice shook uncontrollably.

He laughed out loud. "Sure you are." He stepped closer; his broad chest thrust right in my face, and raised his stained t-shirt, showing me the gun tucked in his waistband. "Well, you're here now. Good timing, too. That little bump got me all turned on; I was about to go mess up my goods."

Suddenly, he shifted to the right, moving so quickly for such a big man. He reached behind me and locked the door. "We're not going to need an audience."

I let out a petrified moan.

He flipped the wrench with the key attached in his hand. "Now, don't make too much noise, you hear? I don't want to have to wipe that pretty smile off your face with this."

Switch with me, the pontianak whispered.

"What?" My knees trembled, threatening to give way.

The man grabbed my chin in his hand. "I said, don't make too much noise."

Switch!

I exhaled, and let go.

CHAPTER 12

I was licking the most delicious jelly off my fingers. Sweet, lifegiving jam, oh, it tasted so good! It was *so* satisfying, the perfect accompaniment to the delicious hunk of shiny purple liver I'd just eaten. I was full. Satiated. *Mmmmm.*

Wait. What?

I looked down at my fingers. I'd almost licked them clean; a tiny hint of jelly was still stuck under one of my ragged nails.

I lifted my fingers to my nose, and sniffed. Not sweet. Tangy, metallic copper.

Blood.

My head reared up; I caught sight of myself in the mirror. My hair was a mess, flying everywhere, and it was inexplicably black… but wait, no… it was shortening, and fading rapidly to its normal bleach-blonde. I gaped at myself in the mirror, seeing my deathly-white skin flood with color, back to my usual rosy complexion. My eyes were wide, and fading from blazing red to my normal ordinary blue.

I took a little breath. Then another. Another.

I looked down at my feet.

Bloody chunks of flesh lay strewn around the bathroom floor. A mangled torso in a stained shirt was wedged in the corner, its head tipped backwards at an impossible, broken angle. Rubbery, bloody intestines festooned the stall doors.

The toilet door creaked open. One leg stump was jammed in the men's toilet.

Mmmmm. He was delicious, the demon sighed.

I exhaled. "Did I… did I just…"

No, child. Not you. I did. I feasted on the flesh of an evil man. It is my nature, after all.

I looked up into the mirror, staring at my reflection. My image shimmered; red smoke filled the mirror, and the pontianak appeared, exactly where I was standing.

She was taller than me, towering above me, almost seven foot, a terrifying, mighty creature. Long, thick wild black hair floated eerily around her in a non-existent breeze. A white gown billowed around her bulging pregnant belly. Eyes gleamed red like fiery coals in her deathly white skin. She tilted her proud chin back, staring down at me, her expression haughty.

She just ate that man. She *ate* him. Tiny bits of him were littered around my feet. The whole floor was saturated in blood. I looked back up, panting in fear, staring at her. I was struggling to find the words to say.

Finally, I found them.

"I'm a *vegetarian.*"

She chuckled. Lifting one arm, she extended a black claw-tipped finger and used her nail to worry at a bit of gristle stuck in her teeth.

In *my* teeth.

"Ugh! No!" I smacked at my own face. "Oh my God!"

You asked for this, child, she said, her voice surprisingly mild. *You invited me in. What did you think was going to happen?*

"I don't know," I moaned. "I don't know! I thought maybe that you would scare Terry a little, like you did the first time."

Liar.

"Okay, fine! I don't know!"

You forget I can see evil intentions, child. I can hear when someone wants to abuse their power. You had *no power. You wanted just a little.* She cocked her head to the side. *Turns out, you didn't need it from me. Not to leave that pathetic bloodsack of a husband of yours.*

I stared at her in the mirror, horrified.

She laughed and shook her head. *No, you did that all on your own. You didn't need me for that.*

I took a few deep breaths. "Okay. Okay. Do you think... do you think you could maybe... leave now?"

Hmmm. No. She frowned deeply for a moment, thinking. Then, she patted my body; the body she occupied. *I don't think I can,* she finally said. *I assume you are stuck with me for the moment.*

I moaned, staring down at the bloody hunks of human man littering the floor.

You should be thanking me, child. He was going to rape and torture you, did you know that?

"Yeah..." I stared back up at her in the mirror. "I had to come in here, though. You said he would kill Ben if he confronted him."

She shrugged. *I mean, he probably would have.*

"What do you mean, probably?"

I'm not a fortune teller.

I groaned. "I thought you were psychic?"

She laughed. *No, I'm not psychic.*

"But you can read minds?"

It doesn't work like that. I can only sense evil intentions.

"You lied to me?"

She shrugged again. *You allowed yourself to be misled. He was evil. I was hungry.* She chuckled darkly. *He was delicious.*

I huffed out a breath. "What are we going to do now?"

That's not my problem, she said idly, inspecting her long black nails. She used the point to dig at another bit of gristle in my teeth. *I'm just the muscle. Mmmm. Muscle. Oh, that heart was delectable.*

I shook wildly. "Listen… demon…"

My name is Mavka. You may call me Mav. Technically, I am not a demon. I'm an archetype. I'm a vengeful spirit from the astral plane. I come in many forms; the pontianak is the most well-known. Her brow furrowed. *Probably because the Indonesian people are smart and know the right things to fear.* She drew herself up proudly.

I squeezed my eyes shut. "I don't really have time for this right now…"

She peered at her nails. *Suit yourself.*

I looked down at the bloody chunks at my feet. I started shivering. "We need to get out of here."

Of course. You're welcome, by the way.

I stared at her with wild eyes. "For what? For eating my potential rapist?"

She scoffed. *No. For not spilling any blood on your clothes. I may be bloodthirsty, but I am a careful eater.*

I glanced down at my body. She was right; I only had a couple of smears of blood on my arm. I rubbed at them with my shirt sleeve, feeling my gorge rise. Luckily I was wearing black.

"We need to get out of here," I whispered.

She tossed her hair. *That would be wise. I am quite full. If the police came now, I might be forced to eat them too. I'm not sure if I could find the room.*

"Excuse me?"

She looked at me imperiously. *What? Do you think I have*

any intention of staying in one of your police cells for an extended period of time? No, indeed.

I stared at her in the mirror, aghast. "You can't eat the police."

Of course I can. I will consume any evil man who abuses his power. She shrugged. *I'm assuming you are aware of the domestic violence rates among that particular occupation. The average constabulary is like an all-you-can-eat buffet,* she added dryly.

I needed to get out of here. I exhaled heavily, looking around. The toilet key, along with the wrench it was attached to, sat in a puddle of blood by the mirror.

No way was I touching that. I pushed open the female toilets with my elbow. Inside the cubicle, above the cistern, a tiny window was propped open. I shot inside and put the seat down, stepped on it, and heaved my belly up onto the windowsill. It was going to be a drop – headfirst into a patchy garden bed.

Luckily, fourteen years of gymnastics training kicked in. As I fell I dived and rolled, landing neatly in a pile of tussock.

I sprang to my feet, looking around wildly. No one was around. I sighed in relief, edged forward and peered around the corner to the store's entrance.

The little truck was still parked outside. A movement caught my eye; someone approaching the door. I ducked back around the corner, and peeked again. It was Antonio, headed inside the gas station store. Was he looking for me?

I must have been gone for too long. He was worried.

Quickly, I ran forward toward the truck and put my ear to the side of the container again. Muffled sobs. A harsh female whisper.

My heart thudded.

There are only women inside, the demon – Mavka – whispered. *They have no thoughts other than survival.*

"I have to get them out."

The door jangled. I moved around the side of the truck.

Antonio looked up; his expression relieved. "There you are! You've been gone for ages."

I ran towards him. "Where's Ben?

"In the car, with Prue and Dexter." He peered at me, concerned. "Are you okay, Sandy? What's going on?"

"I was coming out of the store and I heard someone in this truck, crying," I whispered to him, waving him closer.

He frowned.

"Shush…" I pulled him forward, and motioned for him to put his ear to the side of the truck.

Antonio's eyes widened in horror. He stepped back immediately, checking the lock on the back of the truck. "Get Ben," he snapped. "Call 911 right now."

CHAPTER 13

It was late when we pulled into Cherry Row – the alleyway in Foggy Bottom where my Great-Aunt Marcheline lived. It had been more than three years since I'd been back.

Everything looked different. I couldn't put my finger on it. Before, when I'd lived in Foggy Bottom, our neighborhood was just a bunch of plain brick apartment buildings with narrow cobblestone paths running between them. Our block was a little bit like a labyrinth; the alley didn't run straight, instead, it was as if some maniac of a town planner had plonked a handful of similar three-story buildings haphazardly around and threw cobblestones between them for the roads.

Cherry Row was darker, more colorful and felt far more secretive than I remembered. The alleyways of Foggy Bottom were famous; close-knit communities living together in the old red-brick three story apartment buildings with alleyways running in between them, fruit trees in pots on every doorstep; devil's ivy and fat monstera vines dripping from balconies. The area, of course, had been gentrified in the last few decades, and it was lucky that Aunt Marche had bought the apartment building more than fifty years ago. What was once a ghetto for the immigrants and freed slaves who worked in the hallowed buildings of the capitol, was now a ridiculously hip, cutting-edge neighborhood.

D.C. was a compact city and we were packed in tight. No one seemed to mind, though. The alley dripped in heritage, marinated in a rich and sometimes dark history that was almost tangible in the night air; a misty beast that drifted in like the fog the suburb was named for.

Aunt Marche owned one whole small building – a three-story, cherry red brick apartment block, with two little apartments on each of the bottom two levels, and the third top floor she occupied herself. At some point, Chloe, Prue and I had all lived together, each occupying one of Aunt Marche's apartments, but since then, Chloe's dad had bought another little two-story heritage block and restored it to its former turn-of-the-century glory. Prue still lived on the second floor of Aunt Marche's building. I was glad she was going to be close.

We drove into the alleyway in silence. Ben dropped us at the front door, helped ferry eight gym bags full of gear to the hallway, gave Antonio a kiss, and left.

He had a lot of work to do. We'd left absolute anarchy behind at the gas station, and he had to go back and help the investigators piece together exactly what had happened.

I still couldn't believe how the afternoon had unfolded. Antonio had snapped the lock on the back of the truck with the pair of bolt cutters he carried around in his kit and opened up the back doors to an absolutely heartbreaking sight.

Twelve young women, some drugged unconscious, all in shackles in the back of the truck. A hard-eyed brunette took charge of the rest of the victims, explaining that they were all homeless kids and runaways, all snatched off the streets from Jacksonville, to Savannah, Charleston to Wilmington to Virginia beach, one by one, and put in chains. They were being transported to DC to be sold, she said.

We were still there answering questions when the police discovered the ragged remains of the truck's driver. I even got to see the girl's faces when they were told their tormentor had met a grisly death in the gas station bathroom. The demon inside me purred with pleasure at the sight of it.

The police made noises about getting official statements from us but made it clear they assumed some gang hit was responsible for the man's demise. They didn't even take down my full name. It was obvious that they would never even think that a busty little bleach blonde – a young mom with twigs for arms – would be responsible for that kind of carnage.

I didn't know what to think. They dismissed us, and we drove to Foggy Bottom in near-silence.

Prue and Antonio helped me unpack. Luckily, the apartment was furnished and filled with kooky things painted in odd colors: Three walls painted dusky pink and one exposed red-brick, a glittery gold ceiling, countertops of dark slate marble, the cupboards in a delicate lavender with shiny chrome handles. The appliances weren't white, either – the fridge, dishwasher and oven were all rose-gold.

I glanced into the bedroom. My bed was a huge wrought-iron four-poster, elevated so far off the ground I was going to need a stepladder to get into it. The bedroom included a little antique toddler bed in the corner of my big bedroom.

It was going to be perfect for us. I bit my lip.

"You okay, doll?" Prue patted my shoulder.

I shrugged. "Sort of. It's not every day I wake up from a coma, have a miscarriage, leave my husband, find out my best friend is a skeleton, my great-aunt is a witch and my brother is gay."

What am I, chopped liver? Mavka murmured from deep inside of me. *Mmmmm. Liver.*

"Shut up," I hissed.

Prue glanced at me sharply. "What was that?"

"Nothing." I wrinkled my nose. "I'm a bit overloaded, that's all."

"Well, you'll settle in no time." She gave me a crafty grin. "You know what you need? Work. Mundane, boring, creative work."

"Oh, you think so?" I let out a slightly hysterical laugh.

"Yes, I do. You'll be happy to know that there's a chair at the salon with your name on it. You've got four days a week, that's all you need, anyway, since Aunt Marche has refused to take rent money from you. We'll give you fifty-five percent of all your takings, plus tips. Okay?"

I nodded, pressing my lips together so I wouldn't cry. Jenny gave me twenty percent and insisted on splitting the tips. For every ten dollars I made for her, I kept two dollars, and I opened and closed the salon five days a week. Jenny was a bully. I was a coward that never stood up to her.

Prue took another one of my bags and tossed it into the bedroom. "I've already enrolled Dexter at the Foggy Bottom Love Bugs Daycare, so that's probably where all your pay will go."

"How..." I shook my head. "How did you get Dexter in? There's a waiting list a mile long at every daycare in the city!" I'd checked it out one day, dreaming of a day when I could escape the nightmare I'd been living in.

Prue smiled sadly. "I've had him on the list since he was born. We've been trying to spring you from Terry's clutches for three years, Sandy."

I burst into tears.

"Whoa." Prue patted my arm awkwardly. "Hey now. Calm down. It's okay. Everything is going to be okay."

"I'm sorry," I sniffed, wiping a flood of snot with my sleeve. "I just didn't know how bad it was until right now. They all told me I was lucky; I had a lovely son, a handsome husband, a good job at a great salon. They were all running me ragged. I feel like Cinderella escaping from her step-mother's clutches. Thank you," I held her gaze meaningfully.

"Don't thank me." She slapped my cheek gently. "Thank Aunt Marche. You better head upstairs and say hi to her, then come by the salon so I can break you in. Chloe's there, holding the fort; she's desperate to see you."

"Hold on." I held up my hand. "Chloe."

"What about her?"

"Break it to me gently. What is she?"

"What?"

"Vampire? Siren?" I racked my brains, trying to think what kind of supernatural creature she might be. She liked glitter and pink. "Fairy?"

Prue chuckled. "She's a dumb blonde, that's what she is. She's one-hundred percent human, Sandy. She's got no idea about any of that stuff. She doesn't See anything. Occasionally, she gets a bit confused about all the giant wolves running around Foggy Bottom, and she once saw Scarlett mid-feed, but she brushed it off as a weird giant pet trend, and Scarlett getting kinky. She's the most innocent person in this entire city."

Suddenly, Prue gritted her teeth. "We've got to help her figure out who her blackmailer is, too, and stop them. She doesn't deserve this."

I gave her bony arm a squeeze. "We will. You've already saved one of your friends today. You're on a roll."

CHAPTER 14

My Aunt Marcheline took up the whole top floor of the apartment building. The grand internal staircase – elaborately carved oak, with trees etched into the balustrade and newel posts made up of sneering woodland creatures – led right up to her lavender-painted door. I climbed the stairs wearily, feeling the burn in my thighs, eyeing the fairies and gnomes carved into the staircase, wondering how in the hell I'd never suspected she was a witch before.

I reached the landing, hitched Dexter higher up on my hip and knocked. The door swung open with a puff of smoke. "Darling!"

I coughed, waving my hand to clear the haze away from my face. "Aunt Marche?"

She reared out of the smoke like a Valkyrie riding a storm – tall and regal, with a riot of curly dark gray hair and a mass of wrinkles around her wickedly twinkling blue eyes. My great-aunt looked much younger than a woman in her early seventies, but the thick aura of wisdom that she wore like a trench coat also made her seem centuries older. She thrust forward out of the cloudy doorway and clutched my shoulders in her hands, a huge smile on her face. "Oh, blessed be, my dar–"

She froze. Her icy-blue eyes widened; her little mouth dropped open. "Holy fuckballs!" She abruptly plucked her hands off my shoulders as if they were burning hot.

I frowned. "Everything okay, Aunt Marche?"

There was a pause. She stared at me, her expression wary, then… a flash of something else passed over her. Shock? Guilt, maybe?

Before I could decipher it, she plastered a smile on her face. "I'm just so happy to see you, darling!" She grinned at Dexter. "You too, chuckles." She tickled him under the chin. He laughed, and swatted her with his truck. "You settled into your apartment okay?"

I nodded. "It's like coming home." My chin wobbled. "I should never have left."

"Oh, honey, no," she said, slinging an arm around me. She pushed me inside her apartment. "I'll make some tea."

She led me to the kitchen table and sat me on a chair, and busied herself filling a kettle. I looked around her apartment.

I'd been in her home hundreds of times before, but I'd never really seen it. I wasn't even sure if I'd ever properly looked before. In my memory, it was a normal old lady's house, with funny smells, sewing kits in old cookie tins, lots of knick-knacks, and too many cats.

Now, it looked fascinating, like an Arabian souk, a bazaar somewhere in a rich, ancient land. Thick persian carpets were piled high in random places. The ornately carved and tiled coffee tables were covered in brass trinkets, fat wax candles and leather-bound books. The apartment was lit by glowing antique bulbs, some floating in mid-air, apparently untethered. Portraits of ancestors lined the dark-paneled walls – they were everywhere, staring down at me from every spare inch of space, some eyeing me beadily, looking down their noses, and others smiling at me saucily.

One of them winked at me. I stared at the portrait hard, but he didn't move again. Maybe I imagined it.

I put Dexter down. He immediately scuttled off to confront Aunt Marche's fat tabby, Winifred. She raised herself onto her back feet and batted him like a boxer.

"No claws, Winnie," Aunt Marche said, her back turned.

Winifred whipped her tail around and waved her paws in Dexter's face. He mirrored her, wiggling his butt, and squared up, raising his fists.

"I don't think that's a good idea, buddy," I told him.

"Meow," Winifred said.

I giggled. "That almost sounded like she actually *said* the word 'meow' instead of actually meowing."

The cat looked at me. "What did you want me to say, you dundering clotplate? I doubt your little crotch goblin understands the flowing prose or intricate witticisms of Shakespeare's pastoral comedies. I'm a little limited on material, here."

My mouth dropped open. I stared at the cat.

She looked back at me. "Meow."

"Dexter's fine," Aunt Marche said. "Leave them." She poured hot water and carried a steaming pot over to the table along with two china teacups. "Winifred won't do harm. She can't," she added, somewhat cryptically. "Now, darling." She settled herself into a chair languidly as if she was sitting on a throne. "Let's chat."

I sighed. Mentally, I shoved the fact that the cat I'd patted every morning for three years could talk – and, apparently, give out some serious sass – and sat down at the kitchen table opposite Aunt Marcheline.

She looked at me.

I stared back at her.

She raised her eyebrows. "Is there anything you want to tell me?"

"Oh, you first." I nodded at her sarcastically, taking a sip of tea. It was scalding, and burnt my tongue. "Is there anything you want to tell *me?*"

She sighed out again. "If I told you I was a witch, you wouldn't have heard me. People only hear what they want to hear, you know." She waved her hand around the kitchen, gesturing at the open pantry in the kitchen. The shelves were lined with amber bottles filled with strange things; tiny eyeballs, fat dust puffs, oddly shaped bones.

I gazed around again with wide eyes. Now that I looked at her kitchen properly, she might as well have a sign above the range hood that said THIS KITCHEN BELONGS TO A WITCH.

I looked at the counter. There was a pewter cauldron on a stand. A *cauldron*.

"This stuff has always been here." Aunt Marche shrugged. "You couldn't See."

"That's a terrible excuse. You should have told me. Aunt Marche, you're a witch. You're *the* witch, apparently."

She shrugged. "To be fair, I never hid it. You just didn't want to Hear."

"That's bullshit. I would have heard you if you'd told me."

"Okay. Tell me this." She shifted in her chair, leaning forward, fixing me with her merry bright blue eyes. "Are there any witches in Emerald Valley?"

"No." I shook my head. "Not that I know of, anyway."

She gave me a smug smile over her teacup. "No?"

"No." I was sure I'd never seen anything like this in Emerald Valley.

"You've never ever seen that witch's shop across the road from your old salon?"

I frowned, trying to think of what had been across the

road from Curl Up and Dye. "Oh. You mean Marigold's?" I wrinkled my nose. "No. Marigold is just a local, and her store is a herbal beauty and remedy..." I trailed off.

An image of the pretty blonde shopkeeper swam in front of my now apparently-open eyes. Billowing black gown, covered in crystal necklaces and sacred talismans, triquetra tattoo on her wrist. Pointy hat.

"Oh." I exhaled heavily. "She's a witch."

"A very powerful witch. We are first cousins once removed, in fact. Her mother was my cousin."

I furrowed my brow. "Is that why we don't speak of family very often? Is that why my mom doesn't talk to you?"

Aunt Marche made a face. "Hoo boy. There's a lot to unpack here, darling." She flicked her wrist over and looked at her watch. "I really don't have enough time to cover it, Damon is going to be here in a minute. We've got a Live to do."

I barely heard her. "It doesn't make sense. We've got witches in our family. My mom has always been so religious," I said wonderingly. "She hated you *so* much. When I told her that I'd found you, and I was going to be staying with you while I studied, she flew into the most unchristian rage I'd ever seen before in my life."

I'd originally come to D.C. with a friend from church. It was the only way my mom was going to let me go in the first place. We'd been living at a Christian hostel, when after a month, my friend abandoned me to go on a mission to Kenya, leaving me alone in a dorm with a bunch of very weird young people who scared the absolute crap out of me. I'd packed my bags, ready to go home, and my new beauty-school friend Prue introduced me to Aunt Marche the next day. I was blown away when I found out she was my great-aunt, and that she wanted me to stay with her.

My mother was horrified. She ordered me home, threatened me with all sorts of things. It was the first time in my life I grew a spine and defied her, though. She never said why she hated Aunt Marche, apart from the fact that she wasn't a Christian, so I promised I'd chip away at her and try to convert her. My mother clammed up and refused to speak on it ever again.

"Why did she hate you so much? It can't just be that you're not a Christian."

"The sins of the father," Marche said sadly. "And the mother too, actually. It's a horror story that we've never been able to escape."

I fixed her with a stare. "Tell me."

She studied me carefully. Finally, she shrugged. "Another day, perhaps. I'm just so happy to have you home. I don't want to darken the day with horror stories." She leaned back, and gave me a smile. "Let's talk about you. How have you been, darling?"

"Oh, I don't know. Living the dream?" Dexter barreled into my chair and bounced off. Him and Winifred had started running races around the living room. He shook himself, and took off again.

Aunt Marche took a sip of her tea. "Tell me what happened."

Briefly, I outlined what had happened in the last few days, leaving out any mention of the demon that possessed me. Mavka had been quiet – so quiet I almost forgot she was there. It was almost easy to believe she'd been a figment of my imagination. I finished the story, recounting the part about my collapse and miscarriage, watching a soft empathy bloom in my aunt's eyes, then, a wary suspicion.

"... And then my bone-monster best friend and my gay brother rescued me," I trailed off.

Marche eyed me carefully. "That's it?"

I met her gaze. "That's it."

"Nothing else?"

I shook my head.

Marche leaned in, inspecting my face carefully. "There's nothing else… you want… to tell me?"

I sat very still, watching her expression. There it was again. A faint fear, a touch of guilt crossed her features.

"Aunt Marche?" I peered at her closely. "What have you done?"

Her face went black. "What do you mean, darling?"

I opened my mouth to speak but a knock at the door cut me off. "Marche?"

A young man with a very strong Californian accent loped into the kitchen with a grace so laid-back, it was almost unconscious. He flicked his long, sun-kissed hair out of his tanned face and adjusted his tie-dyed t-shirt over his board shorts. "I hope you're ready for the most bodacious, most kick-ass live spellca–"

He spotted me and trailed off. "Whoa," he said in a surfer dude voice. He stared at me blankly for ten seconds. "Greetings, or should I say, merry meet, my friend." He held out his hand for a fist-bump, and pulled me into a one-armed hug. "You must be Alessandra."

"Sandy." I stared at him. He talked like a ninja turtle.

Deep within me, I felt Mavka stir. She sniffed, grimaced, and settled back down. It seemed that this guy didn't have any evil bones in his body that she could eat.

The young man nodded, using his whole body. "I'm Damon," he drawled. "I'm your aunt's acolyte."

"Acolyte?"

"Her most devoted and loyal student of witchcraft."

I turned deliberately to stare at Aunt Marche. She stared back innocently. "What? Am I not allowed to have students?"

Winifred barreled into the kitchen, bouncing off an armchair and a side table, tearing through to the living room.

"Avast, merry youngling! The footrace is done, I am the victor! Bow to my magnificence, you bull-pizzle brat!"

Dexter pounded after her, thumping his little feet on the floorboards. He was fixated on the cat; he wasn't paying attention to where he was going. He almost ran head-first into a chair.

"Whoa, young dude," Damon's long arms reached out and plucked him by the back of the shirt at the last minute. He held Dex up in the air, using his momentum to zoom him around like an airplane. "You've got some speed in those two little feet."

Dex giggled, and made a cute *vroom* noise.

Aunt Marche smiled at me. "Damon is also studying environmental science at Georgetown. He lives in the apartment downstairs, on the second floor, next to Prue. His mom is an old coven sister from Santa Monica, she's sent him here to learn the craft." She inclined her head towards me. "He's also a qualified manny."

I frowned. "Manny?"

"Yuh," he nodded. "A nanny. But a man nanny. A manny." He hitched Dexter higher, still holding him by the back of the shirt, and swung him around. "Vrooooom!"

"O... kay?"

"He can watch Dexter for you at nighttime, while you're out." She gave me a knowing smile. "Doing whatever you need to do."

She was up to something. I was too tired to decipher what she meant. I sighed. "Aunt Marche... Damon... listen, thanks. I appreciate the offers, but... It's been a very long day, and it's about to get longer. I have to head to the salon to catch up with Chloe and Prue." I stood up and stretched. "I might as well get completely settled in." The sooner I got into a routine, the sooner I could forget my nightmare life as Terry's slave.

"Leave Dexter here," Aunt Marche said fondly, watching Dex whiz around the room on the end of Damon's long arm. "I want to get to know my grandnephew."

"Oh no, it's fine," I said. Damon was a stranger, and I would never leave my kid with a stranger, even if he was my aunt's student. "I don't want to impose."

Deep within me, Mavka sniffed in disgust. *That boy is such a pure soul he makes my stomach churn.*

I almost rolled my eyes. "Okay, fine," I said, watching Damon hold Dex upside down by the feet as he squealed with delight. "That would actually be really handy." I turned to meet Aunt Marche's eyes. "We're not done here, though. We've got more to talk about."

She sighed. "Yeah. I guess we do. There's some things I need to tell you, Sandy," she said wearily. "Come back when you're done, okay?"

CHAPTER 15

I hurried down Cherry Row, following the cobblestone road as it curved around the red-brick buildings. Dodging lemon trees in pots and ducking under trailing vines from low balconies, I took a left, then a right, then finally I was standing on the wide sidewalk of Lumiere Avenue, in between two fat-trunked trees.

Chloe and Prue's salon was on a tiny strip of shops almost smack-bang in the middle of Foggy Bottom, hidden from tourists; a very pretty little one-way street lined with big red maples and scarlet oaks. Lumiere Avenue was a hidden gem, a secret sparkling diamond of commerce. When I lived with Aunt Marche, I used to love coming to this shopping strip. It felt almost like another world, like stumbling into a fascinating alleyway in a fancy rich foreign city street, pretty, clean, quaint, and cutting-edge chic. There was a little bakery and cafe, an organic grocer, a florist with the most exotic displays of blooms in the windows, Scarlett's wine bar, the Dog and Bone pub, and Dominique's, a ludicrously expensive designer that sold bespoke women's clothes.

Prue and Chloe's salon stood in the middle, a stunning

little storefront with blonde wood and floor-to-ceiling glass. The layout was open plan, white polished concrete floors, smooth marble benchtops and vaulted wood ceiling. Over the exposed wooden beams, the girls had engineered a hydroponics unit and netting system, so that the ceiling was a riot of lush green leaves and flowers. It was like looking up at a jungle canopy.

Jenny's salon back in Emerald Valley was all white plastic. It had been cluttered with dusty magazines and discarded promotional haircare cut-outs. It smelled like perm solution.

My heart gave a flutter as I walked into the salon. I couldn't believe I would be living in Foggy Bottom, and working here. It felt like a dream.

The salon was empty; it was past closing time now, and the girls would be finishing up. Chloe stood at the podium near the door, staring at the computer screen and chewing on her bottom lip. At the jingle of the doorbell, she looked up. Her big eyes went round when she saw me.

"Sandeeeee!" She scooted past the podium and charged into me, almost tackling me to the ground. "Oh, Sandy! I'm so glad you're here," she wailed in my ear.

I squeezed her back. "Are you okay, Clo?"

"I got another message," she sobbed. "Another one of my nudes."

"Oh, no!" I pulled her back before her wailing popped my eardrums, and looked her in the eye. "Was there a message?"

She nodded. "Yeah." She pulled out her phone from her back pocket and showed me, sniffing.

The message displayed under the photo of Chloe, topless, smoldering to the camera with one finger in her mouth. *Just be a good girl and everything will be fine.*

My eyes popped. "Good grief, Chloe," I muttered. "That's the worst porn-star pose I've ever seen in my life."

She snatched the phone back. "I was drunk, okay? I was

just messing around and having fun. No one was supposed to see it!"

"I know, honey," I patted her shoulder. "Did you call the number?"

She nodded. "I tried again the second I got the message. It's switched off. No voicemail. The number is different from last time, too. Whoever it is, they're using burner phones for almost every message."

I exhaled heavily. That indicated whoever was doing it was experienced at this sort of thing.

Prue popped up behind Chloe. For a second, I saw her true form; a terrifying animated skeleton rearing up from behind my best friend. I blinked, and it was Prue again; long silky black hair swishing around her pale, sharp boned features.

"That's bad news," she declared. "I looked into it – it's damned hard to get even one burner number these days; most providers need all sorts of ID and security checks. This fucking douchecanoe has gone through three numbers already. Not only do they know exactly what they're doing, they've probably done this sort of thing before."

"I was thinking the same thing." I looked at Chloe. "No demands so far?"

She shook her head. "None. I just don't understand it."

"Hmmm." I was no detective, and I could be stunningly blind when the people closest to me wanted to lie to me and manipulate me...

But I was very good with mysteries. Out of the three of us, I'd always been the most tenacious, the most doggedly determined to work out any riddle. I was excellent at social media stalking, I knew how to cross-reference friend lists to look for connections, and I was fabulous at wheedling information out of fusty old bureaucrats. I'd figured out who was loading our dumpster with junk after piecing together a bunch of ripped up papers and making a few phone calls to various tradespeople, while Chloe charged around like a golden retriever and Prue screamed at all the other shop owners like a premenstrual banshee. I'd tracked down the guy who ghosted Chloe after he gave her chlamydia, so Prue could yell at him.

I probably shouldn't have given her his work address. Then again, he shouldn't have given Chloe chlamydia. I'm sure he'd get another job eventually.

Chloe's blackmailer was a mystery I was sure I could work out.

I bit my lip, thinking. Why would they go to all this trouble and not make any demands? The hacker had let Chloe know exactly what he'd got. He'd picked out the most embarrassing photos to send to her.

I looked up, meeting her eyes. "This has gone on for a couple of weeks, right?"

She nodded.

"He's giving you time to realize that there is nothing you can do about it," I said. "He would have known you'd go to the cops. He wants to give you enough time to understand that you're helpless to stop it."

She let out a little wail. "I fucking hate this."

"He's keeping his language deliberately vague, too," I went on. "The threats are all implied, and could be easily argued against in a courtroom." I let out a little growl of distaste. "This guy knows exactly what he's doing. It's all a big build up to something."

"We don't know if it's a guy," Chloe sniffed.

Prue looked disgusted. "Of course it's a guy."

"It might not be," I said.

Of course it is, Mavka declared from inside me. *All men are inherently evil.*

I froze. The demon bristled inside of me.

A stunning realization hit me. I turned away so the girls couldn't see my face.

Mavka could sense evil intentions. She could literally hear it when someone was planning to do something terrible.

She'd heard that sex trafficker loud and clear, even when he'd been doing something as benign as choosing a drink from the refrigerator. She heard him as clearly as he'd been shouting his sins from the rooftop. She could help us.

Of course, she'd also eaten the man's liver, and sucked his blood off my own fingernails. Inside me, she shivered in delight at the memory.

I pursed my lips, and spoke to her internally. We're going to have to have a talk as soon as we're alone. We need some ground rules.

I am the scourge of the wicked, she growled sulkily. *I don't do ground rules. Ground human flesh, yes. Not ground rules.*

Chloe and Prue were bickering beside me. "He hasn't asked for anything! How do we even know he wants something?"

I cleared my throat. "It seems that the aim right now is just to scare you. Maybe that's the only goal," I shrugged. "That would be the best-case scenario. Maybe it's someone you've pissed off, and they've concocted this elaborate plan to keep you miserable and scared, and they have no intention of doing anything with the photos or your contacts."

"That's the *best*-case scenario?" Chloe wiped the tears from her cheeks, sniffing dramatically. "Best case scenario sucks."

"Worst-case scenario is that he blackmails you, and asks you to do something dangerous. Or illegal. Or dangerous *and* illegal. Right?"

She howled like a sad dog.

I rubbed her shoulder. "Honey, I think it's always good to

think of the worst-case scenario. So you can mentally prepare for it, and so you can understand that if the worst happens, you're not going to die, and we're still going to love you."

"We need to start checking out the suspects." Prue said, cracking her knuckles. "I need to punch someone."

I like her, Mavka murmured.

"Okay. We need to make a list." I walked towards the back room, a large space at the rear of the salon where we stored equipment, supplies, and occasionally downed coffee in between clients. Shelves lined one side of the room, with boxes of hair color and bottles lined up on the mixing bench. A large whiteboard on wheels displayed our client stats, random appointment notes and product information. A little table with a couple of chairs served as the place where we dumped our handbags. We barely ever sat down.

I flipped the whiteboard over to a blank side and took out a marker. "Okay. Let's go over the suspects we've already talked about. Suspect number one. Which one is it? Who do you think is most likely to have done this?"

"If I was going to go on gut feelings, I would say Linus Brady," Chloe said. "He's the guy from the lobby group who is courting my dad for donations. He's a total creep; I get the worst vibes from him. The way he looks at me..." She shook her head and shuddered. "His politics are disgusting, too. He heads up a group called Freedom for Families – they're all uber religious conservative. I'm talking not only complete abortion bans, but contraception bans, too, and making it harder for married couples to get divorced. The last time I overheard a conversation with my dad and Linus, they were laughing about a new bill he'd proposed that would make it easier for under eighteen-year-olds to get married. Said that it would open up my dad's dating pool."

"Ergh," I shuddered. "That's some crazy Taliban stuff, right there."

Prue gave a bitter laugh. "It's *American* stuff, Sandy. Child marriage happens all the time here in the good old U.S of A."

I frowned at her. "What? No. It can't. There's laws against that."

"Child marriage is legal in 43 states."

"*What?*"

"Oh, yeah." She looked disgusted. "Most states have a minimum age of sixteen years old, but some states have no lower limit at all. At *all*," she emphasized.

I shook my head. "That can't be right."

"It is. You just need parental permission, and a judge's stamp of approval. You can imagine there's a lot of conservative judges very happy to grant permission for their fifty-five-year-old golf buddy to marry a thirteen-year-old girl. It happens all the time." She sighed heavily, and shuddered. "It's easy to brush it off as some sort of barbaric foreign country's practice, but it happens here, in America, every day."

Thirteen. Holy crap. I was twenty-five years old, and I'd only just stopped doing everything my mother told me to do. At thirteen, I was a good little obedient girl. Imagine being forced by your parents into marrying a middle-aged man at thirteen. In America!

"Wow," Chloe's face was frozen in horror. "That's… that's…" She swallowed. "I did not know that. And Linus Brady is working on a bill that will take away the need for a judge's approval. Parents will be able to sell their children like objects."

I gave a shudder, and shoved the concept out of my head. "Okay," I took a deep breath. "Linus Brady is Creep Number One. I'll put him on the top of the list. See if you can find out when your dad is meeting with him next, Chloe, and we'll drop in and check him out. We might get some clues." I wrote Linus Brady - Creep Number One on the whiteboard. "Who's next?"

"If we're looking at motive, I would put my mom's assistant next. Her name is Gretel." Chloe wrinkled her nose. "That woman is hell on wheels. She's pushing for my mom to run for office. Her personal motto is 'the ends justify the means.' She'd blackmail me to put pressure on my mom. And she'd release my nudes just for publicity. She's a tyrant."

Prue pursed her lips and looked away. "I like to think she's just proactive."

"Well, we shouldn't discount her just because she's female." I wrote on the whiteboard: Gretel - Hell On Wheels. "Let's drop in for breakfast with her tomorrow," I said. "I'd like to see your mom, anyway."

Chloe's mom was the opposite of mine – soft, gentle, intelligent and understanding. Watching Chloe with her put more cracks in my relationship with my own mother than anything else I'd ever come across. She'd shown me what a loving mother-daughter relationship could be like.

I flipped the marker in my hand. "Who is next? You said some regular from Scarlett's had been hitting on you?"

Chloe wrinkled her nose. "Yeah. His name is Keith – he's an accountant. He hits on me every time we go into Scarlett's. Won't take no for an answer. He's always brushing past me at the bar and rubbing up against me." She shuddered. "He's a creep."

I wrote it down: Keith - Creep Number Two. "What about the bartender from the Dog and Bone?"

Prue made a face. "That's Corey. He likes to flirt with Chloe, but I doubt it's him." She smirked cryptically. "He's on a tight leash."

I peered at her, inspecting her expression carefully. "How do you know?"

She tossed her hair. "I just know."

"Is it anything to do with... I don't know... his boss? The *owner* of the Dog and Bone?" I stared at her pointedly.

Max, the owner of the English-style pub, was in his early forties, a grizzled, hard-muscled man with close-shaved blond hair, constant stubble and thick-striped scars on his arms. I'd noticed that the bartenders and wait staff deferred to him with a very wary respect. I'd wondered on more than one occasion if Max was an ex-con, Irish mafia, or something. Most patrons in the pub seemed a little scared of him.

Except Prue. Nothing scared Prue.

And Max had a thing for Prue. While most men were scared off by her bristly nature and sharp tongue, Max seemed to enjoy their verbal sparring matches. When Prue advised him on the location and force by which he could shove his opinion up his asshole, Max would laugh, and asked if she'd oblige to perform the service herself.

Prue shrugged. "Max wouldn't hire a bartender that he couldn't keep in line." A crafty look came into her eyes. "Put him on the list, though. We can head to the pub tonight to check him out."

I chewed on my lip, watching her. For the first time, the thought entered my mind that she actually enjoyed clashing horns with Max, too. "Okay." I flipped the marker again and wrote on the board – Corey Bartender: Major Flirt. "Who's next?"

Chloe chewed her lip. "That's all I can think of."

"What about the guy you're seeing?"

"Gregory?" She frowned. "He's a sweetheart. It can't be him. He's been so great about all this."

Prue put her hands on her hips. "I thought you were planning on dumping him?"

"No," Chloe said in a little voice. "Well, okay, I was. He's lovely, it's just... I need this support right now, Prue, okay? He knows all about the hacker. He was revolted by it.

Honestly, he seemed so horrified that anyone would do this to me."

Prue curled her lip. "You were going to dump him because he's love-bombing you."

"It's intense! Yes, I was going to back away from him, but I need the support, okay? He's nice. He's lovely!"

I shook my head. "Okay, okay. I'll put him down anyway, I want to cover all bases." I wrote on the whiteboard: Gregory Hedge-Fund, Love Bomber. "Who are we going after first?"

"We can start now," Prue said, nodding towards the door. "Antonio and Ben are going to meet us at Scarlett's later, so we can check to see if Keith, Creep Number Two, is there." Her eyes twinkled. It was only a little shine, but I saw it. "And head to the Dog and Bone to see the Major Flirt Bartender."

"Okay." I snapped the lid back on the marker. "We've got a plan."

CHAPTER 16

I wasn't dressed for going out. I'd swapped my shirt when we'd first arrived at Aunt Marche's, binning the slightly bloodstained black top I'd been wearing, and had shrugged on a plain white t-shirt, but I was still wearing distressed jeans and ankle boots that I'd worn all day. There was no chance I was planning on heading home for a shower and a wardrobe change, however. I could feel a total mental breakdown hanging around the periphery of my psyche, and I was worried that if I was left alone to think for five minutes, they'd find me rocking in a corner, muttering insanely and pulling at my hair.

So much had happened. If I stopped moving, I might have to process it. Processing it meant thinking about it, and if I started to think about all the insane things that had happened in the last forty-eight hours, I'd need Eric the Social Worker to come and lock me up, just like Terry wanted.

I plastered a smile on my face as Prue locked the salon doors. "Right," I said, grinning like an idiot. "Let's keep moving."

We walked a few steps over the road to Scarlett's, the small, uber-chic wine bar just opposite the salon. The folding windows were wide open, displaying the whole bar.

I peered inside. Apart from one well-dressed older man sipping brandy, and Scarlett herself, lounging behind the bar, languidly dragging on a long, thin cigarette in clear violation of the city's non-smoking laws, the bar was empty.

Just then, I remembered that Scarlett was a vampire. I was *not* ready to deal with that information. Not just yet. "Let's head to the Dog and Bone, first," I said. Prue and Chloe agreed, and we changed course, heading down past the florist and the cafe, toward the Dog and Bone.

Whereas Scarlett's displayed the whole bar openly to anyone passing by, the Dog and Bone was far more discreet. All the windows were painted white, like the exterior of the building, so you couldn't see inside. The heavy oak doors were firmly shut, and there was no welcoming signage, no advertisements for beer, nor any other indication that you were allowed to set foot in there.

Unperturbed, with no hesitation, Prue pulled the thick brass handle and stalked in.

I held the door open for Chloe. "Go on, babe."

She took a quivering breath in, visibly steadying herself. "I can't believe we're doing this," she muttered.

I grabbed her hand and squeezed. "It's okay. *You're* okay. We've got you."

"I'm so glad you're here, Sandy. I've missed you so much."

"You too, Clo." My voice wobbled.

She ducked her head and walked into the pub after Prue.

I held the door, pushing it open a little further, glancing down the street as I turned to walk in.

I hesitated. There was a man on the other side of the street, just past the salon, walking this way. Something about him drew my eye.

It might have been his posture, the way he walked with his back straight and his head held high, it made him seem much taller and bigger than everyone else around him. It might have been the way his broad shoulders moved, slightly tense, arms thickly corded with muscle under hard skin, poised, ready for anything, even though he held them apparently relaxed as he walked. It might have been the clothes he was wearing – tan chinos and a light-blue shirt with the sleeves rolled up to his elbows, displaying tanned forearms, an outfit that would have looked chic and stylish on anyone else, but with what looked like scars on his forearms, made him look sexy and dangerous.

It could have been the expression on his face, maybe. He was objectively *ridiculously* handsome. A photo of him would have displayed model-good looks, with slightly disheveled sandy blond hair, carved cheekbones, a chiseled jaw, and full lips that made my heart pulse in a very foreign way. The man would have been almost pretty in his younger days, but he was older now, in his late thirties, maybe, and he was rougher, more grizzled. His expression was too knowing, like he occupied a space no one else could see. His eyes were hard, and filled with darkness.

Too old for you, I told myself firmly. Too old… Too damaged…

His presence was enormous; it took up almost my whole vision. In a busy street bustling with late-afternoon traffic, the only thing I saw was him, and I couldn't look anywhere else. He was a stick of dynamite striding down the street, he was C4, an atomic bomb, dangerous and about to explode into violence at any point.

My eyes caught the glint of a chain around his neck; it pulled at something heavy. My gaze followed the line of the chain down to inside his shirt, and I could see an outline, a faint bulge.

A badge. He was a cop.

I waited for Mavka to growl inside of me. She was silent.

Suddenly, the man looked up; his flinty-blue eyes locked on me. He'd caught me staring at him.

Holy shit.

I froze. All at once, I understood the saying 'deer in the headlights'. This man *was* headlights. He was the sun shining directly in my eyes. I took a breath, blinking furiously, trying to break the spell.

"Are you coming, Sandy?" Chloe had backtracked from the bar.

I nodded, wrenching my eyes away from the man in the street. "Yes." I stepped inside, letting the door slam shut behind me.

CHAPTER 17

The Dog and Bone was a small pub, with a large square bar right in the middle. On the left side, plush sofas and well-worn armchairs were arranged around tables, some occupied with beer-swilling young people talking and laughing happily. On the right were tall tables and high stools, where you could have steak and fries or fish chowder special. There was room for bar stools on the other side, where you could sit and have a drink, alone, or chat to the bar staff if you were so inclined.

Prue had wasted no time. She already had a mojito in front of her, and she was loudly berating the bartender, a tall young man with long, shaggy red hair.

Chloe and I joined her, mid-tirade. "I swear by all that's holy, if I find out that it's you, Corey, I'll rip every single one of your pretty red hairs off your head."

He chuckled lightly, both amused and a little confused. "Prue," he shook his head. "She hasn't even given me her number. I've asked almost every week for six weeks, and she's said no. How could I possibly be sending her awful text messages? What have they been saying, anyway?"

Prue lifted her chin. "None of your business. Just tell me the truth, Corey. Have you been sending Chloe messages?"

"No! Like I said, I don't even have her number."

We should eat him, Mavka growled.

I tensed. Oh, good grief. Did we catch the blackmailer on the first go?

I muttered to Mavka under my breath. "Is he evil?"

Of course he is evil. We need to eat him.

Oh, Lord have mercy.

Corey the bartender turned to face Chloe. "Sorry, babe, it wasn't me, and I'm sorry if some weirdo is sending you dick pics."

I prodded Mavka internally. Is he lying?

She didn't answer. She just gave a low growl.

Chloe blushed. "It's not dick pics, Corey. It's a little more… sinister."

He cocked his head. "Is there anything I can do to help?" He glanced down at Prue, and gave her a suspiciously meaningful stare. "Is there maybe something that Max could do to help?"

"No." Prue said bluntly. "I don't want Max's help with anything."

I cleared my throat, getting Corey's attention. "Hi."

He smiled down at me. "Hi, new girl. I'm Corey. What can I get you?"

Prue snarled. "You can get fucked, that's what you can do. Stop hitting on my friends, asshole."

He turned to her and chuckled. "I'm a bartender, Prue. I'm supposed to ask what she wants." He gave me a wink. "So, what will it be? Sex on the beach? A slippery nipple, perhaps?" He hooded his eyes, smoldering down on me.

I will have your spleen on a bed of parsley, Mav hissed.

"Uh… I'll have a glass of pinot gris, thanks," I muttered,

staring at my feet. Internally, I poked my demon again. Is it him? Is he the blackmailer?

She growled in response. *I must feast.*

Okay, that's not exactly confirmation. Was she being deliberately evasive?

Corey had his back turned, pulling wine out of the fridge behind him. I stared at the back of his head, willing her to answer me. Is it him?

Prue, it seemed, was doing the same thing, but out loud. "You're a pervert, Corey. You hit on anything with tits that walks into this bar. How are we supposed to believe you're above sending creepy messages to Chloe?"

He laughed and uncorked the bottle, pouring it into a glass. "I'm just friendly, Prue. A little flirty sometimes, maybe; it's good for tips. You should try it."

"Over my dead body," she hissed at him.

"Interesting choice of words." He winked at her.

His member would be delicious in a red-wine jus.

I flinched. Urgh. No. Just tell me if it's him or not!

She was silent.

I needed to talk to her directly. "Sorry, girls, excuse me for a second," I muttered, and I turned and hurried away before either of them could offer to come with me.

Kicking open the bathroom door, I quickly checked the stalls to make sure I was alone. The ladies were empty, as usual; the men in this bar usually outnumbered women three-to-one. I faced the mirror and took a deep breath. "Mavka."

Red smoke filled the mirror; suddenly, she was standing right there, exactly where I was, staring right back at me. She lifted her chin and eyed me haughtily. *Why are we not plucking out his kidneys already?*

"You didn't answer my question. Is he the blackmailer?"

She tossed her wild black hair back. *Why does that matter? He's evil. I must feast on him.*

I slumped. "So it's not him?"

There was a long moment of silence. *No.*

I sighed, and put my hands on the basin, staring down at the black drain in front of me. That was a definitive – albeit, very reluctant – answer. It looked like I could cross Corey off the suspect list.

Suddenly, the thought occurred to me that maybe he was something worse than a blackmailer. Mavka said he was evil. He might still need to be brought to justice somehow. I glanced up, peering at her. "So, how evil is he?"

He's a man, she hissed, hair flying wildly around her.

"Yeah, yeah. All men are evil." I parroted her, chuckling darkly. "Is this my superpower? Misandry?"

He is a hound. He will mount any woman if given half the chance.

"What do you mean, 'half the chance'? Does he not get consent?" I tilted my head, glaring at her. "He's a rapist? Is that what you're saying?"

There was another long moment of silence. *No*, she said sulkily. *He obtains the necessary consent.* She looked up and glared back at me. Her voice shook with fury. *But he has no interest in a woman after he has mounted her.*

I stared at her. "Wait." I pointed my finger at her in the mirror. "You think he's evil just because he's a fuckboy?"

Of course, she said dismissively. *He cares nothing for a woman after he has impaled her.*

"Okay," I waved my hand. "Can we dial it down just a notch? Can you… maybe… try not to use inflammatory language, like 'impaled'? You mean slept with. Or made love to. You're confusing me with all the hyperbole. I was almost ready to let you eat him."

Her eyes lit up. *Really?*

I rolled my eyes. "He's not evil, Mavka. You can't eat him."

All men are evil.

"Is my brother evil? Or Ben? You were suspiciously quiet around both of them…"

She laughed scornfully. *I'm sure it's just a matter of time.*

"And Damon? What about him? You said he was disgustingly pure."

She bristled, and looked away.

I took a deep breath. "Listen." I leaned forward, fixing her with a stare. "Can we go ahead and agree that evilness is a spectrum? I can't let you eat Corey just because he likes to hit it and quit it. He's not evil, okay? Yes, it's shitty behavior, but it's not evil."

Well. That's your opinion, isn't it?

"Oh, God." This demon was going to be the death of me. I shook my head, thinking. "Let's try this. Imagine a sliding scale. A spectrum. On one end is Damon; and on the other end is the dude at the gas station. Terry is right in the middle."

She huffed, crossing her arms over her chest. *This is juvenile.*

"Where does Corey sit on the spectrum?"

She pouted. *I suppose... somewhere in between Damon and Terry.*

"Right. Okay. Now we're talking. I need some ground rules, Mav. I need some boundaries, or else I'm going to get confused. Can we agree that you are not allowed to eat anyone less evil than Terry?"

She threw up her arms. *No deal. Your husband was a cockroach. He deserved to be eaten.*

"He didn't force me to do anything. I think that's going to be the yardstick, Mav." I fixed her with the hardest stare I could manage, considering I was looking at a terrifying vengeful spirit in the mirror. "Yes, he manipulated and schemed and took advantage of me, but he didn't force me. Can we just agree that the yardstick is the use of physical force?"

She huffed out a breath. *Fine. That is acceptable.* She stretched her arms up and out, a terrifyingly huge figure in the mirror, and sighed with satisfaction. *This is a big city; a cesspool of dark masculine energy is waiting to be consumed here.*

I blinked. "Er, good. I'm glad we got that straight."

Indeed.

"Thank you for letting me know the truth about Corey. I appreciate it."

She looked up at me, bemused. *I am truth, as well as justice. To acquire vengeance we must have truth.*

I smiled at her. "Does that mean you are incapable of lying?"

She sniffed haughtily. *Lying is beneath me. I have no use for it.* With that, she whirled around in a vortex of red smoke, and disappeared, leaving only the reflection of short, curvy, blonde me.

"Ha." I couldn't help but grin at my own reflection, proud of myself for figuring out a little more about the demon that shared my body. Then, I grimaced and smoothed down my hair. I might be crazy; none of this might be real, but at least I could create some boundaries around my delusion.

* * *

I WALKED BACK into the bar feeling both more confident and more certifiably insane, to find Prue having a screaming match with Corey.

Or, rather, Prue was screaming, Corey was chuckling to himself, with Chloe slumped on a barstool, her face in her hands.

It took a second for Prue's illusion to snap in front of my

eyes; at first, I saw a terrifying bone monster snapping its fingers back and forward in front of the bartender's eyes. "How come you keep asking her, then? You can't take no for an answer, is that it?"

Corey poured her a shot of tequila and slid it over to her. "Of course I can take no for an answer." He turned to wink at Chloe. "She just hasn't said no yet."

"Well, she's saying no now." Prue's illusion slid back in place; my beautiful friend with the long, silky dark hair lifted the shot glass in her fingers and threw it back, slamming the glass back on the bar. "You better get her a tequila shot to say sorry."

He crossed his arms over his chest and stared down at Chloe. "Are you saying no, Chloe?"

"Uh, yeah, I guess," she mumbled into her hands. "No for now, anyway."

Prue turned to glare menacingly at her. "Chloe.... No. You cannot have anything to do with these people."

She shrugged. "I don't have a problem with him."

I frowned. "What's going on?"

Prue lifted her chin, glaring at Corey. "They are animals."

He laughed out loud. "Party animals. Sex animals."

A gruff voice cut through his laughter. "Corey."

The effect was instantaneous. Corey ducked his head down, stooping lower, as Max, the owner of the Dog and Bone, came up behind him. "Sorry, Max," Corey muttered. He disappeared so fast to the other side of the bar I would have missed it if I'd blinked.

Max fixed his gaze on Prue and stalked up towards the bar with an uncanny, feral grace at odds with his muscly bulk. "Prue. To what do we owe this pleasure?"

She made a face. "Pleasure for you; not for me. I'm on a mission, buddy."

He cocked one eyebrow, a slight smirk on his face. "Is that

right?" He turned, and looked directly at me, his hazel eyes carefully assessing me. "Alessandra Montefiore." He smiled wolfishly. "It's wonderful to see you again."

"It's Sandy," I said automatically. "Sandy Becker, now."

God, I remember being in such a hurry to change my name to Becker when I married Terry. An unexpected flush of shame ran through me when I realized how stupid I'd been. I'd done it with the echoes of taunts in my ears; a hundred times some kid had teased me about my foreign-sounding name. I remember being pleased to introduce myself to people in Emerald Valley by my new, generically white married name. Now, listening to my own real name rolling off Max's tongue, I realized how beautiful it sounded.

Prue frowned at me, obviously having the same thoughts. "Is it? No, honey. No. You're going back to Montefiore."

I nodded dumbly. "Yeah. I think I will."

Max turned his attention back to Prue. "A mission, you said? What mission would that be?"

Prue glanced at Chloe. Chloe nodded.

"Someone's blackmailing my girl here," Prue explained. She leaned forward over the bar. I smirked, clocking her new body language. "They've gotten hold of some of her nudes, and they're threatening to post them online."

"Hmm." To Max's credit, he didn't say anything victim-blamey. He tensed, though, a feral glint in his eye. "And you think it might be one of my boys?" He tilted his head. "Corey?"

"Your boys are dirty dogs, Max," Prue purred. "They think with their dicks. I wouldn't put anything past them."

"I keep my employees in line," he said, leaning over the bar to meet her stare, his voice low. "You know that."

"You have a lot of faith in those hormone-filled psychopaths that you call *employees*."

"No. I'm just supremely confident that they will obey me."

I tensed, mentally prodding Mavka inside me. Some of the words Max was using sounded very... mobster. Forceful, even. We'd made a boundary about the use of force.

Mav didn't flinch, though. She was decidedly uninterested. Weird.

Prue languidly took a sip of her cocktail. "Maybe you don't know your employees as well as you think."

Max gave a low chuckle. "Oh, I do." He leaned forward and put his hands on the bar; his forearm muscles bulged. "I know my employees inside and out."

"Inside and out, huh? Sounds like you have trouble with boundaries. Just like Corey seems to. He's got a thing for Chloe, and he keeps hitting on her."

"Ahh, my dear," he leaned forward, his eyes hooded, staring at her seductively. "He's got a crush. You can't blame him for flirting. She hasn't turned him down yet, either, so I'm not going to discipline him for it." He smoldered at her. "And I know you enjoy flirting with me, so I'm not going to stop either."

"You're a dog." She curled her lip.

"And I'd do anything to jump your bones."

I snorted. "Bones?" I giggled.

Both Prue and Max snapped their heads towards me. A yellow light rolled over Max's eyes.

Just then, it hit me. My mouth dropped open. "Oh! Oh my God!" I started laughing. Once I started, I couldn't stop. Oops, here comes the mental breakdown!

I clutched my sides. My abdominal muscles started to spasm, but it only made me laugh harder.

Max turned back to squint at Prue. "She can See?"

Prue rolled her eyes. "Sandy, can I talk to you for a second?" She grabbed my elbow. "Max, get Chloe a shot. Reassure her that none of your boys did this to her."

"I am your humble servant," he rumbled, leering at her.

CHAPTER 18

Prue led me back to the bathroom and slammed the door. “Right, girl. Pull yourself together.”

I couldn’t stop laughing. “It’s just so insane, Prue! Come on! All these years of him making jokes about wanting to jump your bones... he’s a werewolf, isn’t he?”

“Urgh, Sandy. Yes, he’s a werewolf.”

I dissolved into laughter again. “That’s why he’s got such a raging hard-on for you. He’s a...” I snorted, trying to get enough air in my lungs. “He’s a dog. And you're a *bone!*”

She giggled, and punched me on the arm. “You have no idea how many times I’ve heard that one. I swear, the mileage they get out of dog-with-a-bone jokes...”

“That’s why you always got free shots here! That’s why all the line cooks literally salivate whenever they see you.”

She shook her head. “Well, yeah. But they’re line cooks, Sandy. Line cooks are horny bastards. That’s their default mode.”

“But they’re wolves, aren't they? This whole bar is staffed with werewolves.”

"Yeah," she huffed out a breath. "I'm surprised you didn't notice before. They all sit up and beg when I come in."

I dissolved into side-splitting laughter again, and found I couldn't stop. Hysteria had well and truly set in. Prue giggled along with me for a moment, but her laughter ebbed away slowly, replaced by a look of concern. "Sandy…"

I collapsed on the floor.

"Sandy, are you okay?"

I wiped away tears. "Obviously not." My voice cracked; I started crying.

She got down on the floor and pulled me into her bony arms. "It's okay, babe. It's okay. Everything is going to be okay. I know it's a lot to absorb, but you'll get there."

"It's not that," I sniffed. "It's… Honestly, Prue, out of everything that's happened to me today, the thing that gets me the most is finding out that Terry deliberately got me pregnant so he could manipulate me into marrying him. You being a skeleton, Aunt Marche being a witch… even these guys all being werewolves; it all pales in comparison to losing my dream." I wiped my cheeks. The tears just wouldn't stop. "All I wanted was for Terry to be a good husband, a good father. I wanted him to be the loving, happy, fun guy he pretended to be. I wanted a simple life and a family."

She rubbed my head and made soothing sounds.

"The honest truth is this: I felt like the baby I was carrying was going to be the thing that flipped my dream into action," I sniffed. "I'd been so stubborn about everything. When Terry got me pregnant, he made me so many promises. I put the vision of being a little soccer-mom, and a salon owner, with a happy life, directly into my head, and I *wanted* it."

"I have to admit, I was confused about that," Prue muttered. "I wondered why you stuck it out with Terry for so long. You're so tenacious when you want something."

"I was chasing something that didn't exist," I sobbed. "He promised me the dream, and I got a nightmare."

"He fucked you over, Sandy. Let him go. Find a new dream."

I sighed deeply. "It's all I ever wanted."

"You didn't make those decisions in a vacuum, Sandy." Prue's voice had a little bite in it. "Can I just remind you that you've been brainwashed by your mom for the last twenty-five years?"

I paused. "What do you mean?"

"Having a family and looking after them was *her* dream, not yours. Babe, the world has just completely opened up for you. You can do whatever the hell you want."

"Oh," I said in a little voice.

"So... what do you want?"

To consume the flesh of evil men.

I cringed, and shushed the demon inside of me. "Oh, good grief, I have no idea! Prue, it's insanely hard to get rid of the idea that all I should aspire to is to have a family."

"You can still have that, you know. You're only twenty-five, doll."

"Single mom," I said sadly. "I'm going to be dodging my own mother's calls forever. According to her, all single mothers are useless evil sluts who can't take care of their families. I could do without the lecture about how I'm going to burn in hell." I chuckled lightly, albeit a little bitterly.

Prue peered down at me. "That's... that's not really funny, love. It's not normal, you know."

I glared up at her. "Your mom left you to drown in the bath and bound your spirit to your dead body," I said. "Your mom is not exactly normal either."

She shrugged. "Touché."

"At least I've got Dexter." I wiped my nose. "I might not

have the handsome, helpful husband or the three hellraiser children, or my own little salon..."

"You've got me," Prue kissed me on the forehead. "And Chloe and Aunt Marche and Antonio."

I sat up abruptly. "Oh, shit! I forgot! My fucking brother!" I scrambled to my feet. "Talk about emotional overload." Suddenly, I was desperate to see him. "Him and Ben will be at Scarlett's, is that right?

"Yeah." Prue got to her feet and stretched up, smoothing her hair and adjusting her skimpy top. "We might as well head over there. I think we can cross Corey off your list. Although I might go back and yell at that dog a little more before we leave."

"Creep Number Two might be at Scarlett's," I said.

We walked out of the bathroom and back to the bar. Instantly, I noticed that the atmosphere in the room seemed to have changed. The air was charged with expectation, with a sense of danger, like something was about to explode.

Warily, I walked up to Chloe. "You okay, babe?"

She looked up at me; her eyes were slightly bleary. "Er-yuh." A half-dozen empty shot glasses were lined up next to her elbow. "Immmagood." She sat up straighter, knocking one of the glasses off with her elbow. "It's not Corey," she said, brushing her blonde hair off her face.

"Yeah, we know." Prue shot a glare at Max, who stood facing away from us, talking to someone on the other side of the bar, with his huge arms crossed over his chest. His posture was odd; he held himself stiffly, as if he were on-guard. Prue frowned. Max didn't turn to look at her.

He moved to the side slightly, and suddenly, I could see who he was talking to.

My breath left my lungs in a sigh before I could stop myself.

The cop.

He sat there on a barstool, like a god trying to pretend to be an ordinary man. He was as explosive now as he had been when I saw him walking down the street; a veritable supernova of whirling, intense energy wrapped up inside the lithe, handsome grace of an apex predator. Everything about him was a contrast; a contradiction; his hyper-sexy full lips and strong, chiseled jaw, his beautifully tailored light blue shirt and the thick scars on his muscular forearms, the power and knowledge in those flinty blue eyes, and the way he commanded Max's attention like a tsar. Rasputin himself would bow down.

I waited for Mavka's growl. She would eat every single part of this man and suck his bones dry.

I bit my lip. Maybe I could negotiate with her on the terms of 'sucking his bones dry.'

But Mavka was oddly silent.

Prue plucked at my sleeve, eyeing Max apprehensively. She couldn't see the cop from where she stood, but she could obviously feel the change in atmosphere just like I could. Chloe was already too drunk to notice. "Come on, Sandy. We should go."

I nodded dumbly, and let her lead me out the door.

CHAPTER 19

The cold night air blew out the fog in my head as quickly as we used the blow dryers to blow away our farts in the salon. It did Chloe some good, too. As we walked out of the Dog and Bone, she threw back her head and breathed in deeply. "Oh, God," she moaned. "I shouldn't have done four shots in a row."

"No, you shouldn't have," Prue snapped. "That was silly, Chloe. We're meant to be on the job. We're investigating."

"Like Charlie's Angels," she hiccupped.

I chuckled. "Exactly," I said. "Just like them. Except none of us speak any other languages, other than English."

Chloe shrugged. "I can't even speak English properly."

"And none of us can shoot. I don't even know how to hold a gun. I can't abseil out of a helicopter. Or do a split."

"I got kicked out of Tae Kwon Do when I was seven," Prue said morosely.

"What for?"

"Biting."

I giggled.

"Honestly," she huffed. "I don't see the point in martial

arts, anyway. They have no real-world applications. I mean, if a giant, violent asshole was trying to grab me right now and haul me away, do you think he's going to stay still long enough for me to get into the right posture for a front kick? No."

"I tried Jiu Jitsu once," Chloe piped up. "I got cuddled very firmly on a mat for half an hour. It was actually quite nice."

I grinned at her. "Did you learn anything, though?"

"Yeah. The only thing I learnt was that if someone bigger than me decided to beat me up, well," she shrugged. "I was going to get beaten up."

"That's what I mean!" Prue punched her on the shoulder. "They *should* have been teaching me how to bite! It would have been way more helpful. Luckily," she said, baring her teeth, "I've learnt how to bite properly since then. I've had to teach myself." She ran her tongue over her slightly pointed canines. "We should teach other women how."

"You're not wrong, Prue," I smiled at her. "We should do our own martial art. We'll call it the Art of the Red Flag."

"Our first move would be to teach how to recognize when someone is going to cause you harm."

Amateurs, Mavka muttered scornfully.

I ignored her. "Then, where best to bite. How to use coconut oil as a lubricant so you can wiggle out of anyone's grasp. Then, the art of running away."

"Or we could just invest in some tasers," Prue said.

"That could be included in our study units. How to use a taser."

We strolled slowly past the cafe. The florist next door had a seriously insane window display; a huge flowerbud in a pot which looked suspiciously like the alien plant from Little Shop of Horrors. I paused to look at it for a moment, waiting to see if it would move, slightly disappointed when it didn't. It had been that kind of day.

Prue tugged me away. "Come on. Antonio is sitting in the window."

Scarlett's Wine Bar had filled up in the forty minutes that we'd been inside of the Dog and Bone. The place was packed with beautiful professionals in sharply tailored suits and cocktail dresses, as well as handsome older men and women in structured gowns and flamboyant jackets that screamed fashion, money and influence.

Antonio sat on a chair looking out towards the street, with a glass of wine in front of him, chatting easily to the couple next to him. Out of uniform, I got to marvel at how insanely handsome my brother was. He got the lion's share of handsome Italian good looks in the family; the strong jaw, thick brows, and roman nose. He wore a plain, crisp white shirt, just a fraction too tight.

Ant spotted me and raised his glass. "Chablis, darling?"

Chloe waved merrily. "Hi Ant! Where's Ben?"

"He got held up at work. He might not make it."

"We'll be over to join you in a second." Prue tugged us both inside. "Remember," she hissed. "We're supposed to be on the job." She craned her neck, looking at the throng of people that filled the little space. "Chloe, is Creep Number Two here?"

"Uh…" Her eyes quickly darted left and right. "I don't think so."

"Chloe…" Prue's voice held a warning.

"Urgh, fine." She deflated a little. "I'll look properly. He's just so horrible, though. I really don't want to talk to him."

"You don't have to." I rubbed her arm. "Let's just see if he's here. If he is, we'll all go over and ask him some questions, maybe threaten him a little. See if he breaks."

Prue cracked her knuckles. "If not, then we'll break him."

"Or bite him," I winked at her.

"Either way is fine with me."

Chloe, using her superior Nordic height, scanned the room, and slumped. "He's here. Over there, in a booth at the back."

Prue squared her shoulders. "Let's go."

Keith – Creep Number Two – certainly looked the part. Creepy. He looked like a short guy trying to cosplay as Loki. Longish, greasy black hair slicked back, pale skin, pointed chin. His suit was impeccably tailored, screaming of money. It did a fabulous job of making him seem taller and more muscular than he really was.

There were two other men in the booth with him, sitting on his left. From the way Keith positioned himself, with his whole body turned so he could face them, leaning forward, eager expression on his face– he was comparable to a Jack Russell dog trying to appease his master.

The man to his left looked a little younger; mid-twenties, perhaps, with hooded dark eyes and heavy brows. He wore a black shirt with a blood red tie. He lounged back in the booth, relaxed, not looking at Creep Number Two at all. An arrogant smile sat on his full lips.

The other man was hard-faced, blond, craggy, and dressed in a suit jacket with a shirt underneath. His eyes swept the bar restlessly, never settling on anything.

We walked forward. The younger man in the middle noticed us first; his eyes expertly sweeping up and down, appraising the three of us like he was inspecting horses. The arrogant smile turned into a smirk.

Creep Number Two – Keith – turned his head to see what his friend was looking at. "Chloe!" He rose up in the booth. "Babe. How are you doing?"

The younger man shifted in his seat, resting his elbows on the table. "Who's your friend, Keith?"

He grinned happily. "Kane, Ivan, this is–"

Prue cocked her eyebrow and sneered at him. "We're not your friends, Keith," she snapped.

The younger man – Kane, raised an eyebrow. "Look here, sugartits. Who the hell do you think you–"

I didn't hear anything else. A blinding rage overtook me; I froze, unable to move, unable to even see. Blackness flooded my vision as Mavka seethed inside of me.

Evil men, she hissed. *Hearts of darkness, souls filthy with abuse and sin. Their flesh calls to me, I must consume them!*

Her sudden rage was so violent I could barely pay attention to what was going on around me. I could hear Prue's voice, as if screeching from the end of a tunnel. "We're the ones that are going to fuck you up, that's who we are! Keith, you little bitch, where did you get Chloe's number from?"

The men laughed, slow, lazy and condescending.

I must feast! They are oppressors, they are torturers.

"Okay, little Skinny Minnie," Kane chuckled. "Sure. Oh, you're a firecracker, aren't you?"

"I don't have Chloe's number," Keith whined. "I haven't sent her any messages."

Their blood is thick with evil intent, Mavka snarled. *I must quench my undying thirst with it.*

I clamped down on her hard, trying to get a hold of myself. I spoke to her internally. Okay, Mav, calm down.

I am the tempest that sweeps clean the evil of men. I will not *calm down.*

Is it him? Is it Keith that's blackmailing Chloe?

Worse.

I blinked.

The three men at the table were all staring at me. Keith raised his eyebrows. The arrogant one – Kane, laughed softly. "What's wrong with your friend, Skinny Minnie? Is she retarded or something?"

Rage blinded me again.

Calm down, I hissed internally.

That wasn't me. That was you. Apparently, while you need a second opinion on rape and murder, you draw the line at him using slurs.

There was an awkward silence. I realized everyone was still looking at me. I chuckled nervously. "Uh, excuse me for a second." I turned and shuffled my way through the crowd of people, ignoring Chloe calling behind me.

The bathroom was a single, thankfully. I slammed the door shut, locked it, and took a deep breath. The little stall's walls were painted a dark ruby red; the floor was black tiled. A single candle illuminated the space.

I almost rolled my eyes. All trendy bars were the same. For some reason, it was chic to pee in near-darkness. An ornate gold mirror above the basin threw my reflection back at me, then swirled with red smoke. Mavka appeared, impossibly tall and glaring at me with undisguised fury.

Why are we here? We must feast. Their kidneys are thick with the evil of their many sins.

"Yes, yes," I nodded. "I just wanted to get a few things sorted out, first. Now, which of them are evil?"

All of them.

I raised my eyebrows. "Is Keith the one blackmailing Chloe?"

She pouted. *No.*

Damn it. I guess I could cross Creep Number Two off my list. I frowned, and rubbed my chin. "Back to the drawing board, I guess."

Rallying again, she pointed a long, black nail at me. *As I said, they are worse.*

"Worse, how?" I peered at her in the mirror.

They are men, she hissed, turning away from me and crossing her arms.

"Mav." She didn't turn around. "Mavka..."

She huffed out a breath.

"Remember our spectrum of evil?"

Reluctantly, she nodded.

"Where do they sit on the spectrum?"

They are all different.

"Well, what about Keith?"

He has darkness in his heart. His hatred for women is blooming like the corpse flower.

"Can you... I don't know... be a little more specific? It would be helpful."

Fine, she sighed. *You have no patience for the beauty of the language of vengeance.* She stared at me peevishly. *It is tiresome.*

"Please," I begged her. "I can't let you eat people that haven't done anything yet. Has Keith done anything illegal?"

Not yet, Mavka admitted. *But he will. And the two men beside him are so filthy with corruption their blood sings to me. I must devour it.*

"Can you focus, please? What is Keith planning on doing?"

He is buying pills from them that will render his feminine victims unconscious, so that he might spend himself on them without their knowledge.

I frowned, translating her words in my head into something I could understand. "He's buying date-rape drugs? Is that what you are saying?"

She nodded imperiously. *Your friend Chloe is one of his targets.*

"Oh. Sheesh." I shivered. "He's getting them from those other two? Kane, and... the blond guy? Ivan, was it?"

The candle in the bathroom flickered; her eyes flared brighter red. *Their diabolical intentions waft off them like vapor. Oppression, destruction. They seek to enslave women; they seek to control them. They think of themselves as Kings.*

I waved my hand impatiently. "Okay, okay, Mav. Listen. What have they actually done?"

She crossed her arms again sulkily, and huffed out another sigh. *Organized crime, you peasant. The one on the end, Ivan, is a mob enforcer. He has committed multiple murders, and he has terrorized women on many occasions.*

"And the other one? Kane?"

His heart is made of darkness, she hissed. *His intentions are that of a murderous tyrant.*

"There you go again with the intentions," I muttered.

She arched a brow, staring down at me. *You promised I could eat anyone on the scale from Terry upwards.*

"And these guys definitely are as bad as the Sex Trafficker Guy?"

They will be.

"Urgh, Mav. It's not enough! Intention to commit crime isn't as bad as actually doing the crime.

Of course it is.

"It's not!"

Well, they've already done some heinous stuff. It's worth a little evisceration, at the very least.

I took a deep breath. "Mav..."

They have illegal pharmaceuticals on them, child. They have illegally manufactured pharmaceuticals and unregistered firearms on their persons right now. I can give you a list of exactly what they are holding. They are currently committing crimes. In fact, all three of those men are planning on dropping those pills into the drinks of women in this very bar, so they can take them home and rape them. They have the women picked out, she snarled.

I exhaled heavily, letting the breath leave my body in a whoosh, and bent over the basin.

The door handle rattled.

I flinched. "Just a minute!"

I looked up, and met her eye. "Okay."

She perked up. *I may feast?*

I shook my head. "No. Mav, listen. If these guys are as bad as you say they are, I need to get them arrested. They need to be held to account."

I will suck the marrow from their bones. That *will hold them to account.*

"Mav, no. Can we…" I rubbed my brow. "Can we please do this my way this one time? You can't go around eating every man who has shitty thoughts about women, okay?"

I can, actually. It's my nature. You might as well tell a bird not to fly and a fish not to swim and a cat not to be such an asshole.

"If they're planning on doing something terrible, let's get them caught in the act," I said. Their victims need closure, okay?"

She eyed me beadily. *I think you underestimate the evil in their hearts.*

"Yes, yes, I get it, they're men, they're evil," I nodded, placating her. This bitch thought that she deserved to eat Corey because he was a fuckboy. "Look, thanks for the information. Let me run with this one. I'm sure we'll find someone else more evil to eat by the time the day is over."

She turned her back on me with a huff and disappeared into a cloud of red smoke.

* * *

I LEFT the bathroom and hurried back through the crowd, thinking furiously. I needed the police. Luckily, I knew someone. I made a beeline towards the folding windows. Antonio was still draped over the windowsill, chatting to young people walking by. "Ant," I tugged at his arm. "Is Ben here yet?"

"He's not going to make it. He's too busy." My brother

frowned deeply. "What am I, chopped liver? We haven't caught up properly yet."

"Uh, yeah. I was just… wanting to get to know the man you were dating, that's all. Y'know, to show you how cool I was with your lifestyle choices."

He snorted. "Okay, you weirdo. He can't come, though. He's been recalled for more questioning about that little incident with the trafficked women and the dead trucker dude in the bathroom." He made a face. "Apparently they gathered up all his body parts and tallied them up, and there are a lot of his insides missing. Organs, to be specific. Ben's gone to answer some more questions about it."

"This morning?" I exhaled heavily. "That was only this morning?" It felt like a whole lifetime had passed.

"Time flies when you're having fun gathering up body parts, I guess." Ant took a sip of his wine. "Here. Try this merlot."

I took a sip. Almost immediately, I felt the alcohol hit my empty stomach, and all of a sudden, I was tired. Bone tired. My lids felt heavy, almost impossible to keep open. For a wild second, I thought I might have been drugged myself.

Nope. Just good wine on an empty stomach. I took another deep sip and sighed heavily.

Even though I couldn't see my friends, I could hear Prue over the buzz of the crowd. She was threatening to set Keith's car on fire. Keith protested his innocence. Kane was laughing like he was genuinely amused. The third guy, Ivan, was deathly silent.

I needed the police. Pulling out my phone, I stared at the screen blankly. My lock screen was a photo of Dexter licking a window. My heart squeezed. I missed my little guy.

Concentrate, Sandy.

I could call in an anonymous tip to the local police department. Those dirty bastards might be long gone before the cops showed up, though. Slunk off to their lairs with unconscious women slung over their shoulders.

I needed a cop *now*.

Tiredness overwhelmed me, fogging my vision again. One more thing. I'd do one more thing, then I'd go home and sleep. "Do you have a pen on you?"

Antonio nodded and pulled a little black permanent marker out of his pocket. "Here."

I scribbled a note on a cocktail napkin. "I'll be back in a second. Can you keep an eye on Prue and Chloe for me?"

Ant peered over the heads of the crowd. "Uh. I don't think Prue needs any help." He narrowed his eyes. "Although someone might want to take that charcuterie board knife off her. She looks like she's going to stab someone."

I quickly scuttled out the door, my mind curiously blank and focused. I didn't really want to think about what I was about to do.

I ran the few yards past the florist and cafe, and hauled open the door to the Dog and Bone. Like Scarlett's, the pub had filled up in the last half an hour.

He was still here. I could feel him; the atmosphere in the bar was still charged, still excited and on-edge. I barely even had to look for him, I was drawn to him like a moth to a flame. He sat at the bar, as still as a marble statue, contemplating a thick-cut crystal glass of amber liquid in front of him.

I didn't hesitate. I was too tired to think about it too much, anyway. I dropped my note in front of him, right next to his glass, and walked away as fast as I could.

CHAPTER 20

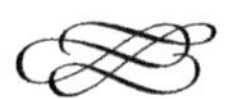

Antonio insisted on walking me home. As soon as I got back to Scarlett's, he took in my haggard, dead-eyed expression, and all but ordered me home to bed.

I refused at first. I didn't want to leave just yet; I wanted to stay and make sure that the Three Creepy Amigos got what they deserved. I wanted to be sure that the insanely, unbearably sexy cop in the Dog and Bone followed through on my tip.

I wanted to see him again, too. From a distance. He scared the shit out of me.

For some strange reason, I was positive he would come. He was waiting for something in that bar, I was sure of it. That man's presence was thick with anticipation, like a powder keg begging for a match. Even his scent was explosive; dangerously sexy, like whiskey and fireworks.

I wanted to see what would happen, but I knew if I stayed I'd have to answer his questions. And there was no way in hell I could even think straight looking into those flinty-blue eyes.

Chloe had already disappeared. Unbeknownst to us, she'd texted Gregory, the Love Bomber, demanding French fries and burgers, and he'd swooped straight in to Scarlett's, picked her up and took her straight to Burger Edge.

I was a little annoyed. I wanted to question him, but I figured any boy that would drop what he was doing and rescue the girl like that was either fantastically romantic, or just a little pathetic and desperate.

Prue harangued the Three Creepy Amigos for a little while longer, but ran out of steam after Chloe left. She was satisfied Keith wasn't Chloe's blackmailer.

"He's too much of a weasel," she said. "And he doesn't have the patience for that sort of thing. If it was him, he would have demanded a blow job by now."

I agreed with her. After extracting a promise from her that she'd stay away from Keith's creepier friends, I left her, deep in argument with a couple of stockbrokers.

So Antonio walked me home, gave me an awkward but nice hug, and told me he'd catch up with me in the morning.

I was dreading walking up three flights of stairs to collect Dexter from Aunt Marche's apartment. I was so tired I thought my legs were going to fall off. To my surprise, as soon as I let myself into the ground floor of the building, the door of my little apartment opened and Damon stuck his head out.

"Sandy, dude," he drawled. "He's in here. Little man got the yawns big time, so I brought him down and put him to bed."

It took me half a second to decipher Damon's California Surfer accent. "Oh," I said. "Dexter's in bed already?"

"H-yuh. I rubbed a warm flannel over his face and hands and he put his jammies on himself. I got two pages into The Hungry Caterpillar before he fell asleep."

I bit my lip; tears welled up in my eyes. "Thanks." My voice came out in a rough whisper.

"Aunt Marche wanted me to tell you to come up to talk to her," he said. "She said there was something she wanted to tell you."

I nodded, and blinked. A tear overflowed and ran down my cheek.

Damon peered at me. "You okay, Sandy, doll?"

"Uh, yeah," I walked into the apartment, blinking furiously to clear my eyes. In the corner of my enormous room, on the beautiful antique toddler bed, Dexter lay fast asleep. His pajama buttons were done up all wrong, and he'd put his night-time diaper on backwards. I stared down at him; more tears welled up in my eyes and I quickly brushed them away.

Terry never put Dexter to bed. He didn't have the patience. He'd either hype the kid up so much that he got wired and overtired and wouldn't shut his eyes, or he'd get bored and annoyed, and just shut the bedroom door on him, leaving Dex to cry himself to sleep. It broke my heart so much that, like everything else, I just did it myself. "It's just... it's just that..."

"He's a great kid," Damon rescued me.

"The best," I said vehemently. "He's the best kid. I love him with all my heart and soul. I wish–" I swallowed the lump in my throat. "I just wish I could have given him the life he deserved."

The last vestiges of my dream burned away and flew off, like ash into the wind. My old life was gone. It was a shitty life, but I'd held on to so much hope that it could be exactly like I wanted, eventually. A handsome, helpful, happy husband. Three hellraiser children, and a business that fulfilled me, both creatively as well as financially.

"Naw, Sandy..." Damon nudged me. "You already gave

him everything he could possibly want. He's got you." He shrugged. "That's all he needs."

A sob escaped my chest, and suddenly, I couldn't stop crying. Damon pulled me into a very chaste hug and patted my back gently, in exactly the same way he would soothe a distressed toddler. I held onto him and cried and cried.

Mavka didn't make a sound.

CHAPTER 21

Breakfast with Linda – Chloe's mom – was a bust.

Gretel, Linda's assistant, was indeed Hell on Wheels. Pushy, loud-mouthed and snappish, wearing the most hideous denim overalls and striped sweater combo which made her look like an overgrown Chucky doll. She never tore her eyes away from her phone, and she never stopped haranguing Linda on strategy and alliances.

Mavka, surprisingly, was completely silent the whole time. We stumbled through a breakfast of waffles and orange juice in Linda's spacious kitchen in Columbia Heights, listening to Gretel bitch about rival candidates and polling figures. She paced back and forth in the kitchen in her socks and Birkenstocks, barking into her phone and using annoying buzz phrases like 'crystal-clear messaging' or 'paradigm shift' and 'move the needle.'

Several times, she suggested Chloe's mom should use underhanded tactics to smear her rivals. She was awful, and I could definitely see her blackmailing Chloe to get what she wanted.

Although, from what I could tell, the only thing she

wanted was for Linda to succeed. Linda was her hero, that was obvious, and while she was probably happy to stick the knife into her rivals, I doubted she'd go so far as to hurt Chloe.

When I excused myself so I could go to the bathroom and interrogate Mav, the demon advised me that she couldn't tell whether Gretel had evil intentions or not, because she was a woman.

I have no idea what her plans are, Mavka said, blithely inspecting her long black nails. *Her current incarnation is one of female energy, so I do not know.* She gave an idle shrug. *And I don't really care. To be honest, she could be planning on slaughtering the whole of congress, and I wouldn't raise an eyebrow. Only twenty-eight percent of them are women anyway, so she'd be doing my work for me. It's not my business,* she added. *Gretel might be evil, but at least she's not a man.*

"Seriously, Mav? Just because she's got a vagina, you don't care if she's evil?"

She pursed her lips. *Oh, she's definitely evil. Did you see she's wearing socks and sandals together?*

"Mavka. Come on."

I cannot read her. But if that outfit is anything to go by, the only danger she presents is carpel tunnel from making you sign too many petitions.

I rolled my eyes, gave an overly dramatic exasperated huff, turned my back on her and slammed the bathroom door on the way out.

Prue met me in the hallway. She grabbed my shoulders and looked me dead in the eye. "Sandy, we need to leave immediately, or I might punch that woman in the mouth."

"Okay... I don't blame you, but why, exactly?"

She frowned. "She keeps asking me to help with the Asian-American demographic, and if I can record a message of support in Cantonese."

Prue's family had been in America since the gold rush in the mid-eighteen hundreds. Her grandmother sounded even more California surfer-dude than Damon did. Despite Prue being able to trace her American heritage back almost two hundred years, and the fact that her great grandmother had native American blood, some assholes still occasionally told her to go back where she came from.

"Oh," I said out loud. "Well, she found the fastest way to piss you off."

"The irony doesn't help. If anyone could actually see me properly..." She sighed. "I keep asking Aunt Marche to put an off-switch on my permanent illusion so I can scare the racists, but she won't do it."

Just then, I remembered I forgot to head upstairs to talk to Aunt Marche last night, like she asked me to. She said she had some things to tell me. I'd have to head over after work. "Gretel's not racist, though... is she?"

"She saw my face and 'othered' me," Prue said. "It's a microaggression. It's not as bad as outright racism, but there's always that insinuation behind it; the suggestion that I don't come from here, and I'm not really American." She frowned. "White people don't get it, and they probably never will."

I thought about it. My grandparents had come from Italy, more than one hundred years after Prue's great-great grandparents had. No one ever asked me where I was from. I think if anyone ever did ask me, I might be a little confused. If people *constantly* asked me where I was from, I'd be insulted.

"I kind of get it," I said. "But I don't understand. No one ever understands this stuff until it happens to them." I grinned. "I remember Jenny went to Paris for a week on vacation – she came back absolutely spitting mad because every single French person was rude to her, and called her an ignorant American, and told her to go back to where she came from."

Prue raised a brow. "Based on what you've told me about her, I'm sure she did a bunch of stuff to deserve it."

"Oh, absolutely. So yeah, you're right, it's not the same. I think she caused a fuss in a few stores because she didn't get why she had to change her money to Euros. She honestly thought she could use U.S. dollars and get normal change back. She complained at the Louvre because the line was too long. She complained about the Mona Lisa, said it was too small, and demanded to see the bigger version."

Prue giggled. "What a fucking idiot."

"She's been calling me non-stop since I left," I sighed. "I never handed in my notice. She keeps leaving me voicemails asking when I'm coming back to work."

"Sandy, she literally left you bleeding on the floor of her salon, in a *coma*." Prue stared at me. "For a whole hour. You should go and burn down her house."

I chuckled and shook my head. "No, that's not necessary."

"It is. In fact, I'll do it for you. A little vengeance is good for you."

Exactly, Mavka purred.

Hush, you, I mentally jabbed at her. "We need to get out of here," I said out loud. "Gretel really is the most abrasive person I've ever met in my life."

"She's good for Linda, though," Prue admitted, grimacing. "Linda needs a bulldozer in front of her, and Gretel is a regular one-woman John Deere T2 crawler."

I giggled. "Do you think she did it, though? Blackmailed Chloe, I mean?"

Prue shrugged. "I don't think so. She's a crafty manipulative bitch, but honestly... it doesn't feel like something she would do."

"Hmm." I frowned. "Chloe seems to think she would. We need to try and find out. We'll have to think of a plan B."

"Well, we're not going to find out today. We've got to hustle back and open the salon." She smacked me on the butt. "Your first day today, babe! Your online bookings have popped off already."

I gave a tentative smile. "I'm nervous," I admitted.

"You'll be fine." She hooked her arm through my elbow and we walked back to the kitchen.

Linda and Chloe were still chewing on their waffles. Gretel stopped her pacing and turned to us. "Oh, there you are. Sandy, I was wondering if I could get you on this focus group."

"Not a chance." Prue pulled Chloe off her stool. "Sandy's too busy with her kid and work and settling back into D.C. Go find another white Christian girl between twenty-one and twenty-nine." She gave Linda a quick air-kiss. "We've got to run. Thanks for breakfast!"

Chloe's mom yawned, gave Chloe one more hug, and we were on our way back to Foggy Bottom in her little blue Audi. Prue, as usual, drove.

"Your first day." Chloe beamed at me happily in the car. "I've dreamed of this, you know. I've dreamed of us three working together again, in our own salon." Her eyes widened. "I think I manifested it!"

Prue muttered something from the driver's seat. It sounded suspiciously like "...Marche... did more than just..."

I looked at her sharply. "What was that, Prue?"

"Nothing," she said innocently. "Bring up the bookings on your tablet, Chloe. I want to see if I can squeeze your mom in for a gel mani somewhere today. Maybe she'll bring Gretel with her, and I can steal her phone off her and check it out."

"You'll have a hard time prising it away from her eyeballs," I said wryly.

"Yeah." Prue took a left hand turn far too fast. "We need to get better at this investigation shit. We're getting nowhere."

"Well," I said. "I thought we'd done quite well so far, for amateur sleuths. We've already crossed Corey off the list, and Keith too. Haven't we?"

"Corey, yes." Prue took a deep breath and shivered dramatically. "I don't know about Keith. He's obviously far dirtier than we thought he was."

I heaved out a sigh. "Are you going to tell me about what happened last night?"

"No!" She turned to stare at me.

"Prue, traffic!"

She pulled the wheel back into her lane. "Sorry. And no, I'm not ready to describe it yet. Honestly, Sandy… the things I saw last night…" She sighed dramatically. "I'm still processing it. I might have to process it some more, tonight, alone, with a glass of wine." She smirked. "And my vibrator."

I sighed. Prue was a drama queen, but she had told me first thing this morning that Keith and his two friends were arrested the second they stepped out of Scarlett's wine bar. And, coincidently, the two women who they'd sweet-talked into going with them to a second location had passed out during questioning, within minutes of the arrest, right there on the pavement.

At least I knew the cop followed through on my tip.

Deep inside me, Mavka growled. *Those men were sweet and ripe with unholy sin.*

I directed my thoughts at her.

And now they're in jail, Mav. Where they can face their victims, and get justice, and hopefully repent.

I could have bathed in the bloody juice of their corruption. They may be only hatchlings now, but their teeth are sharp, and somewhere close to them their sire stirs and thickens.

What the fuck are you talking about?

I felt her heavy sigh. *How would you say it? Let me rephrase.* Her voice grew babyish, mocking me. *Instead of letting the great and terrible vengeance of Mavka bring them to their final justice, it's better to pop them into a jail and let them out within thirty seconds, so they can scuttle back to their elders, who are far more corrupt and malevolent than they are.*

It seemed that Prue wasn't the only drama queen in the car.

"We're fully booked," Chloe announced, checking her tablet. "Sandy, we're tag teaming all day. You've only got one cut, a new client. A men's cut, it's just booked online now."

I grinned. I preferred to color, she preferred cuts. This was a dream scenario for both of us – we worked so well together and complemented each other nicely. "I can't wait."

She looked up at me and smiled back. "Me neither." Her tablet dinged; she looked down, and her face fell. "Oh no!"

Prue swerved the car back into our lane. "What is it?"

"Another text!" She wailed. "Oh, God, another photo. It's the joke one I took on my hands and knees... oh God, no!"

I patted her knee. "Is there a message with it? A demand? Something?"

"Uh, yeah." She wiped her eyes and clicked on the screen. "It just says this: 'It won't be long now. Stay on your knees.' What in the hell does that mean?"

Prue snarled from the front seat. "He's stringing you along, keeping you scared." Her voice dropped to a low tone. "When I find out who is sending those damn nudes, I'm going to rip off his arms and shove them up his ass."

I slid the tablet off Chloe's knee. "We'll get him, Clo," I said. "We'll find out who it is."

* * *

We got to Lumiere Avenue in record time thanks to Prue's questionable aggressive driving skills. I unpacked all my gear into a spare trolley, while Prue rubbed chamomile and lavender essential oil on Chloe's wrists and tipped half a bottle of CBD oil down her throat. Soon, she was a lot calmer, and we opened the salon together.

I couldn't stop grinning. It was everything I ever dreamed of in a working environment. No juggling multiple clients at once, plenty of service time, the highest-quality products, clean surfaces and equipment. There was no Jenny yelling at me to hurry up, no Kerry crying into the bleach powder and ruining highlights, no clients complaining that I'd cut an inch off their hair after they'd requested, quite specifically, to cut an inch off their hair.

And no Terry dumping Dexter on me so he could go fishing. No mountain of housework waiting for me when I got home.

If it wasn't for Chloe's blackmailer – and, I supposed, the fact that I had a demon sharing my body who loudly growled whenever a man walked by and insisted on being allowed to eat him because he ghosted the last girl he talked to – I would think my life was perfect.

We didn't have any assistants, but we didn't need any. We took turns to answer the phone, sweep up, and greet clients at the door. Prue, the nail wizard, had her own shit covered. Because of the type of high-end nail art she did, she only had three clients the whole day – all ridiculous wealthy, flamboyantly fabulous people who had their appointments booked months in advance.

While I worked on a new client, creating an icy blonde babylighted money piece that would grow out perfectly, Chloe came to chat with her about her cut. "I'm so glad you're here," she sighed at me when she was done with the consultation. "This is perfect. I forgot how well we work together."

I grinned at her. "I just have to finish this money piece, and it should only take half an hour processing time."

"I'll rinse the color off for you. You can check it at the basin. I think you have your new men's cut coming in a second."

A tear welled up in my eye; I blinked it back. "You're the best."

"No. You're the best."

"Cut it out, you two," Prue said from the podium, wiping her cheeks. She'd just checked out her lunchtime client; three hundred dollars for two hours work. "You're making me all sentimental."

I giggled, and went back to concentrating on my foil work.

I loved babylighting. You took the finest slices of hair and did the tiniest weaves, placing all the foils back-to-back, folding the aluminum foil neatly so they all stacked up in a pile all over the head. It was fiddly, time consuming and detailed work, but I loved it. The results were fabulous. If it were done properly, the average person wouldn't be able to tell that it wasn't natural. I took one more slice, weaved out half the hair, and scooped up the last bit of bleach with my brush, ready to saturate the foil with bleach, when I heard the doorbell jingle and Prue gasp.

"What the–"

Heavy footsteps walked towards the podium.

A low, rough, and very masculine voice floated over to my ears. "I have a two o'clock appointment with Alessandra."

I didn't turn. Only one more foil to go. I painted the hair with the bleach and carefully folded up the foil.

Chloe walked behind me; I saw her in my periphery, in the mirror in front of me. She looked up at the podium, stopped dead in her tracks and dropped the bottles of shampoo and conditioner. They both bounced loudly and rolled away.

I turned around. “You okay, Chloe?”

She seemed to have frozen. Bending down, I scooped up the bottles and thrust them back into her arms.

She was still staring at the podium. Frowning, I followed her gaze.

Prue stood there, her mouth wide open, gazing at the man who had just walked in.

My next client.

The cop.

CHAPTER 22

Prue managed to close her mouth. "Uhhhh. Did you have an appointment?"

The cop stood, arms by his side, the hard lines of his body almost relaxed compared to the coiled intensity of last night. But nothing could disguise those biceps bunching underneath that plain white shirt, the hard, wiry muscles of his forearms, the compact stomach. He wasn't bulky, like Ben, who was built like a linebacker, nor deliberately sculpted like Antonio. This was a body built for combat, for killing, every muscle programmed and primed to deliver a hard, brutal justice. And that was just his body.

His *face*, oh God, he was magnificent, an almost otherworldly beauty, like a Viking warrior, some ancient fae king just strolling off the battlefield, having slaughtered every enemy barbarian on the field single-handed. His aura felt as dangerous and as explosive as ever, like a tangible thing, a separate entity inside the salon. It felt like a lion had strolled into our workplace, rumbling deeply, and we were just supposed to act natural.

His deep blue eyes stared at Prue, assessing every movement, cataloging every little feature, watching her carefully. Those eyes had seen things. Bad things. I could tell.

"You're— you're—" Prue swallowed roughly. "You're Detective Conrad Sinclair," she finally forced out.

He nodded.

I knew that name. I knew it from somewhere. My brain was refusing to cooperate.

It was a name that had been dropped on me easily, along with a bunch of information, nearly inconsequential in a day where I'd found out my husband had manipulated me, my best friend was a skeleton, my aunt was a witch, and my brother was gay.

The way his name had been mentioned before, it was almost inconsequential. Mere additional information, nothing important. Oh, but it *was* important.

This man's name was a title. It deserved to be announced by a herald on a horse, bearing a flag of hard blue and white. Detective Conrad Sinclair. The Enforcer.

This was the cop who had rescued Antonio from the vampire. The human cop that everyone was scared of, including supes. The one with no fear. The one that seemed to be completely human, yet he was always exactly where he needed to be, perfectly executing the killing shot with godlike efficiency. The one that everyone had a crush on.

My stupid, irrational brain. I should be screaming inside, frozen with terror, freaking out: Why was he here? How did he find me? Did he know about Mavka? Was he here to kill *me?*

No. Those thoughts danced around the back of my subconscious barking for attention while my body betrayed me, forcing different thoughts to the forefront of my mind.

An insane, senseless longing. A fiery burn so intense I almost felt like I could burst into flame. Instead of being scared, I was smoldering with feverish, pathetic desire.

I'd never understood the sin of coveting before. I understand it perfectly now.

What would it be like to have a man like *that?* To have him look at me, right in the eyes. To touch his chest, to run my hands along the stubble at his hard jaw, to cling to his bulging biceps, to let my fingers wander down his waist, curling around, feeling the strength and power in that body...

Terry had been handsome; most people said so, anyway. He was tall, generic looking, and he still had all his hair.

This man wasn't handsome. He was jaw-droppingly, terrifyingly gorgeous.

And dangerous.

My hands started to shake.

Prue looked down at the computer screen and tapped the mouse with a shaking hand. "Conrad Sinclair. You booked under C Sin."

"Maybe there's something wrong with your computer."

"It's fine." She snatched up a clipboard with our client forms on them. "I could have used the warning, that's all," she muttered, a hint of her usual sass creeping in. "Sandy is looking after you today. Follow me." She turned away from him and looked at me pointedly, her eyes wide.

I needed a moment. I forced my legs to move and willed an easy smile to my lips. "I'll be with you in a minute," I said out loud. It came out in a pathetic croak. Gathering up my color bowls, I headed to drop them in the sink at the back of the salon.

Prue followed me, walking stiffly, as if she'd forgotten how to walk naturally. "What the fuck, Sandy?" she hissed under her breath, her words completely at odds with the happy, mindless smile she'd plastered on her face. She was as good as faking calm as I was, clearly. "What the actual fuck? Why is Detective Conrad Sinclair in our salon?" She grabbed a color bowl from me and started rinsing. "Bitch, you've been here three hours, and already the hottest and most terrifying man in the whole of D.C. has strolled in for a haircut with you?"

I swirled a tint brush around the bowl unnecessarily. "It's nothing to do with me. He had a booking," I said. "He booked in online."

"I can't cope with this," Prue muttered, her generic smile slipping. "I'm still not over what happened last night. When he walked in just now, I thought my fantasy was coming true."

"What fantasy?"

"Last night I had front row seats to the most sexy thing I'd ever seen in my entire life."

"Were you ever going to tell me about that?" I shook the bowl out and put it upside down to drain by the sink.

"That guy with Keith – Kane, I think his name was, and the big blond one, Ivan. Sinclair stepped up to them right outside Scarlett's as they left, and stared them down. The blond one pulled a gun. Sinclair took it off him as easily as taking candy from a baby, drew his own piece, and forced both of them on the ground with their hands on their heads, while Keith peed his pants in the doorway. Within two seconds he had them all cuffed, and had pulled a bunch of drugs and weapons from their pockets." Prue's fake smile slipped; her eyes narrowed. "And the girls they'd picked up both passed out cold. Drugged," she added. "I can't imagine what they were planning on doing with them. The guy's a hero."

I nodded. "I'm glad he got them."

Her smile wobbled again. "That could have been us, Sandy,"

I met her eyes. A whole conversation passed between us. Finally, I gave a wry smile. "Well, at least we know that Keith isn't Chloe's blackmailer. I doubt he'd be out of jail yet; he wouldn't have access to a cell phone."

"Yeah." She dried her hands. "You better get moving. This needs to be the quickest haircut you've ever done, because I'm not going to be able to concentrate with that premium specimen of masculinity in my salon."

I gave her a wobbly grin. "Girl, get the bandages ready. My hands are shaking so much I'm about to nick my knuckles bloody." I turned, walked back to my station, took a deep breath, and tried to steady myself.

I stood behind the chair and looked at him in the mirror, hoping some of his intenseness would get dulled in the reflection.

It didn't. He met my gaze steadily, not a hint of recognition or expectation in his eyes.

"Hi! I'm Sandy," I said, wincing at how perky I sounded to my own ears. I flicked my shears around in my hands nervously. "What were you thinking of doing today?"

He held eye contact and he watched me in the mirror carefully. His gaze was too intense. I felt like he could see straight through me.

Could he? Mavka had been suspiciously quiet. Mentally, I poked her. She bristled very slightly, as if she were annoyed I'd bothered her, like a cat that resented being moved off a fluffy robe while napping. She clearly wasn't bothered by Sinclair.

"Just a trim." Oh, his voice. That deep vibration thrilled right through me, almost rocking me to the core.

"Okay." I looked down at his hair, and gave myself a good talking to.

Get it together, Sandy. You're a professional. Get it done. You'll be fine. Everything will be fine.

Slowly, tentatively, I ran my fingers through his thick dark-blond locks, feeling the texture of it, exploring, relaxing slightly as I let my work brain kick in. Dense hair, fine, not too coarse, far too long to look neat and tidy. His last cut would have had to be at least three months ago; a square cut that would have highlighted his beautifully chiseled jaw and sat perfectly back from his proud brow.

I worked my fingers through his hair, getting familiar with it, exploring with the pads of my fingers, checking his skin underneath, when suddenly I felt an intense jolt of feedback from the way he'd shivered almost imperceptibly when I raked my fingernails over his scalp.

I tensed, eased back, and retracted my nails. Because if I did that again, I might explode.

Taking a tiny breath, I tossed his hair this way and that, exploring his growth patterns and watching the way the bulk of it fell as I moved it from side to side.

"Well, it looks great at this length," I said, not looking at his face. "You'd look great with it short, too, but a little longer really works for you. I can neaten up the sides, give it a little more shape, and get some texture through the top so it sits a little better."

"That sounds great to me," he said, almost lazily.

I made the mistake of looking into his eyes. Those deep blue irises bored straight into me. I blinked and looked away. "Follow me to the basins, I'll shampoo you."

I turned away so I didn't have to watch him stand up, but I could feel him behind me, towering over me. At the basin I wrapped a drape around him and let him settle back.

"So," I said, wincing again at how perky I sounded. "Do you live in Foggy Bottom?"

"No."

I tested the water temperature on my wrist. When it was perfect, I started wetting his hair down. His dark blond hair turned almost golden in the water. "Do you work around here, then?"

"No. I'm at the Met department."

"Oh." I pumped some shampoo into my hands and started working it through his hair, scrubbing hard, building up a lather. I scraped my nails on his scalp; he jolted, and let out a low, intensely male growl.

I froze. A warmth pooled at my core, shocking me almost rigid. Shame and adrenaline quickly doused the fire.

Stop it, you hussy, I hissed at myself internally. You're supposed to be a professional.

I pulled myself together and started rinsing the shampoo, watching it run the suds off his hair and down the drain. Quickly, I smoothed some conditioner into his hair, and hesitated. This was the part where I was supposed to do a two-minute head massage. I was excellent at this bit; my fingers were strong and I knew intuitively which spots to rub into for the ultimate relaxation.

But touching this man was starting to feel like throwing a gas can on an open barbeque.

Tentatively, I started to gently rub the back of his scalp, looking away. Chloe was cutting her client's hair, deliberately and very carefully concentrating on what she was doing. Her head was shaking with the effort of not turning to look at us.

Prue, still standing at the podium, stared at us intently. I gave her 'fuck off' look, and swung my gaze deliberately to a safer spot, staring at the wall instead. "I suppose the Met is not too far away from here."

"It's about an hour, in traffic, at this time of the day," he said, his voice husky.

I forgot myself, and started to dig my fingers in, the way I normally did. Sinclair let out another manly noise.

"Why would you drive all this way?" I murmured stupidly, staring at the eggshell colored walls.

"I came to find you."

I looked down. "Why?"

"I think you know why."

"I don't." I turned on the hose forcefully, sending a jet of ice-cold water straight into his head.

He didn't even flinch. I rinsed the conditioner from his hair, squeezed it out perfunctorily, and wrapped a towel around his head in a turban savagely, hoping it would dampen his masculinity.

It didn't. It made it worse.

I stalked to the chair, leaving him sitting at the basin. "This way."

He followed, his movements relaxed, almost graceful, walking with an air of intense superiority, as if he were stalking his prey and he knew there was no hope in hell of it escaping. I sat him down in the chair, roughly towel-dried his hair and attacked it with a comb, sectioning it precisely and carefully.

He watched me in the mirror as I worked. "I wanted to thank you for the note," he said. "I've been trying to bag Kane Hogan for months, and you delivered him right to me, and gave me a tip that would keep his defense lawyers off my back. Not only him, but Ivan Milosevic too. He's a Russian import, a standover man, on loan from the Petrovskis."

I pulled up my first section and cut my guide. "I don't have any idea what you're talking about."

"You don't have to pretend with me," Sinclair said, dropping his voice low. "Your note told me where they were, what they were planning, what weapons they had on them and what drugs they were carrying. You told me everything I needed to get their car searched. I've got enough illegal weapons and drugs to get them tied up in court for a long time."

Fumbling my next section, I combed his hair back down and re-sectioned it, looking for my guide again. I found it and quickly finished up the sides, moving around to the back.

He had beautiful hair. So thick, with a slight wave that gave it shape and movement without me having to over-texturize it. I trimmed the length and took the corners off, and accidently caught his eye when I glanced in the mirror to check the balance of the cut.

He was staring at me. "Are you going to tell me how deep you're in?"

"I don't know what you mean." I avoided his eyes, looking in the mirror, pulling the lengths through my fingers, checking to make sure both sides were the same. They were. God, he was beautiful.

He grabbed my hand. The movement was so quick, so forceful. My breath left my body.

His eyes bored into mine. "Listen, Alessandra." He pulled me a little closer. "I can protect you, if you need it."

Impertinent. Mavka finally woke up and growled. *We don't need protection.*

"I'm fine," I said, ripping my hand out of his grasp. "What makes you think I need protection?"

His eyes hardened. "If you're associating with Kane Hogan, you're in over your head."

I frowned. "I don't know him."

There was a slight pause. "I don't understand. You gave me that note."

"I never met him until last night."

His brow furrowed. "How did you know about the drugs? Or the weapons?"

"Oh." Suddenly, it all fell into place. I let out a tiny snort of slightly hysterical laughter. "Did you think I was some sort of gangster moll or something? You thought I was a mobster girlfriend, and I got scared, turned snitch and dropped a note to the first cop I saw?"

He didn't say anything. He watched my face carefully, waiting for me to fill the space with words. Waiting for an explanation.

I had less patience. "Is that what you thought?"

"Yes."

I shuddered. "As if I'd go near a scumbag like that. No, I have better taste in men. I like my men on the right side of the law, for starters." Staring at his face was becoming too intense for me. I turned away and whipped out my dryer, setting it to low, so I could comb his hair into place.

"It was the logical conclusion," he said, watching me intently. "Most people know me; they know what I do. I assumed you knew, too."

"Oh, I didn't know who you were." For some reason, I felt like dumping cold water on his ego. "I'm new in town. I just needed a cop quickly, so I could give him the tip and run."

His dark-blue eyes flashed. "I came here to rescue you," he said softly. "I assumed that you were one of Hogan's girl-friends, or something. Someone in too deep, with insider knowledge. I thought Hogan's goons would have realized that you were the only person who knew about the exchange, and now that he's been busted, they would be after you."

Standing behind him again, I massaged some wax through my palms and lightly brushed it back through his hair, letting it fall perfectly in place. "Well, you know what they say about assumptions," I said brightly. "It makes an ass out of you, and umption." I brushed my fingers lightly through his fringe, pulling it off his face. "Sorry to disappoint you. I'm no gangster moll. I don't know those creeps, and I can't testify to anything."

He narrowed his eyes. "So how did you know about Kane Hogan?"

Having a toddler taught you how to handle interrogation.

I considered my options, and pulled out the uno reverse card. "How did you find me?"

For the first time, his intense expression eased somewhat. The hard line of his jaw softened ever so slightly. "It took me around three seconds. When I saw you in the Dog and Bone, you were with that hellcat Prudence Nakai, known associate of Officer Ben Dempsey and his boyfriend, Antonio Montefiore. You look very similar to Montefiore, and I immediately guessed you were his sister."

"Hmmm. I guess I should thank you for introducing them," I cut in dryly. "So, did you interrogate Ben to get my location? Or did you shake Antonio down?"

"No. Prudence put me on the salon's mailing list after I rescued your brother. I got an email this morning, introducing you to the salon." There was no hint of a smile on his hard face. "There was a photo of you in the email and everything."

He was not smiling at all, but the tension around his eyes had eased. He was amused. I got the feeling he didn't get amused very often. "There was even a 'book now' link under your photo," he added unnecessarily.

I very exaggeratedly turned to stare at Prue, standing at the podium, still watching us.

She wasn't even blinking. She had popcorn in her hands. *Popcorn.* Slowly, she lifted another handful and put it in her mouth, crunching.

I sighed, and turned back to Sinclair. "Well, I'm sorry you wasted your time, but at least you got a good haircut out of it." I whipped off his drape and showed him the back of his head with a little hand mirror, holding it this way and that so he could see it from all angles.

He didn't even look. He watched me instead, in the mirror, while I brushed off his neck with my fluffy brush and smoothed his collar down.

"If you don't know Kane Hogan... How did you know about him? How did you know all the things in the note you gave me?"

"That's not really your concern."

He lowered his voice. "Is it anything to do with your friend Chloe, and the blackmailing complaint that she filed?"

I scowled. Abruptly, I sat down on my stool and wheeled myself closer, until our knees were almost touching. Another day, another life, and I might be shaking from the proximity to this absolute primal beast of a man. "You know about that? About Chloe's nudes?"

"Of course. I looked up all your known associates right after I made this appointment. Did you think Kane Hogan might be blackmailing her? Did you go out last night to confront him?" He shook his head and glared at me. "Are you insane? You can't go after gangsters like this. It's too dangerous. You have no idea what you're getting yourself into."

"Well, the cops aren't doing anything about it," I said brightly, with a slight sting in my tone. "So I guess we have to. And we weren't going after Hogan," I added. "We thought it might be Keith, the accountant. He'd been hitting on Chloe whenever she was in Scarlett's, and being really sleazy."

"Oh, that guy. He's a cockroach. A bottomfeeder. He's been hanging on the edges of the Hogan mob."

He fixed me with an intense stare. "That still doesn't explain how you knew about Hogan's drugs and weapons. He's discreet; I've had a hard time getting anything on him." He leaned slightly closer. "How did you know?

I took a deep, deep breath. Then, I blew it out. No lie came to mind. I didn't want to lie, anyway. Lying to this man felt a little like lying to a priest. It felt like a sin. "I just... knew."

"You just..." He shrugged. "Knew?"

I looked at him. My face was blank. "Yeah."

A long moment passed. Finally, he nodded, and exhaled. "Okay."

"Okay?" I frowned. "You're okay with that answer?"

"Yeah." He stared back at me.

Silence descended for a whole minute. Neither of us moved. We were so close, sitting with our knees entwined, not touching, but his presence was so enveloping I felt like I was sitting in his lap. The intensity built, almost overwhelming...

Then I heard a crunch. Crunch, crunch.

I cringed. Goddamn Prue and her popcorn.

It broke the spell. Sinclair tilted his head up, looked at me thoughtfully. "So, who else is on your suspect list for Chloe's blackmailer?"

I smiled, showing my teeth. "Why do you want to know?"

"I could help you," he said. "I might be able to give you a little information, if I know any. If you'd asked me before last night, I could have told you Keith was a weasley little cockroach who wouldn't have the balls to do something like that."

"Well, hindsight is wonderful, but again, we didn't have any police resources to help us with our investigations," I said tartly.

He ignored my tone. "So who else is on your list?"

I hesitated. Mentally, I poked Mavka again. She didn't even feel slightly interested in Sinclair.

"Fine," I sighed. "We had Keith on the list, as well as Corey, the bartender from the Dog and Bone. We've already ruled them out."

"Mmm. Not Corey. Max keeps his boys on a tight leash."

"Yeah. We got that already." I remembered that Ben said Conrad Sinclair was one-hundred percent human. No supernatural features at all. No vamp skills, no fae blood, nothing. But he must be able to See, because he cut a swathe through both human and supernatural villains alike.

I leaned in a little closer and narrowed my eyes. "You're not at all fazed about the fact that they're... werewolves?"

"No."

That was simple, blunt, and definitive.

"Why... why not?"

"Because it makes no difference to me, Sandy," he said roughly. His gaze dropped to my lips, just for a second, then ran up, tracing the line of my jaw, gently caressed my cheekbones, and finally, he met my eyes again. "It makes no difference at all."

"But they're stronger, and faster than most humans..."

"Almost twenty years in special ops has taught me a thing or two," he murmured, his eyes hard. "Besides, a little extra strength and speed means nothing when you consider their weaknesses. Everybody has their Achilles Heel, no matter who they are." He leaned back, a picture of relaxation. "It kind of levels the playing field."

"Right." I couldn't imagine fighting a vampire. But Sinclair had done it. He'd probably done a lot of it, if the stories about him were true.

He lowered his voice until it was a rough whisper. "It doesn't really matter to me what *anyone* is. Witches, shifters, vampires, those damned pixies that keep swarming in Rock Creek..." He shook his head. "We're all sentient creatures. We all belong here on Earth. We're all roughly humanoid, at the very least. We all know good from bad." His eyes tightened. "And there's good and bad in every species."

"I had you pegged for a supe-hater," I said. "To be honest, this is kind of refreshing. You're an equal-opportunity bad-guy hunter."

"Naw." He shook his head slowly. "People only hate what they're scared of."

"And you're not scared of anything?"

He tilted his head. "What do you think?"

His eyes were so hard. Twenty years in the special forces... My eyes dropped, and I caught sight of his arms, the tanned skin striped with thick scars here and there. "There's no point being scared of anything," he said, his voice rough. "Only pain and death. Pain is easy. Death means nothing."

My eyes widened. "Okay. That sounds... a little dark." This man had seen some shit. It made me feel a little like a perky idiot. The most pain I'd ever been in was childbirth, and I'd wanted to kill myself and everyone around me.

This man stared death in the face on the regular. "I'm not sure it's healthy not to fear anything," I said. "Especially when there are so many monsters out there. Have you... I don't know...considered therapy?"

"There's nothing to fear. Power is a spectrum, and everyone falls on the spectrum somewhere. What someone is doesn't matter. Knowledge is what matters. Ivan Milosevic is human, you know, and he's killed more men in hand-to-hand combat than the black plague. Your friend Prue over there is a supe, and the only thing I'm in danger from her is getting a rude email, and maybe some popcorn crumbs in my shirt."

"She bites pretty hard," I told him. "I'd stay away from her teeth, if I were you."

He didn't laugh. "There's no point trying to divide people up into good and bad based on their species, when humans are the worst. Actions are what matter, not the shape of their DNA."

"But some of them are so dangerous..."

"Everyone is dangerous, and no one is, that's the real truth. Everyone has their weaknesses. Vampires are easy; they've got tons of allergies, and you only have to jab them in the chest with a toothpick and they're dead. Anyone with a tiny bit of fae blood can't cope with touching iron. Wolves have trouble with their sense of smell – anything stronger than Ax Body Spray will send them crazy. Blood witches are arrogant and mostly insane. They're quite easy to manipulate." He shrugged. "Besides, there's not a spell in this world that can be thrown faster than a Winchester jacketed hollowpoint."

I huffed out a chuckle. "I see what you mean."

He leaned towards me. "They're all the same, Sandy. People are all the same. It doesn't matter if you've got any extra senses. If you're good, you're good with me. If you're not…"

I bit my lip.

I had ripped a man apart and ate his liver inside a gas station bathroom. I was *not* good.

Of course we are good, Mavka drawled from inside of me. *There is no difference between vengeance and justice. There is no good or evil either, just order and chaos. I bring order.*

"Shush."

Sinclair raised a brow. Whoops, I said it out loud. I wondered if he registered my distraction when Mav spoke to me. Goosebumps rose on my skin. He studied me silently.

"So tell me," he finally said. "Who else was on your list?"

I jolted. "What?"

"Your suspect list. For Chloe's blackmailer."

"Oh." Irrationally, I wondered if I should drag him back to the storeroom and show him our Blackmailer Suspect Board. "Uh, we've got Chloe's mom's assistant, Gretel. She's a pushy, hell on wheels type. She might be doing it for publicity for Linda. We checked her out this morning, but came up with nothing. I don't think it's something she would do, though."

Sinclair nodded, but said nothing.

"Then, we've got the guy she's seeing now, some preppy hedge fund wizard called Gregory." I held up a finger. "Not a real wizard. I just mean he's good at his job."

"I got you."

"Okay. Apparently, he's normal and boring, and he knows all about the blackmailing, and he'll stand by her if anything comes out. We call him the Love Bomber."

Sinclair shifted in his seat. "He'd be worth checking out anyway. With most crimes, it's usually the person closest to the victim who turns out to be the perp."

I nodded. "Finally, the guy on the top of the list is some lobbyist that is courting Chloe's dad. We're heading out to his place tomorrow night for dinner to check him out. Chloe says he gives her the heebie jeebies."

There was a long pause. Sinclair had gone very still. "What is his name?"

"Uhhh... Linus. Linus Brady."

His eyes sparked, a flash of intense darkness. "No. You're not going near him."

I frowned. "Why?"

"He's not safe."

"I think that goes without saying. If he's blackmailing Chloe, he's definitely *not* safe."

"No. Just... just leave him to me."

I cocked my head. "Why? What's so dangerous about Linus Brady?"

Sinclair didn't say anything, so I nudged him. "Is he a supe? I thought it didn't matter?"

Finally, he shook his head. "I have Linus Brady as a suspect... for something else."

"You're investigating him already?" I squinted at him. "What for?"

He didn't answer.

I waited. And waited some more. Finally, because I wasn't good at awkward silences, I said again. "What for?"

He frowned. He wasn't going to tell me.

Luckily, I'd had lessons from a master interrogator, so I knew exactly what to do. Dexter had taught me well. I stared

Sinclair in the eyes, not blinking, and started chanting. "What for what for what for what for what for what for what for what for what for what for what for."

He ground his jaw and interrupted me. "I could just leave now, you know."

"I've finished your haircut, so you're free to go. As long as you pay me. And leave me a tip."

He fixed me with a hard stare. "Stay away from Linus Brady," he growled.

I leaned towards him. "No." I imitated his low growl perfectly.

He looked away for a second, furrowing his brow, then turned and fixed his eyes back on me. "Are you... are you *mocking* me?"

I shrugged. "Maybe a little. The whole supe-killer Rambo thing you've got going on is a little over the top."

He gave me a hard stare. "I could throw you in jail right now, you know."

"You think that's a *threat?*" I chuckled. "Honey, I've got a toddler who eats everything he gets his hands on and wakes up at least three times a night. I spend at least an hour in the early morning lying in the dark singing nursery rhymes. You send me to jail, someone else makes my food for me and I'll get to sleep in for the first time in years." I grinned at him. "Find a better threat."

He shook his head and blew out a breath. "You are the strangest girl I've ever met in my life."

"You need to get out more." I batted my eyelashes. "Tell me. You said before that you'd share information if you thought it would help in catching Chloe's blackmailer. So, what have you got on Linus?"

There was another long silence while he stared at me, clearly very deep in thought. Finally, he seemed to reach some sort of decision. He looked away, and muttered something under his breath.

I leaned closer. "What was that?"

"Nothing."

"Well, it sounded like you said I was a dead woman walking anyway..."

"When I asked you how you knew what Kane Hogan was up to," he said ignoring me. "And you said you *just knew*."

I eyed him warily. "Yeah...?"

"Can you do that with anyone? I mean, get close to them and just... know things?"

My equilibrium shook, as if my body thought I was teetering on ice skates and about to fall on to very thin ice. I swallowed down the feeling, and took a deep breath. "It depends," I muttered. "Sometimes, I guess."

He shifted in his chair, straightening up. "If I take you to see Linus Brady myself... will you share the things that you know?"

He was asking for my help.

He thought I was a psychic. That I could read thoughts, or something like that.

We can, Mavka whispered.

There was a slight difference between what Sinclair *thought* I could do, and the truth. If he found out the truth - that I had a demon inside of me that killed and ate men - he might kill me. Was it worth the risk? I chewed on my bottom lip, thinking.

I had to help Chloe. Evil or not, Mavka was a gift.

After a long, long moment, I held out my hand. "You help me, and I'll help you."

Sinclair stared at my outstretched hand. "I'm going to regret this," he muttered, not moving.

Suddenly, Prue was beside us. "Ah-hem."

We looked up.

"Sorry to break up the party, but Sandy, your two-thirty is here, and you need to stop Chloe before she cuts any more off your client's bangs. She's too scared to interrupt you, so she's been trimming the same spot for the last twenty minutes."

I glanced over at Chloe. She was very slowly combing down our client's hair and cutting another one-twenty-eighth of an inch off. Her whole head was shaking with the effort of not turning around to look at us.

"Okay, thanks Prue."

She snapped her teeth at Sinclair and walked away, shaking her ass. I met his eye and held out my hand again. "Deal?"

He took my hand reluctantly. I flinched when our skin touched; a shock ran up my arm and buzzed straight down my spine, like I'd been mini-electrocuted.

"Deal."

CHAPTER 23

Detective Conrad Sinclair told me he'd pick me up later that night to take me to meet with Linus Brady. I refused the ride, based on the fact that I thought I'd explode if I was in an enclosed space with him for too long. Being close to him made me feel wild and out of control, and that idea alone put me off sharing a car ride with him. Also, there was the fact that he'd kill me if he knew there was a man-eating demon inside of me.

Sinclair insisted on driving. I insisted on meeting him there. Stubborn was my middle name. Along with perky. It was an odd combination, but he'd have to get used to it.

Luckily, Prue inserted herself right between us and demanded I drive Chloe's car to meet him instead. With gritted teeth, Sinclair gave me the name of a bar in the city and told me to meet him out front. "Brady has a meeting there tonight," he said, by way of explanation. "He won't be expecting us."

I smiled at him. "Fine. I'll see you later." He left.

Prue sagged with relief as soon as the door shut. "Oh,

Lord have mercy!" She took a shuddering breath in. "I thought I was going to choke on testosterone."

Chloe scuttled up to the podium to join us. "I thought my internal organs were going to start falling out my vagina. I had a wide-on."

I snorted. "A wide-on?"

"Like a hard on, but for your vagina."

I burst out laughing.

Prue smacked me on the back. "Sandy, you need to calm the fuck down. You've literally been single for three days and you've already got a date tonight with the sexiest, most mysterious, most dangerous man in the whole of D.C."

I clamped my mouth shut. "It's not a date."

"What is it?"

I turned away. I couldn't tell them about Mavka. Even I wasn't dealing too well with her presence inside my body. Telling someone about her felt like it would be admitting I had a mental illness, or confessing I was a serial killer. A little of column A, a little of column B, I guess.

I wasn't ready to make it real.

And I wasn't ready for the loony bin if it turned out to be all in my head.

I turned back to Prue, who was waiting expectantly. "Fine, it's a date."

"Wa-hoo!" Chloe gave me a high-five, then hustled back to her client.

Prue watched me, her dark eyes suddenly wary. "Be careful," she said. "No one knows much about Detective Conrad Sinclair, other than the fact that he's the Enforcer."

"What does that mean, anyway? No one explained it to me."

"Most supes take care of their own bad guys," she said. "Blood witches get taken down by good witches, the Vampire King keeps his vamps in line. Shifters have a very rigid hierarchy, and no one in a pack will usually dare defy their alpha. But occasionally, a vamp will go rogue from their nest, a lone wolf might go berserk, or a blood witch might just get too powerful for a coven to take down by themselves. Or the three factions might be warring with each other, I don't know." She shook her head. "Sinclair has been rubber-stamped as the go-to guy to take the rogues out if their own can't do it. Or won't," she added darkly. "He's human, he's impartial. He's an absolute weapon, and he wins every time. He's got the blessing from the Vampire King, and the Shifter Queen. Even Aunt Marche adores him." Prue huffed out a laugh. "She's scared of him, too. Everyone is."

She grabbed me by the tops of my shoulders and stared at me in the eyes. "Promise me you'll be careful."

My stomach was churning. "Okay," I said softly. "I'll be careful, I promise.

* * *

WE CLOSED UP, and I rushed off to pick up Dexter from daycare. He'd had a great time, I could tell as soon as the staff handed me a plastic bag with his wet, muddy and paint-stained clothes.

I loved picking up my son. I always missed him so much it hurt. He covered my face with slobbery kisses and chatted happily on the walk home. With a sad pang, I realized he hadn't mentioned his daddy since we left. I hadn't heard from Terry, either. No calls, no messages. I wasn't sure what to think about that.

The only person that had been calling me with single-minded persistence was my mom. She'd left numerous messages, too. I hadn't listened to any of them yet.

She called again as we were walking home. My brain called me a coward as I sent her call to voicemail one more time. My heart called me brave for setting boundaries. I wasn't ready to talk to her yet.

Dexter and I walked down Cherry Row, hand in hand, and I let us into our apartment. As soon as I opened the door, I spotted all the notes that had been shoved under it.

All were from Aunt Marche. It seemed she was desperate to talk to me, too.

It would have to wait. I had the usual pile of guilt about leaving my son with strangers all day, so I needed to work through that, as well as revel in the beautiful squishy feeling I got from spending alone time with Dexter.

He played happily at my feet as I made pasta for both of us for dinner, told me wild stories of dinosaurs and fairies while we ate, and reenacted a bloody pirate battle during his bath.

By the time I'd rubbed him dry and he'd pulled on his PJ's, both tops and bottoms inside out and back to front, he'd started yawning and nuzzling into me. And by the time I'd read three pages of *Desmond the Donut Destroyer*, he was asleep.

I messaged Prue, who had agreed to babysit for me, and she walked downstairs from her apartment wheeling a suitcase behind her.

"What's that for?" I asked her. "I'm only going to be out for a couple of hours."

"It's for you, idiot," she snapped, flipping the case open. "I'm doing your makeup before you go on your date."

I cringed. "That's not necessary..."

"Shut the fuck up." She waved a makeup sponge in my face. "Submit to me, and this won't hurt."

"Prue." I put my hands on my hips. "No. This is silly. He can take me as I am, or not at all."

She frowned. Her bottom lip wobbled. "I don't get to do

this to myself, you know. I just have to will an illusion of makeup in place."

I sighed, and sat down. "Fine."

The frown disappeared. "Ha!"

For the next half-hour I let her attack my face with little brushes, and wrestle me into a cherry red dress, instead of the usual jeans-and-white-t-shirt combo I was planning on wearing. The dress was fitting, cinching in at my waist, and halter-cut, the neckline wrapping around the base of my throat. The hem fell to just below my knees, so despite the vivid color it was at least quite modest.

Prue eyed me critically. "I don't understand it. Your boobs are completely covered, but I can't stop staring at them."

"Maybe I should change," I said, looking into the mirror and biting my lip. She was right. I looked stupidly glamorous. If I committed to the look, I'd give myself a pin curl set and a swipe of bright-red lipstick, and I'd look exactly like Marilyn Monroe. "This is meant to be a casual drink."

"I will cheerfully murder you if you get changed," Prue said, grinning. "I'd give anything to have your boobs. Detective Conrad Sinclair will eat you alive." She licked her lips.

"God, I hope not." Metaphors like that were really starting to take on a new meaning since Mavka moved into my body.

There was a soft knock at the door. I opened it. Damon stood on the landing.

"Sandy, duuuuude." His eyes bugged wide. "You look amazing."

"Thanks, Damon."

"I don't want to interrupt, but your Aunt Marche is desperate to talk to you. Do you think you could come upstairs for a chat for a few moments?"

"Ah, it's not really a good time right now."

"She insisted."

"I've kind of got to be somewhere..."

"Just for a moment?"

I faced him. "I'll come up later tonight, okay?"

He looked comically sad. "Okay. I'll let her know."

Prue handed me the car keys and smacked me on the butt. "Now go forth and sin, my child."

* * *

I HATED driving in the city. I didn't have Prue's driving skills. The bar was only a few blocks away but it would have been faster for me to walk. My tennis shoes would not go with the dress, though, and I couldn't walk far in the heels that Prue had bullied me into wearing.

The traffic, as usual, was diabolical, and more than once I congratulated myself for avoiding Aunt Marche and leaving early. If I had gone upstairs even for a quick chat, I would be running late by now. And something told me that Aunt Marche wanted to have a little more than a quick chat.

I tried not to think about Detective Conrad Sinclair too much while I drove. Whenever his image came into my mind, my chest flushed, and I felt a little hot. Just once, I allowed myself to think about what it would be like to actually be on a date with him, and I had to squeeze my legs together for a minute to get rid of the bubbly feeling.

This wasn't a date. It was serious. I needed to find out if Linus Brady was Chloe's blackmailer. Sinclair seemed to think he was rotten to the core. If he was bad enough that a guy like Sinclair was on his tail, he would definitely be bad enough to hack Chloe's phone and lift her nudes.

I found the address where we were supposed to meet and drove around for another fifteen minutes, trying to find a park. Eventually, I jammed the car into a tiny spot underneath a hotel nearby, paying a fortune for the privilege of leaving it there for two hours, and scuttled out.

Detective Sinclair was waiting for me on the street, leaning against the side of the building, eyes roaming around the street restlessly. He'd swapped his shirt and jacket for tan chinos and a dark-blue sweater, perfectly tailored to his gorgeous body.

My gut flopped over when I saw him; that weird mix of intense, sinful longing and overwhelming despair – the kind of feeling I imagined a teenager would get meeting their celebrity crush. It wasn't fair that he was so magnificent. It wasn't fair that I could never have someone like him.

His gaze passed over me as I walked towards him; his eyes instantly dismissed me, moving on to look down the street. A pang of despair shot through me so violently that I wobbled on my stiletto heels.

I took a breath, and kept moving.

He looked at me again. This time, he focused on me. Did I imagine the slight widening of his eyes, the tiny jolt of surprise when he saw me? He pushed himself off the side of the building and walked towards me.

"Hi," I said, giving him a big smile.

He looked down at me, almost glaring, his brow deeply furrowed. "Why are you dressed like that?"

"I thought we were going to a cocktail bar, so I wore a cocktail dress. I didn't want to stand out."

He clenched his jaw, looking away. "Then you should have worn something different." He sounded pissed.

"I'm sorry it doesn't meet your expectations," I said sweetly, even though my stomach churned. "This is my first time as a… sidekick? Honorary detective?"

"You're a consultant. For now." He looked down at me again, his gaze running down my throat, following the line of fabric as it curved around my breasts and cinched in the waist, then down to where it hugged my thighs, and he sighed. "This was a bad idea. Maybe you should go home."

"Why?"

"These are dangerous people, Alessandra." His voice caressed my name so gently I almost stopped breathing. "If Linus Brady is as bad as I think he is, then getting on his radar is not a good idea."

I held his stare. "I have to find out if he's the one blackmailing Chloe."

"Blackmail is the least of our problems," he muttered, looking away again.

"What? What do you think he's done?"

Sinclair glanced back at me. He was silent for a long time. Finally, he wiped his mouth. "Murder."

"Murder!?"

His eyes rolled slightly. I probably shouldn't have gasped and clutched my chest. "Yeah, murder. Amongst other things." His expression darkened again. "I suspect that Linus Brady is part of a cartel…" He stopped, and frowned. "I don't think it's safe if you know too much."

"Detective Sinclair." I gave him a wide smile, well aware I looked a little crazy. "I'm here because I *know things*. If you want me to help you, you're going to have to get comfortable with a whole bunch of stuff really quickly."

"Fine." He scowled. "Did you bring a jacket?"

"No." I shrugged. "It's warm out."

"*Fine*," he said again, his voice almost a growl. "Come with me."

We walked into the building, headed for the elevators. Once we were inside, he hit the button for the rooftop and we lifted off so slowly that I probably could have crawled up the stairs faster. "This bar is owned by associates of Linus Brady," Sinclair said quietly as we moved. "He's comfortable here; he will be relaxed. He's meeting with old school friends tonight. It's nothing to do with business, or his lobby group." He glared straight ahead at the closed doors of the elevator, not looking at me. "All of that business is conducted in secret, behind closed doors. This is the first time I've managed to get access to him in a public place."

"Okay," I nodded. So this was a rare opportunity for Sinclair to get close to Linus without setting off warning alarms for him. I understood why he wanted to take this chance.

"It would be best if we weren't seen to be together," he said.

Stupidly, my chest ached. This is not a date, you idiot, I seethed at myself.

"Brady knows who I am," Sinclair went on. "He'd notice you with me. Especially in that dress," he muttered under his breath. Louder, he explained, "Anyone close to me would be seen as a potential target; a bargaining chip, or a source of information. You'd be in danger."

I plastered my smile on my face, while inside, I seethed with anger. For a second I thought it was Mav, but no. This was all me. It rankled to be reduced to something as lame as a bargaining chip.

"How close do you need to be to... *know* things about him?" Sinclair asked me.

I bit my lip. "I'm not sure. It's a little trial-and-error." Mav didn't chip in to help me. She was suspiciously quiet around Sinclair. The only thing I got from her was a faint bristle of resentment.

"Okay. You go in first and grab a drink at the bar," he ordered. "Pretend to be waiting for a date, or something. Do you know what Linus Brady looks like?"

"Yeah." We'd printed off photos to go on our Blackmailer Suspect Board. Linus was tall and quite thin, with generically white skin, brown eyes and dark-brown hair that he cut in a classic slicked-back dapper style. He was objectively quite handsome, but even his photo gave me odd vibes. It was his eyes, I decided. I might be projecting based on what Chloe had told me, but I could sense madness just beneath the surface.

Sinclair raised a brow, apparently surprised I knew what Linus looked like. "Try and find a seat at the bar as close to him as possible, and see if you can do your thing. Don't do anything to get yourself noticed by him. Don't approach him. Don't try to get closer."

"I got it. Stay away, but get close enough."

Sinclair pinched the bridge of his nose. "We shouldn't be doing this," he growled into his hands. "It's not safe."

"Relax, Detective Grumpy-Pants," I elbowed him in the stomach. I winced, and rubbed my elbow. Good grief, those abs were like concrete. "I'll be fine. I'll scan the place when I go in, sit close but not too close, and see if I can do my thing."

He glowered down at me. "If any man approaches you, tell them you are a lesbian."

"And what if a lesbian approaches me?" I asked sweetly.

He glared down at me. "Tell her you're *not* a lesbian."

"You don't *know* that I'm not a lesbian," I sang under my breath.

He turned and grabbed my shoulders, forcing me to meet his eye. "This is serious, Alessandra," he said, his dark blue eyes almost black in the dim light of the elevator. "I don't want to scare you, but this guy is like nothing you have ever seen before. There is nothing funny or playful about this situation. You screw around with these guys, you die."

I met his gaze steadily. "I got it."

The elevator dinged. The doors slid open.

I turned on my heel and walked out, shaking my ass a little for good measure.

CHAPTER 24

I walked into the bar with my head held high, leaving Sinclair looming menacingly behind me. "Okay, Mav," I breathed out. "It's party time."

The rooftop bar was glass on all sides, providing a panoramic view of Washington's skyline. The building was no skyscraper; D.C. wasn't known for its towering cityscape, but being enclosed on all sides by twinkling lights of the buildings surrounding us kind of gave the place a New York feel.

The bar was square in the middle of the room, a structural marvel of glass and steel, lit by amber and red glowing lights, with bar stools all around. The rest of the room held luxurious dark-green suede armchairs and scarlet chaise lounges, perfect for lounging on while holding a twenty-four year old scotch in your hands and chatting to your senator buddies.

Two security guards on either side of the door gave me a quick glance, eyes scanning my body, noting my tiny clutch, only just big enough for a phone and keys. They dismissed me as any kind of threat immediately. "Good evening, miss."

One guard nodded at me disinterestedly. His eyes looked past me immediately and hardened.

I nodded back and walked inside.

Being the mom of a toddler made you prepare for any eventuality, and I'd already run through a few worst-case scenarios in my head. I'd looked up the bar online, hoping to familiarize myself with the layout as much as possible, trying to prepare for any sort of situation. I knew where the bathrooms were; unisex single stalls down a small corridor to the left of the entrance, hidden behind a chrome sculpture of a bull. I knew where both exits were: the one I'd just come in, and another one through a door at the end of the bathroom hallway, which led to the rooftop fire escape.

I even knew the menu inside and out. I almost had a heart attack at the prices. One single gin and tonic would set me back twenty dollars. Sinclair better reimburse me for this.

I paused just before I reached the bar, letting myself gaze around the room at every face, not hiding the fact that I was looking at everyone. Sinclair might cringe at me being so obvious, but I figured that a girl who was coming to a bar to meet a date would definitely walk in and look around. It would be suspicious if she didn't.

The bar was comfortably filled with people already, young city-dwelling professionals enjoying an evening drink; sharp-suited lawyers spitting words at each other like gunfire, older men chuckling good-naturedly with each other. Smug grins and smirks, flinty eyes, scornful looks, disgust, envy, it all wove around me, mixing together in an atmosphere drenched with old money and new ambitions.

This place is thick with evil intent, Mavka purred inside of me. *It is all around us. The power-hungry oppressors spill their essence into the air like the perfume of jasmine in the night air.* She inhaled deeply. *Oh, it is delicious.*

"Hold that thought," I muttered, not moving my mouth. I

was getting good at this ventriloquist thing. "We're looking for one dirtbag in particular." I edged around the bar, looking at every face.

That one, there, he is cheating on his wife and his mistress, with his own stepdaughter, she growled, willing my head to turn towards a middle aged, slightly paunchy man in a dark blue suit. *And that one next to him is drugging his rich wife without her knowledge so she stays docile and agreeable. He is draining her fortune right before her eyes.*

"Scummy behavior. Not what we're looking for, though." I couldn't see Linus Brady anywhere. Maybe he wasn't here yet.

One group of men caught my eye, though. A cluster of very arrogant-looking young men sat in a circle of plush armchairs in the far-right corner of the bar, dressed in tweed and aged brown leather, clothes far too mature for their youthful appearances. There were no women among them at all. Could this be the old school friend group Linus was meeting? They definitely gave off elite private-schoolboy vibes.

Linus might not have arrived yet. I quickly scanned the rest of the bar, and decided that this group was my best bet.

Sinclair hadn't come inside yet either. I let myself look deliberately towards the entrance and spotted him being patted down by the security guards. They were giving him an intense screening, checking for weapons, carefully scanning his ID, and muttering into their earpieces. Apparently, they thought Sinclair looked a lot more like a threat than I did.

I finished my circle of the bar and let myself slump slightly, giving off a dejected air. Anyone who was watching me would think I'd just realized my date wasn't here yet, and I was disappointed. Then, I lifted my head, took a breath, and made my way over to the bar at the far-right corner, closest to the group of young men, pulled out a barstool, scooting my butt up onto it.

The bartender approached me immediately – a smooth looking young man with a mustache. "Good evening, madam. What can I get for you?"

This one seduces the rich women that he meets here and takes their jewelry when they are sleeping.

I gave him a wobbly smile. "Gin and tonic, please."

He got busy with the glasses, flipping a shaker and juggling ice cubes, making a production of the most simple cocktail on the menu.

I give thanks to you, child, for bringing me to this den of sin, Mavka inhaled happily. *The smell of evil blood alone is thick and satisfying. I will have my pick of corrupt man-flesh in here. I imagine this is what they mean when they say 'I feel like a kid in a candy store.'*

"We just need information, Mav," I muttered. "What do you make of the group of men in the armchairs behind us?"

Revolting. She licked her lips hungrily. *They are all baby oppressors, sons of damned men, but they are as corrupt as their fathers and abuse their power as if it were their right, like the kings of old. Slumlords, sweatshop owners, media manipulators; they keep women firmly under their heels.* She exhaled greedily. *Oh, they will be delicious.*

"Information, Mav. I'm looking for one man in particular."

It is hard to concentrate with the scent of so much evil blood in the air.

The bartender placed my drink in front of me with a flourish, took my fifty, and put the change on a tray in front of me. I left him a tip and out of the corner of my eye, noticed that they'd finally let Sinclair in. He stalked straight inside and took a barstool almost directly opposite me on the far side of the bar. I could barely see him through the glinty lights and bottles. He was facing away from me, staring out the window with a moody expression. He looked like a knight with no dragon to slay.

Maybe his information wasn't accurate. Maybe Linus Brady wasn't going to show. I might as well enjoy my drink.

I took a sip; the tonic danced a tingle on my lips. It was delicious. The pantomime with the shakers and ice clearly worked some kind of magic.

"Why, hello, young lady," an older short man wearing an almost-comical shirt and bowtie combo sidled up to me and gave me what he probably thought was a sexy, cheeky grin. "Are you here all by yourself?" He waggled his eyebrows, leering at me.

"Oh, no," I gave him a well-practiced smile.

I'd worked on my smiles a million times. This one was designed to let the recipient know that I was a nice, friendly girl, but sadly taken, and extremely loyal. "I'm meeting someone," I told him. "He's not here yet."

The man chuckled. "Well, I hope he hasn't stood you up."

"No, he's just running a little late," I let my smile droop slightly – a careful, slightly self-deprecating quirk of lips that said 'my date is very important and I'm more than happy to wait for him.'

"Well, if he doesn't show up, come sit with me," the man said, pointing to the other side of the bar. "I wouldn't want to tread on anyone's toes, but a beautiful girl like you shouldn't be spending the evening alone."

"That's sweet of you," I replied, and pointed to my phone. "He said he'd be here soon, though."

The man retreated, clearly not wanting to be caught talking to me in case my date did show up and turned out to be someone that he shouldn't be messing with. I patted myself on the back for a job well done.

Linus Brady was still decidedly absent. On the other side

of the bar, I noticed Sinclair looking at me out of the corner of his eye. I couldn't decipher his expression; it was an odd mix of frustration and satisfaction. Two beautiful women in sharply tailored suits, both around his age, had parked themselves next to him and were chatting to each other animatedly. They held their body positions open; a subtle invitation. I could tell they hoped Sinclair would join their conversation soon.

I felt a pang of jealousy. The women were so confident in their skin; both lithe and well-muscled, their hair and makeup perfect, their suits screaming of money and power. Alpha females. Top of their game. They were more suited to Sinclair than me, a curvy little blonde hairdresser, a single mom. I took another big sip of my drink.

You have as many skills as they do, Mav said smoothly. *This modern society places value on odd things. Your ability to multitask is beyond exceptional.*

"Thanks," I muttered under my breath.

Now, can we eat that man in the corner?

I gritted my teeth. "No."

But he chokes his lovers mid-coitus, without permission, she growled. *He does not care how dangerous it is. He likes to see them struggle underneath him. One day he will do permanent damage.*

I sighed and took a big swallow of my drink. Too late, I realized I'd drained it. Should I order another one and wait a while longer?

Mavka was getting restless. I weighed up the need to keep a grip on my mental faculties with the need to blend into my surroundings. The mustached bartender caught my eye and inclined his head. "Another one?"

"Why not?" I nodded and fiddled with my coaster. Mavka was inside of me, after all. Maybe she'd mellow out after a couple of gins.

I quickly glanced at Sinclair, still facing away from me.

He had stiffened; the hard lines of his body coiled with tension. The women still chatted happily beside them.

Suddenly, a surge of rage almost catapulted me out of my seat.

A spike of adrenaline quickly followed; I dropped my coaster and clamped down, holding on to the bar. I froze.

At the same time, the bartender placed my drink down in front of me. I panted, trying to keep control, as Mavka thrashed inside of me, absolutely incoherent with rage.

A cool, smooth and undeniably arrogant voice spoke up from just behind me. "Put that on my tab, Jasper."

The bartender nodded, and immediately retreated.

A hand touched my bare shoulder, resting there lightly; it was too hot, unexpected, I clamped down hard so I wouldn't flinch. I wanted to tear the hand away, tear it off its wrist, and shove it down the owner's throat.

"A beautiful young woman like you should not be paying for her own drinks."

Finally, Mavka found her voice. *Murderer! Torturer, slaver! Most depraved, most corrupt! I must feast!*

Her scream was so loud I could barely concentrate. I swallowed, as the man moved from behind me, and slid himself up onto the barstool next to me.

I clenched every single muscle in my body tightly, set my jaw, and turned to face him.

Linus Brady stared at me, a light smirk on his face. "What's a pretty young thing like you doing in a lion's den like this?"

I managed to move my jaw. "I'm waiting for someone," I muttered.

He is pain, he is suffering! He uses women like tools, like toys, he will drain them and dump them and leave them to sink into the sludge at the bottom of the river.

"Well, it looks like your boyfriend isn't here," Linus said

smoothly, resting an elbow on the bar. "You shouldn't be drinking alone. It can be dangerous, in a place like this."

My smile – my well-practiced smile, had completely abandoned me. Mavka's screams overwhelmed me. I gritted my teeth. "I'm fine," I stuttered. "He'll be here shortly."

"Is that so? Well, I'll keep you company until he gets here," Linus murmured, smoothing his dapper hair back. He gave me a toothy, predatory smile. It didn't reach his eyes. They were stone-cold. Soulless. "Someone should give him a piece of their mind, leaving a pretty thing like you all alone." He leaned in so close I could smell him, a musky coppery scent with a sickly sweet afternote that turned my stomach.

He is a blood witch, Mavka seethed. *You can smell his corruption, the stench of ultimate evil. His kidneys will be dense with vice. His liver is saturated with unholy degeneracy. I must feast on his flesh!*

He was a witch? Sinclair didn't say he was a witch. I turned away for a second, desperate to take a fresh breath of air to clear my nose of that sickly scent, silently begging for Mavka to listen to me. Details, please, Mav, I begged. This is the one I need. Please give me details!

Fuck the details, she hissed. *I must eat him! I am vengeance – I am justice!*

Please, I begged her.

I turned back, facing Linus directly, and smiled. "Honestly, I'm fine," I said, my voice firm. "I'd prefer to wait for him alone."

"Oh, no, I insist." He put his hand on my knee. I froze. My skin crawled.

You want details? He has murdered at least a dozen women in the last two years, Mavka snarled. *He captures runaways, he buys sex slaves. He does not use them the way a man usually would; rape does not interest him. Only torture satisfies him; screams of innocent women charge his depraved soul. He drains them,* she growled, her voice hoarse with naked need. *He tortures them and drains their blood, and uses it to charge his spells – more power, more corruption. He believes women to be slaves, kept underfoot and stabled like cattle, and he will act to bring this depraved vision of feminine enslavement to the rest of the world. He is lost to the nothing, the darkness. And he does not act alone,* she added, her voice lowering, vibrating with intensity. *He is one thread in a spiderweb. One line in a net.*

I swallowed. I needed more.

He was waiting for a reply. I dropped my voice to a whisper. "My date might get upset if he sees me talking to another man."

Linus laughed out loud. "I hope he does." His chuckle echoed coldly. "I like a challenge."

More? There is more, so much more, he is fat and ripe with evil intentions. Fine. You wanted details, child? He is meeting with his coven later tonight; they are being delivered fresh female flesh to sacrifice in their underground lair.

I cocked my head and smiled at Linus. My lips felt brittle; like I was going to crack any second. "That might not be wise for you," I said, trying and failing to keep my voice smooth. Internally, I begged the demon inside me. More details!

Linus Brady chuckled haughtily. "It might not be wise for *him,*" he said. His hand, still resting on my thigh, squeezed. "You obviously don't realize who I am."

It revolted me. "Please take your hand off my leg." I kept my voice pleasant, but firm.

"Or what?" He smirked at me. "What will you do? What will *he* do, this mysterious boyfriend of yours?"

He is thinking of it now, Mav hissed. *He would love to bleed you on the rack tonight, too. He imagines himself slicing off your breasts while your imaginary boyfriend watches. He imagines the power that your suffering and blood will bring him.*

More details!

His minions wait for him now, in an old place, an old farm down by Founder's Park, where they practice their spellcraft. Mavka writhed inside of me, frenzied with hunger. *On the banks of the Potomac. Their shipment of victims will arrive by boat at one hour before midnight.* She trembled, concentrating fiercely. *The building's name is the Old Gray. You will find horrors there.*

Linus laughed coldly again. "Cat got your tongue, little mouse?" He squeezed my leg again, so hard, I jolted in fright.

"That hurt," I snapped.

His soulless eyes sparked. "It was supposed to."

"Take. Your. Hands. Off. Me."

He leaned forward, smiling like a snake. He exhaled as he spoke, sending a hot breath directly into my face. "Make me."

Suddenly, the temperature dropped. A voice like pure ice, vibrating with intense menace murmured from behind me. "Please. Allow me."

Conrad Sinclair was behind me.

He reached down to where Linus Brady's hand gripped onto my thigh, curled his own huge hand around Linus's wrist and very, very slowly bent it backwards. I sensed the struggle, the competition for supremacy as Linus battled to keep his hand on my thigh, but Sinclair was far too strong. Linus was forced to release his grip on me.

His eyes flashed with anger. "Sinclair," he snarled. "What are you doing here? You don't belong here."

"I'm off the clock, Brady. A man's allowed to have a little downtime." He lounged easily next to me, relaxed, an absolute beast of a man; a lion taunting a slippery snake.

"Leave us alone. You are interrupting us."

"I don't think I am," Sinclair said, his voice dangerously mild. "I think you were harassing this young woman." He turned to me. "Is that right?"

I nodded dumbly.

Linus thrust his chin up. "This is none of your business, Sinclair. Be smart for once in your life. Listen to your *superiors*," he drawled, dark eyes filled with spite. "Turn around, and walk away. Before you do something you regret."

Sinclair shook his head, a faint smile curving up his lips. "Not happening, Brady. I won't let you harass women right in front of me. She doesn't want you here. Leave her alone."

Mavka battered at the edges of my psyche. *We must feast! We must. We cannot let him get away!*

My grip was shaking. It was becoming harder and harder to keep a hold of her. As well as words, she battered me with images; a dark paneled room lit with candles. A rune on the stone floor, drawn in blood. A circle of hooded figures, chanting in low tones. A shadowy figure in the middle, a void, an endless black hole...

My vision swam; I stumbled off the bar stool and onto my feet.

Both men turned to stare at me.

"Okay." I adjusted my dress frantically and picked up my clutch and phone from the bar. I waved my phone around. "Oh, look, a message. I've been stood up after all. I'm going to go. Uh. Bye, I guess."

Abruptly, I turned around and marched away, walking stiffly, desperately trying to hang on to the raging demon inside of me before she exploded and ate every man in the room.

CHAPTER 25

I took the stairs. I needed to keep my legs moving.

No! Mavka screamed. *Go back! We must feast!*

"Not today, Mav." I walked down the stairs carefully. One foot after the other. One foot after the other.

Linus Brady is death; he is destruction! He sows the seeds of chaos along with the rest of his coven. They will bring darkness into this world!

"Well, you're not exactly Pollyanna yourself, are you?" I muttered under my breath.

I am vengeance. I am justice! Go back. Let me feast!

I gritted my teeth, ignoring her. One step at a time. My head was whirling with information, and that sick churning feeling where you knew something terrible had just happened, and you were powerless to stop it.

I reached the bottom of the stairs, pushed open the door, and clomped unhappily across the ground floor lobby. An enormous presence loomed behind me.

"Don't turn around," Sinclair murmured. "Keep walking. Head to the car park in the building opposite us. Basement one."

I trudged forward, trying to ignore Mav, who was still frantically willing me to turn around. I walked outside the building onto the sidewalk and realized Sinclair was no longer behind me. My legs kept me walking, though, following his instructions, and took me across the street, and through a side door in the building opposite with a P emblazoned near the handle.

One short flight of stairs later and I was in basement one. There was no one around.

A squeal of tires sounded in the silence; a black Lexus screeched to a halt in front of me, with Sinclair at the wheel. "Get in."

I shook my head. He filled the whole space of the car with his presence; a man-god, squished into a high-performance car. "No," I said. I was tired.

He narrowed his eyes. "Get in," he repeated.

"I'm going home," I said. "My car is parked underneath the hotel next door." I turned around.

"It's not safe," he growled. I heard him pull the handbrake and open the door.

Wearily, I turned back. "Where is safe? Nowhere is safe; that's the harsh truth. The whole world is filled with monsters and demons."

I was one of them.

Sinclair stared at me, his blue eyes alight with concern. I swallowed. "I'm a little overwhelmed. I'm sorry."

He moved around the car and came towards me, thankfully keeping three feet of distance between us. The heady scent of his whisky and fireworks aroma made me dizzy. "Alessandra…" His eyes bored into mine. "Please. You have to come with me. Brady would have told his goons to follow me just in case, and knowing him, he'd send someone to try and track you down, too. Even if he was convinced we weren't together, you'd be unfinished business to him."

He didn't mean that as an insult, but I took it as one anyway. I was sick of being described as an object. "Unfinished business. A bargaining chip. A target." I hitched up my shoulders and chuckled humorlessly. "If only you knew."

He furrowed his brow and leaned closer. "If only I knew what? Alessandra, he scared you badly. I could tell. What did you find out from him?"

"I.... I..." I shook my head. There was so much.

He exhaled heavily. "Please. Get in the car. I'll drive you to your car, and you can tell me what you got from him on the way."

Mavka was kicking my ass. I could mentally feel her, pulling at me, trying to force me back to the bar so she could eat.

I huffed out a sigh. "Fine." I got in.

"Buckle up."

Driving with Sinclair was worse than I thought. He was a masterful driver; he worked the car like it was his job, like an expert; an F1 driver or something, split-second timing and smooth turns, his hands caressed the wheel firmly but gently. I faced the windscreen, trying not to look at him. It just wasn't fair that someone should be so insanely attractive, powerful and mysterious.

Speaking of mysteries...

"You should have told me Linus Brady was a blood witch," I muttered.

His head whipped towards me. "You got that from him?"

"That, and more. He's in some sort of death coven; he's been murdering women for the last few years. *Exclusively* women," I added. My voice was toneless. "I got hints that he's been draining women for power spells and dumping their bodies at the bottom of the Potomac."

His eyes pinched shut. "I *knew* it." He punched the steering wheel; an explosive display of frustration that made me jump. Taking a breath, clearly mindful that he was scaring me, he clenched his fists instead. "I knew it was him."

"There's more. He's got more victims being delivered to him tonight by boat, at eleven PM. His coven meet at an old farmhouse somewhere in or near Founders Park. The building's name is The Old Gray." I shuddered. "Apparently you will find horrors there."

Sinclair pulled into the underground park of the hotel and slammed on the brakes. He turned to face me. "Tonight? This is happening tonight?"

"Yep."

"You're sure."

"Positive." Mavka couldn't lie. Besides, I trusted her. Which was weird, considering she was a man-eating demon. She'd gone quiet since I'd gotten in the car with Sinclair. She wasn't screaming at me to go back anymore.

He exhaled heavily. "I have to go." Pulling out his phone, he started tapping out a message. "I'll have someone come and tail you home."

"No need." I gave him a sad smile. "I *know* things, remember? And I know I'm going to be safe tonight."

Sinclair paused, his phone forgotten, and gave me a hard stare. "Are you sure?"

"Yeah."

There was a long moment of hesitation, while he looked at me. Finally, he nodded. "Okay."

"Okay?" I huffed out a chuckle. "Can I just say how weird it is that you're cool with all this?"

"Let's just say I have some experience with this kind of weirdness," he muttered, tapping his phone again.

"O-kaaaaay." I cracked my knuckles. "Well, this was fun," I said stupidly. "Thanks for a lovely evening. My car is just there." I pointed to the corner of the building. "I guess I'll be heading off now."

"Wait." His voice was gruff. Still tapping out a message, he got out, walked around the car, opened my door and held out his arm. "I'll walk you to your car."

I didn't take his arm. I couldn't. I didn't trust myself not to cling to him like a pathetic piece of cooked spaghetti. Instead, I smoothly put my clutch in the hand closest to him, avoided his eyes, and launched myself out of the Lexus, marching straight towards my own car. Sinclair moved in front of me instinctually, covering me. The protective thing made me sway on my stupid heels. His phone rang once while we walked, and he gave a series of intense, incomprehensible military orders in a low tone to whoever it was that called, while inspecting the backseat and trunk of my car for monsters. He hung up, and turned to me.

"I'll be in touch, okay?" The way he stared at me; the way he held eye contact… It was almost more intimate than a kiss. He bent down towards me. "Alessandra… thank you." He put his hand on my shoulder, and I almost peed my pants. "I know tonight was frightening for you, but I appreciate you being so brave."

"Yeah," I croaked awkwardly. I coughed to clear my throat. "*So* brave. Actually, just one more thing."

"What is it?"

"I got the feeling that whatever Linus is a part of, it's much bigger than just him."

Sinclair's eyes darkened. "Oh, it is. Linus Brady is just the tip of the iceberg." He ground his jaw, and looked away. "I don't want to scare you anymore than you already are, but there's something big happening here in D.C." His voice lowered to a whisper. "Something very evil is shifting chess pieces into place, gathering soldiers and gaining power. There's a darkness; a black vortex here, and it's drawing all the dirty malevolent creatures closer."

I remembered the vision Mavka had shown me. A black hole, a swirling, pulsing pit of despair.

Chaos.

I swallowed roughly. "Yeah. I kind of got that."

He glanced down at his phone. "Alessandra… I have to go. If we're going to have the team assembled, and get there in time to raid that farmhouse…"

I nodded. "Oh, yeah. Okay. Go on. Have a great time," I added lamely.

He opened my door for me. I started the car, gave him a wave, and drove off.

I watched him in my rear mirror. He didn't move until I'd turned out of the carpark entrance and driven away.

CHAPTER 26

Mavka started screaming at me again as soon as we hit the street. *Stop! You must stop immediately, child. Halt this vehicle, post haste!*

Confused, I indicated to turn into a miraculously free space, just a few spots down from the hotel. "Why? Mav, what's going on."

We must go back! She tugged at me, willing my hands to stop the car. *We do not have much time!*

I forced my hands back on the steering wheel. "Back to the rooftop bar, you mean?" I shook my head. "Mav, it's in the police's hands now. We have to leave it with them."

Damn you, child. We cannot. You must go back. We must face him now!

"Detective Sinclair is going to take care of it," I tried to reassure her.

Idiot girl, she seethed. *He is in grave danger. You do not understand.*

A chill ran down my spine. Sinclair was in danger?

I moved the rear-vision mirror down so I could see my own face. Immediately, the glass filled with a red smoke, and

Mavka's gleaming ruby eyes stared back at me through her wild hair.

I glared at her in the mirror. "Explain it to me. Now," I added, a little snarl to my voice.

Linus Brady is but a mere cog in the machine, she hissed. *There are many other cogs, and many more important parts. Then, there is the driver...* The vision of the seething pit of chaos and despair swam in front of my eyes again.

I shook my head to get rid of it. "Mav, I don't understand what you're saying."

He has kicked the hornet's nest, and it is our fault. He will be stung.

"Okay, so are the bad guys robots, or are they wasps, Mav?"

She shuddered. *You have no sense of poetry, child. Put the pieces together. Sinclair is in danger. We have already meddled by giving him information to apprehend the vampire.*

I gritted my teeth. "Okay, Mav... stop. Just stop, and speak plainly. Now, what fucking vampire?"

Kane Hogan, she hissed back. *Kane Hogan is a vampire, and we gave Sinclair information to take him down. Kane Hogan and his masters are rogues, just like Linus Brady and his masters are rogue black witches. They are part of a new cult, a coven of men that worship the darkness. They call themselves the Blood Kings.*

"B–Blood Kings?" That didn't sound good.

They are following a path that ends in unending chaos. Detective Sinclair has heard whispers of it, and he thinks he is moving in secrecy, but the second he apprehended Kane Hogan, he was noticed.

"I mean, it would be kind of hard not to notice an arresting officer..."

You don't understand, child. Linus Brady wanted you. I hid the worst of his intentions from your mind, but he desired to use you in unimaginable ways.

I shuddered. "Yeah, I got a little hint of it."

Linus Brady always gets what he wants, Mav growled. *Always. Conrad Sinclair thwarted him tonight. He imagined you on the rack, as a blood sacrifice, and he was enjoying the idea of taking a knife to the softest parts of your flesh.* Her ruby eyes sparked with fire. *Sinclair has denied him his pleasure. He will be stewing upstairs at that bar, and it won't be long before he takes his revenge. When he mentions Sinclair's name to his masters, it will be too late. Conrad Sinclair will be eliminated.*

No.

Oh, Jesus, no.

"I can't let that happen." I exhaled shakily. "No."

She tugged at me again. *We must go. Now.*

I locked my legs in place. "Mav… I can't…"

I can. I will. Vengeance is justice, Alessandra.

"What do I do?"

Switch with me, she purred.

"I don't want to black out again," I whispered. It had been horrifying waking up to a sea of gore in a gas-station, licking blood off my fingers. "I don't want to black out."

Let me drive, then.

"What?"

Your body is a vehicle, Alessandra, she said, her voice almost gentle. *Stay in the seat. But take your hands off the wheel.*

I panted, staring her in the eyes. She stared back.

Let go.

I took a deep breath, and let it all out.

I let go.

CHAPTER 27

avka

I GLANCED DOWN AT MYSELF, frowning. This body seemed far too small and soft to house my magnificence. Yet it was relatively pleasing; with strong limbs, gentle curves and an admirable hard core.

The red dress was a bit much. I preferred black. I patted myself down, familiarizing myself again with this body I inhabited.

I felt a pang of wild despair as I ran my hands over my full breasts; these were perfect for suckling a babe; a sacred duty that not only I would never perform, it was the reason I was dreamed into being in the first place.

That was who I was. An archetype; a goddess, of sorts. I was the spirit of one who would never give birth; the goddess of women who were never supported, who were oppressed, who were taken advantage of. I was the one who avenged those who were enslaved and used as mere incubators for the tools of men.

I was the manifestation of the rage of millions of female victims. I was vengeance. I was justice.

A gentle prod inside me snapped me out of my brooding. Alessandra, my hostess. Oh yes. That's right. I had a job to do. I licked my lips.

I opened the door of the vehicle and got out, stretching my neck, feeling the buzz of strength in my arms and the pulse of the muscles of my legs. Oh, she was more lovely than I thought. This would do nicely.

The rooftop bar was only across the street. I started to walk, swinging my hips on these ridiculous high heels. They made my buttocks sway in a way I imagined that men would find very enticing. Idiots.

Crossing the street, I strolled into the lobby of the building and walked to the elevators, my feet making a strangely hypnotic tap sound on the marble floor. I hit the button for the rooftop bar.

A man stopped directly behind me as I waited. I could hear his thoughts as loud as if he were shouting directly into my ear.

Nice ass. I'd like to bite it. Oh, Jesus, Nathan, stop it. You're getting married in a week. You can't do this anymore. Although... if Cindy didn't know... it wouldn't hurt her. Would it? Probably not. Would I feel bad about it, even if she didn't know? Ha ha. No.

I chuckled darkly. The arrogance, the entitlement of men would never cease to amaze me. This idiot behind me had already decided I would let his teeth near this derrière...

The elevator door chimed; the door slid open. I walked in and turned around. The man – predictably dull, with no commendable features and an unsurprisingly tedious demeanor – attempted to follow me in, but I slammed my hand against the doors, blocking him, halting his progression.

A spark of both anger and intrigue colored his uninteresting features. *Oooh, this chick is feisty. Maybe she's one of those crazy ones. Ha ha, I likey. Crazy in the head, crazy in bed...*

I smiled, and licked my lips. "Mortal men," I purred. "Your foolishness will never fail to amuse me."

He frowned. "Uh… thanks?"

I leaned closer, and let a hint of ruby fire color Alessandra's blue eyes. "You are a slug; a mere speck of dirt, unimportant, uninteresting, unworthy of your fiancé. To compare you to a dirty dishcloth does a severe disservice to the dishcloth," I added dryly. "I hope Cindy comes to her senses quickly."

His eyes flared wide; he took a step back, horrified. The elevator chimed; the doors closed. I laughed in his face as he disappeared from sight.

That was …fun. Maybe there was more to this mortal existence than pain and suffering. Hmmm. Interesting.

The elevator moved slowly upward. Maybe I should have let the man share the elevator ride with me. That might have been even more fun. Oh well. Maybe next time.

The bell chimed again; I'd reached the rooftop. I strolled out of the elevator and back through the entrance to the bar. The two guards inside cast a cursory glance at me, instantly dismissing me. I smiled at them as I walked through.

Oh, this bitch is back again, one of them thought idly. The other gave me no consideration at all.

I was nothing to them. Just an object; a body reduced to its parts. Not even a worthwhile object, in fact, judging from the idle, uncharitable scorn in the guard's thoughts.

How different this mortal existence would be if everyone could hear the things I heard, the dark whispers and seething hatred in the thoughts of men.

Alessandra mentally elbowed me. *Not all men.*

I hushed her. "You are scared of snakes, are you not?" I murmured to her. "Well, not all of them are venomous. It is unfair to snakes to be scared of them."

She pushed a vision to the forefront of my mind. Detective Conrad Sinclair. I paused at the entrance of the bar, idly surveying the scene in front of me.

Sinclair was odd. He held no dark thoughts towards women at all. None. Oh, he wasn't pure, like that odd Damon creature, and he wasn't good, like Alessandra's brother and his boyfriend. It was strange that Alessandra, a damaged young girl, had somehow surrounded herself with men who didn't detest womankind.

Sinclair was the strangest of all. He was a veritable powerhouse of violence and rage, but it was all directed at other men.

It seemed we had a lot in common.

I lifted my chin and strolled into the bar, making a slow, lazy circuit. Many heads turned my way; many sets of eyeballs mentally undressed me and had their way with me.

Ah. *There.* Linus Brady, the blood witch, the piece of excrement who dared call himself Blood King. There he was, reclining in an armchair in the corner, a glass of dark amber liquid in his hand and a sulky expression on his face. His school friends surrounded him, laughing uproariously, telling inane, unimaginative stories of their precious time at their elite boarding school. Linus glared into his whiskey. I slowed, listening to him furiously.

He wanted to leave, but he couldn't. Not just yet. Someone would be picking him up from here in less than thirty minutes, to take him to the coven meeting this evening. Someone he was afraid of. His master. He itched to rebel, though, to find that girl, to squeeze the cop's head until it exploded. His hands twitched involuntarily. He wanted to go now.

I walked slowly past, swinging my hips. One of his hideous school friends noticed me; his head turned towards me. Linus Brady saw the movement and followed his friend's gaze.

I turned my head towards him, looking back as I walked past. I met his eyes.

The effect was electric. Linus Brady's sulky expression disappeared; he sat up straight and narrowed his eyes. His prey was back.

I considered a flirty smile, a wink, maybe a subtle nod towards the bathrooms, where he would get the idea to follow me. Anyone else maybe, except the filthy sewage of his thoughts told me that wouldn't be satisfying for him. He wanted to hunt me.

He didn't want me to enjoy this. He wanted me to be scared.

I let myself flinch under his gaze. Immediately, I lowered my eyes, turned, and hurried away, stumbling once on my high heels. Brady's predatory thoughts followed me as he watched me scurry towards the bathrooms. He was up and out of his seat before I disappeared behind the enormous chrome statue of the bull.

The hallway was empty; all the stalls were unlocked. I listened carefully, waiting to hear his footsteps, then, I moved inside the first stall and locked the door behind me.

The little room was dim. A soft amber glow came from an antique bulb suspended above. The bathroom contained only a commode, a sink and a gilt-edged mirror.

I waited patiently. Within seconds, the lock on the door clicked back. The handle turned.

I edged back, and let out a squeal as Linus Brady let himself in with a master key.

"What are you doing?" I gasped theatrically, clutching my heaving bosom. Alessandra's body was perfect for this sort of caper. I was almost enjoying myself.

Linus smiled like a snake. "Oh, this is your fault, you know. You come into this place, in that dress, sitting all alone." His thoughts ran foul like raw sewage from his brain as he slowly examined my body. *I'm going to enjoy carving those heaving tits off that chest, piece by piece. Disgusting. Women shouldn't be allowed to be let loose like this, they should be kept in place, I'll teach her...*

I lifted my chin. "Get out." I let my voice tremble. "Now."

"Oh, I don't think I will." *Roofies in my pocket; that will do the trick. Make her eat them, carry her out, say she's drunk. We'll bleed her out tonight. At least she'll be good for something.* Linus smirked. "I think I'll stay right here. And you'll do what I tell you to do." *I'd love to have that cop watch this, maybe I'll film it, play it for him later, he seems to be sticking his nose where it doesn't belong, Lord Seth's not worried about him yet but he should be, I'll tell my master, he'll tell the Lord, I'll get the credit, he'll bless me...*

Inside me, Alessandra breathed a sigh of relief. The Enforcer was safe for now. And we had more information. A name. Lord Seth.

Linus Brady turned and locked the door behind him. Slowly, deliberately, he turned back and pulled out a knife from a sheath in his jacket; a strange piece with a black matt finish and runes embedded in the handle in gold. That was no ceremonial athame. That was a tool of darkness. "Now, be a good girl." *Disgusting whore.* "Swallow these." He held out his hand, his palm littered with tiny pills.

I shook my head, feigning panic. The athame did give me cause for concern, however. A blood witch with his experience would wield considerable power. "No," I said breathlessly. "No, I won't. I'm not stupid."

Oh, yes you are. You're a fucking idiot. He lowered his head and fixed me with a hypnotic stare. I felt the magical pressure behind his gaze; a compulsion. "Open your mouth," he growled.

My lips fell apart softly – oh he was strong! Quickly, I clamped my mouth shut and turned my eyes away from him. "I won't. No. I'll… I'll scream!"

He laughed, and took a step closer. "Not now. Maybe later." He reached out and took my chin in his fingers, clamping down on my skin hard. It hurt. "Open your mouth," he said softly. He raised the black knife, and ran it softly down the side of my cheekbones. "Or I'll cut your lips off."

I moaned in terror, panting, my eyes wide and turned away, clearly scared out of my mind. An Oscar-winning performance, surely.

Alessandra twitched inside of me. *Stop playing with your food, Mav. We got what we wanted.*

Wait.

"No, we didn't," I said out loud.

Linus Brady cocked his head, confused. "What?"

I stared at him in the eyes, pushing back on his compulsion with a little effort. "Did you hack Chloe West's phone? Are you the one blackmailing her?"

He paused. *What the fuck? What is this stupid bitch talking about? Who the fuck is Chloe We– oh yeah, that dumb blonde daughter of Harry West.* His thoughts shifted away from Chloe immediately, a vision of her father in his mind's eye instead. *He'll be ours, soon,* he thought triumphantly.

That was interesting. And not in a good way. I frowned. "I'm going to take that as a no."

He thrust his face into mine, hissing. "Open your mouth, bitch." The knife came at me, he wedged the point in between my lips.

Mav…

I rolled my eyes. "Okay, fine." I reached up with my hand and grabbed the handle of the knife, enclosing my palm over his, letting my strength sink into Alessandra's body, and I very, very slowly pushed the point away from my lips.

Linus Brady's eyes narrowed; he gritted his teeth. My strength shocked him, but he was not concerned yet; merely infuriated that a woman might have the strength to push him back. He flexed, using some of his dark magic reserves to try and hold me. "What do you think you're doing?"

I smiled at him; a wide, happy smile, showing all my teeth. A ruby-red sheen ran over my eyes as I shielded myself from his compulsion. His magic was strong, but he was only human.

He wielded magic; I was made from it.

I leaned closer to him. "I think your time is up, Linus," I said, purring with satisfaction.

His eyes flared wide. "Who the fuck do you think you are?"

I laughed. "Who am I?" I moved closer and closer until his back hit the stall door, still holding his hand, clamped around the knife. He twitched, trying to let it go, but I squeezed it until I heard bones break. He let out a shriek; and furiously slammed his magic down on me, trying to push back.

"I'll tell you who I am," I murmured softly, holding his hateful stare. "I am *vengeance*. I am the wild spirit of a million feminine screams. I am the manifestation of their pain and suffering." I bared my teeth. "I am *justice*."

His face trembled in rage as I pinned him against the door. His thoughts snapped at me, filled with incoherent hatred and spite, *how dare she, how dare she?*

He still didn't understand. I frowned. "You don't get it, do you?" I tilted my head. "Maybe I should show you?"

Red smoke wafted around me as I let my physical form bloom out of Alessandra's body. My black hair swallowed her blonde, streaming out around me; my white, terrible face replaced her soft perky one. Linus Brady's eyes flew wide as I grew in height, one foot, then another, until I was towering over him.

He started to shake. "No. *No....*"

I held his gaze, and pushed the knife slowly towards his gut. There was a twitch inside me as Alessandra checked out.

I was glad. She was still innocent, this beautiful girl whose body I inhabited, despite all she had endured and seen. She still had hope for mankind; she believed in second chances and redemption.

I enjoyed the novelty of her thoughts, as foolish and naive as they may be.

But, for now…

I licked my lips. This monster wanted to feast.

Linus Brady started to scream.

CHAPTER 28

andy

I HAD to stop twice on the way home to throw up.

Mavka purred happily inside me, like a cat who had gotten not just the cream, but had swallowed the entire dairy cow.

I moaned as I retched again. "Did you have to eat the whole thing?"

Of course I did. He was delicious. I haven't had a man like that in centuries. I find it hard to compare the delicacy of evil man-flesh to any of your mortal treats, but perhaps try and imagine eating your favorite bar of chocolate on the first day of your period.

I groaned again.

Calm down, child. This way, his body is gone. There is no trace of any remains. No evidence. No harm, no foul, as they say, she said, picking at her teeth.

I looked down at the little yellow puddle of bile in the

gutter. "I don't understand. If you ate him... why aren't I throwing him up?"

What I consume goes to the lower astral plane. That is where my spirit resides, and it fuels me there.

"Oh. Well, that's handy, I guess." I wiped my mouth. None of that evil bastard was inside of me. That made me feel better.

You can still consider yourself a vegetarian, Mavka chuckled darkly.

Exhaling shakily, I got back in the car and slammed the door shut. It was only a short drive back to the apartment; the traffic had thinned out. "We still don't know who is blackmailing Chloe," I muttered. "We seemed to have skipped over the little personal problem I was trying to help with, and we've leapt right into a massive evil global conspiracy to unleash chaos on Earth."

Whoever this Lord Seth is, he will be a dark beast indeed. Even I would be wary of the master of evil men such as Linus Brady.

I sighed, and pulled the car into the little underground park under my building. I got out of the car, bone-tired. "I guess we'll have to keep pulling the threads, see what we unravel," I said to her, locking the car wearily.

"Who are you talking to?"

I yelped in fright and spun around. Aunt Marche was standing next to me, wearing a pink fluffy bathrobe. Her hair was a tangled mess, her eyes slightly bloodshot. A cigarette smoked in her hand.

"Good grief!" I caught my breath. "Give a girl a little warning, would you? This is an underground car park, Aunt Marche! It's already scary enough without you popping up to scare the poop out of me."

"Yes, but it's *my* underground car park," she said testily. "There's nothing scary about it." She took a puff on her cigarette.

I sniffed suspiciously. "Are you smoking a joint?"

"I've been very stressed lately." Her chest puffed out as she inhaled. "My darling niece has been dodging me, and I'm very worried about her."

"I'm fine, Aunt Marche."

She eyed me beadily. "Who were you talking to?"

I mouthed stupidly for a moment. "Myself," I said.

There was a long, loaded silence. Aunt Marche watched me carefully, and sighed. "Come on up to my apartment. We've got some talking to do."

We walked up the stairs, Aunt Marche wobbling a little. "Sorry for the mess," she said, kicking a ring-light out of the way in the entrance. "I've just finished up three hours on YouTube. So many blessings, so little time."

I chuckled. "I honestly can't believe you're on so many social media platforms."

"Where do you think I get all my money from, love charms? I make a fortune from content creation, you know. Some platforms are rotten as sin, but I'm reaching a helluva lot of kids." She took another big puff on her joint and held it out to me. "Do you want some?"

I shook my head. "I'm good."

"Fine. More for me." She put it in an ashtray and gestured towards the kitchen table. "Here. Tea."

She bustled around me, pouring a steaming cup, then sat down and faced me directly. "Now." She stared into my eyes. "Who is she?"

I looked at her blankly. "Who is who?"

"Hmph." Aunt Marche hesitated a moment, took a deep breath, and sighed it all out. "Sandy, I'm tired. And… I'm sorry. I was only trying to help." Her eyes softened. "It seems I've burdened you with a heavy load."

"I don't know what you're talking about."

Mavka shifted inside me, stiffening. *She knows.*

My mouth fell open. "You know?"

There was a long silence. Aunt Marche watched me carefully, her expression cautious.

I peered at my great-aunt. "Did… did *you* do this?"

"I only wanted to help," she said, her voice a whisper. "I've been watching you, you know, watching you struggle in Emerald Valley with that bastard of a husband and your goddamn Serena Joy mother for three years. I wanted to open you up to the idea that your life didn't have to be like that." She chuckled bitterly. "Bless your heart, Sandy, you're a sweet girl, but you would have swallowed their lies and died of exhaustion in a few short months."

She wasn't wrong. I ended up in hospital, in a coma, miscarrying a child. Tears pricked at my eyes when I remembered.

It was so strange. Sometimes, I forgot about the baby I'd been carrying only a few short days ago. That baby had been a symbol of what I had wanted my life to be.

No wonder it had gone.

But… did she do that? I cocked my head, glaring at Aunt Marche. "What did you do?"

Not that. No, the baby was not meant to be. She did not cause you to miscarry.

My glare softened. I should have known. Aunt Marche was vehemently pro-choice, something that I had vigorously debated with her in my early days of living here. I thought I could change her mind on the subject. She had better arguments, though, and I couldn't fault her logic.

She thinks she summoned me, Mavka chuckled. *Foolish woman, although her heart is in the right place.*

Oh.

Aunt Marche sighed. "I spelled you. Around a month ago. A little ritual for opening your eyes, so you could see you were being manipulated and used. I didn't realize the spell would draw a feminine spirit to inhabit your body." She slumped in her chair, clearly exhausted. "So, who is she? If we know who she is, I can help you get rid of her."

"I don't think I want to get rid of her." The words were out of my mouth before I even thought about it. I cocked my head, surprised at myself. "I mean…she's not *bad*." Not unless you counted the fact that she'd eaten two evil men in two days.

Justice, Mav whispered.

"She's kind of… helpful, actually," I told my aunt. "She senses bad thoughts. She's been helping find Chloe's blackmailer."

Aunt Marche leaned closer, her eyes wide. "Honey, you don't have to play it down for me. I can sense her power in you. It's like a wild torrent; like an avalanche." She shook her head and exhaled in wonder. "How are you even managing her? That kind of force should be tearing you apart. Yet, you're sitting there, drinking your tea calmly, as comfortable as ever."

I shrugged. "We all have our demons, Aunt Marche. I'm just… making friends with mine, I guess."

Her bloodshot eyes bugged out; she let out a bark of laughter. "Ha! Oh, honey, I underestimated you," she chuckled. "I'm so sorry." She gazed at me fondly, and brushed back a lock of my hair. "I'm so glad you're here. Even if you have a powerful astral spirit trapped in your body." She patted my hand. "When you're ready, I'll help you get rid of her, okay?"

Pah. Tell her it was your fault. You ate the banana.

I chuckled awkwardly and took a big sip of my tea to hide my face.

CHAPTER 29

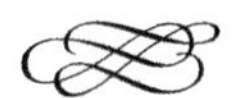

Scarlett's wine bar was packed with beautiful people. It was Friday, a warm late-spring evening, and the folded windows were wide open, letting in the whole sight of Lumiere Avenue.

I sat in the window with a perfectly chilled glass of pinot gris in my hand, watching the world go by. We'd closed the salon half an hour ago. It was a great day at work. I was tired, but good-tired.

Dexter was home making brownies with Aunt Marche and Damon. They'd shooed me out the door to have a drink with my friends.

My brother Antonio sat on one side of me, drinking a Belgium craft beer with a very frothy head. It was nice to finally be able to catch up with him. We'd fallen instantly back into our sibling familiarity, mostly sitting in companionable silence, every now and then teasing each other or making a few snarky comments.

Ben, Antonio's boyfriend, sat on the other side. There was an insanely odd moment when Scarlett herself sidled over in all her young, smooth-skinned and cutting-edge French chic gorgeousness. She gave Ben a cuddle, a kiss, and ruffled his hair up.

I'd forgotten she was his mother. It took me a second to regain my equilibrium.

In a week that was so bizarre, so insane, where so many terrifying and horrifying things had happened, one little thing would penetrate the metaphorical cotton wool I wrapped around my psyche and send me reeling.

I looked to my right, where Chloe slumped on the bar stool, her head in her hands. My heartstrings twanged. "Babe," I rubbed her arm. "We'll figure it out. I promise."

She'd gotten another message. Another nude photo. No demands. "This is torture," she moaned. "They're trying to torture me to death."

Prue, on the other side of her, ground her teeth. "I want to punch someone." She threw her glass of red back into her mouth and swallowed roughly. "Someone get me another drink, or I'll head over to the Dog and Bone and punch someone."

"We've still got a few suspects," I said, trying to keep optimistic. "We haven't ruled out Gretel, your mom's assistant, have we? It could still be her."

"It's not," Prue said bluntly.

Chloe lifted her head and peered at her with bleary eyes. "How do you know?"

"I shook Gretel down yesterday." Prue hesitated, then frowned. "Well, I promised to record a message of support for your mom, as an Asian American," she said, making a face. "On the condition that she'd let me rummage around in her purse. She yeeted it at me so fast it was obvious she had nothing to hide. She's got no extra phones, no VPN, nothing. It's not her."

Chloe's bottom lip wobbled, and she threw her arms around Prue. "Thank you," she whispered, kissing her forehead. "You're the best friend ever." She sniffed and wiped her nose.

"I failed, you idiot."

"You tried. And I appreciate it."

I sighed heavily. Back to the drawing board.

A thought occurred to me. "Chloe," I said, tapping her shoulder. "Do you think you could ask your dad to help you? You don't have to tell him exactly what's going on. Maybe just say you're getting some threatening messages. He might know someone who could help…"

We needed to find out more about this shadowy Lord Seth. If Linus was deeply committed to bringing Chloe's dad in their path of chaos, we might be able to get some more information.

"Maybe." She bit her lip. "As a last resort. Honestly, I'm worried he might kill someone."

Suddenly the air around me tingled. I shivered slightly, shifting restlessly in my seat. It wasn't cold; in fact, it was a beautifully warm evening. Strangely, it felt like all the atoms in the air were charged; like a thunderstorm was on its way. I winced, bit my lip, and looked down surreptitiously at my boobs.

My nipples had hardened with the change in atmosphere, and my bra was too thin and lacy to hide them. They stuck out like marbles shoved down my top. Prue and Chloe had talked me into wearing this floaty, low-cut white dress; it did nothing to rein my nipples in right now. I was suddenly on full-beam, and sitting in the window at Scarlett's, on display for everyone to see. All we needed now was for Mavka to do her smoke and light show and it would be like Amsterdam's red-light district around here. Damn it.

I quickly clamped my hand over my breasts with one arm, sandwiching them together, hoping desperately no one would notice me holding on to my tits and wonder what the hell I was doing.

Maybe Ant had some Band-Aids on him. Sighing, I looked up, and froze.

Detective Conrad Sinclair was standing on the street, staring right at me.

"Oh.... God..."

A flush of mortification burned right through me, so hot I thought I'd burst into flame. I could feel the blood bloom in my cheeks and rush over my chest. Thinking about it made everything worse. My skin throbbed. My whole face must be flaming scarlet.

Sinclair tilted his head, staring at me. The tiniest, faintest smile softened the normal grim, hard line of his jaw. "There you are," he said in a gruff voice. "I've been looking for you. Do you ever answer your phone?"

"I–I–I–"

He's not looking at your breasts, child.

I clenched my teeth and internally seethed at her. Why is he almost-smiling, then? I've only known him a couple of days, and I know he doesn't smile. He broods and he glowers and he kills things.

He was worried about you. He's... happy to see you. Mavka sounded surprised.

Oh.

That's weird. "I–um... Yeah, I do answer my phone," I said out loud.

He did that weird crooked non-smile thing again. "You're not answering when I call you."

I frowned. "Uh, you haven't called me."

He rattled off my phone number. Off by heart. A weird, excited pulse shot through my gut, and exited out between my legs. "That's your number, is that correct?" He lowered his head and fixed me with an intense gaze.

I chewed on my bottom lip. "Stop sounding so much like a cop."

"I am a cop." He crossed his arms over his chest. "Is that your phone number, or not?"

"It is, but you haven't called me."

"I have. At least twenty times."

I shuffled my phone out of my purse and checked it. "I don't see your number."

"It's unlisted."

"Well, that's the problem, then. I don't answer calls if I don't know who's calling."

He furrowed his brow. "Why not?"

"It might be a telemarketer, or a charity mugger, or something."

He paused for a beat. "And?"

"And… and… If I answered my phone, I'd have to talk to them," I said lamely.

"Why?"

"Because I can't be rude to them."

"You could just tell them not to call you, you know."

"What do you think I am, some kind of monster?"

There's two types of people in the world. The ones who relish telling unsolicited callers to fuck off, and the ones who will either concoct ridiculous stories to get them off the phone, or fold and buy whatever cleaning products they're spruiking.

I'm the second type. Chloe is even worse than me. Prue is the first. She doesn't even get any calls anymore. I'm pretty sure she's been put on some kind of telemarketing blacklist.

Sinclair sighed, and tapped on his phone. "Okay."

My phone buzzed. A number came up. "Is that you?"

"No, it's Tania from Incommodus Communications. She wants to know if you have time to answer a few quick questions about your phone bill."

I gasped theatrically and clutched my chest. "You have a sense of humor, Detective Sinclair?"

"Not usually." He glared at me for a second, then, suddenly, his gaze softened. "Listen, we need to talk."

Oh, he meant privately. "Excuse me for a second, guys." I turned to my friends.

The seats were empty. Prue and Chloe had disappeared.

"Ant? Ben?" I looked around. They were gone, too.

I glanced back, confused. "Where did they go?"

Sinclair raised an eyebrow. "They took off the second I arrived."

I laughed. "What are they, scared of you or something?"

He shrugged. "Most people are."

I laughed again. Sinclair didn't smile. My chuckle faded awkwardly. "Oh, you're not joking."

I'd been scared of him, once. I still was. There was always the chance he'd find out about Mavka, and feel the need to kill me out of a sense of duty to his role as Enforcer. She was a bloodthirsty monster, after all. But I was more scared of making a fool of myself in front of him, and that fear weirdly seemed to have overridden everything else.

Yes, he might kill me. But also, I might try and kiss him, and he'd gently reject me, and I'd die of shame. Which is a *lot* worse.

I bit my lip. "Well, I guess we can talk now, then. What's up?"

He moved and came in through the door. The crowd in Scarlett's parted like the Red Sea as he walked through. He took the seat next to me. "We raided the farmhouse," he said. "The Old Gray. We managed to get there in time to rescue the trafficking victims as they were being transferred from the boat. Linus Brady wasn't there, though," he said, his face darkening. "He seems to have disappeared."

"But you got the other bad guys, didn't you? There must

have been some at the farm, transporting the victims. You'll be able to get information out of them. Pull the threads, start to untangle this weird Blood King conspiracy, right?"

His expression grew stony. "There were some men there. Underlings, minions at best. They're no longer with us. They all shot themselves in the head as soon as we raided."

"What?" I gasped. "Are you serious?"

"I don't think I need to tell you how bad that is," Sinclair said. "When the grunts kill themselves rather than be captured, it means that they fear their masters more than they fear us, or death."

"That's… not… great."

"No. We got the victims freed, though."

"What about the property? And the boat? The owners?"

"Shell companies inside of shell companies," he said, looking away. "Both the property and the boat seemed to be owned by at least a hundred different corporations. There's nobody to take any responsibility there." He glanced back and caught my eye. "There's… a lot of evidence to sift through in the farmhouse, though."

One of the visions Mavka had shown me popped into my mind. I shooed it away and pressed my lips together, feeling sick. "I don't think I want to know."

"You don't," he said roughly. He took a deep breath. "The good news is that we've got leads with Kane Hogan. They're still active."

"The vampire, you mean." I pursed my lips. "You could have told me that part." I turned away and took a huge sip of my wine.

"It didn't matter," he said gently. "Remember? What someone is doesn't really matter. It's applicable now, because he's part of a nest, and he has a maker who is pulling his strings." He stared into my eyes, suddenly looking uncertain. "I think I need you with me on this."

I choked on my wine. It went straight up my nasal passages, stinging my sinuses. Some of it came out of my nose.

Dignity, child. Have you heard of it?

Sinclair ignored my spluttering. Mercifully, he acted like I wasn't snorting pinot gris out of my nose. "You got me Kane Hogan *and* Linus Brady," he said. "You saved those girls at the farmhouse from a horrible fate. You've done more to crack this Blood King conspiracy than I've managed to do in months," he said, gritting his teeth slightly. "The new lead we've got from Hogan isn't pretty. I know that some of his nest buddies have been crashing sorority parties. Coincidentally, I've had three girls from Greek houses show up in the hospital, catatonic."

I huffed out a breath. "Oh. Shit."

"He's doing something to them," he growled. "I'm sure of it. I need to figure out what's going on." He pulled a piece of paper out of his jacket pocket. "The commissioner has granted you a consultancy contract," he said. "I'm to retain your services for whenever I need you."

I wiped my nose on a napkin. There was still wine dribbling out of it. "Oh, wow. Thanks, I guess." Half of me was jumping up and down in joy. The other half was shitting herself. "I mean, I'm happy to help out. I still have clients at the salon, but–"

Mavka suddenly pushed an urgent thought towards me. *He's here.*

I frowned. "What?"

Listen. There's a man who has just walked in, a disgusting little weasel. He's thinking of Chloe's nude body, and how fun it is to scare her.

My mouth dropped open. "Who?" I barely noticed that Sinclair had stopped talking and was watching me warily.

Over by the bar. Black suit, neat dark-blond hair, Mavka

growled. *He's trying to decide which one of her nude photos he'll send her next.*

I looked. A man in a suit stood by the bar, ordering a drink, a smug smile on his face.

A surge of intense black rage swelled through me, propelling me off my seat. "Mother*fucker*," I snarled.

I charged through the crowd, knocking people aside. Adrenaline flooded through me, surging through my muscles, melding perfectly with the fury whirling through my brain.

I didn't know who this guy was. I'd never seen him before. It didn't matter. Mavka's strength and fury was flooding through me. She was going to kill him.

I reached the bar, and grabbed hold of his arm, and tugged him roughly around. "Hey, asshole!"

He whirled around. Generic looking guy, not handsome, not ugly either. Bland. He looked a little confused. "Um. Hi. Can I help you?"

I stepped closer, pushing him into the side of the bar. "Yeah, you can help me. Why are you blackmailing my friend?"

True fear sparked in his eyes. I saw it flash as clearly as a lightning bolt in the night sky. Quickly, he masked his expression. He peered down at me, clearly offended. "Excuse me?"

I laughed bitterly. "I saw that, you coward. That's what you are, aren't you? A fucking coward. You're screwing with her, keeping her scared, building up to some kind of awful demand or something." I shoved him in the chest, pushing him back. He hit the bar.

The stranger shook his head. "I don't know what you're talking about. Who the hell are you?"

"I'm your worst nightmare, that's who I am," I snarled. "I'm the one who's going to fuck you up."

He held up his hand, trying to push me back. "Listen, I don't think that–"

Grabbing his hand, I twisted it, and pushed it towards the inside of his forearm, applying pressure until he squealed. Classic gooseneck wrist lock. I remembered something from self-defense classes after all. Thanks, Mav.

"No!" He squealed. He went to push at me limply with his free hand, but stopped the second I applied more pressure to his locked wrist. Haha.

"What are you doing? You're going to break my wrist," he shrieked.

"Good." I glared at him. "Now, give me your phones."

Panic flared in his eyes again. "No!"

I twitched his locked wrist, applying more pressure, more pain. "Do it."

Suddenly, I felt a tap on my shoulder. "Uh, Sandy…" Chloe was standing next to me, staring at me with wide eyes. Slowly, she swiveled to look at the stranger, then back at me. "Sandy, babe… What are you doing?"

"This is *him*, Chloe." I twitched the man's wrist again, and he squealed.

"Ouch! Chloe, get her off me!"

"Yes." She nodded carefully and deliberately. "That's him, Sandy."

My mouth dropped open. "Do you know this asshole, Clo?"

"This is Gregory," she said patiently, as if I'd gone crazy. "My boyfriend. He's here to take me home."

Another surge of rage overtook me, so forceful that my vision sharpened to superhuman clarity. Mavka clearly had some bones to pick. "He's the blackmailer, Clo," I growled, forcing him further back over the bar. "It's him."

"*What?*" That was Prue, stalking in from the other side. "He's the asshole who hacked your phone? *He's* the one blackmailing you?" Looking around for a weapon, Prue picked up a beer bottle by its neck and went to smash it down on the bar. Scarlett, appearing out of nowhere, snagged the bottle before it hit the wood, flipped it in her palm, and walked back down behind the bar, muttering in French under her breath as she strode away.

The fear in Gregory's eyes blossomed. "No. No… babe. It's not me. Of course it's not me. I love you. I would never…"

"It is." I pushed my face closer to his. "And you would. I'm an expert when it comes to what some men will do to keep their woman under their boots, you know. It was you all along." I thrust my chin at Prue. "Search his pockets."

Prue cracked her knuckles and thrust a hand into his pants. She pulled out two phones. Gregory let out a low, terrified moan.

"Two phones? Why do you need *two* phones, Greg?" Chloe sounded outraged.

"Babe… I'm sorry." He started sobbing. "I'm so, so sorry. I just wanted to keep you close, that's all. I love you so much, I wanted to keep those pictures of you with me always, that's why I took them. You always refused to send me any, you know, so this is kind of your fault. And I wanted you to know how much I loved them, but I knew you'd be mad… so… so… AAARRRRggggghhhhh!"

A bone cracked under my hands.

Gregory's face twisted with anger. "You broke my wrist! You… you fucking broke my wrist!"

I bared my teeth at him and growled. "Oops."

Prue held up one of his phones. "It's him, alright. He's got all the photos saved in this phone."

"Babe… Baby, please…"

"Honestly, Greg." Chloe shrugged. "I didn't even like you very much. You knew that, didn't you? That's why you did it." She tilted her head, regarding him thoughtfully. "I guess I'll have to call Daddy and tell him what you've done." Slowly, she turned her back on him. "Maybe he will get the pool tiler to sort you out."

Gregory froze. His face turned bone white. "Chloe," he whispered. "Chloe. Baby."

I turned around too. My job here was done. Gregory's goose was well and truly cooked.

"Thanks, Mav," I muttered under my breath.

Why are you thanking me? I didn't do anything.

I frowned. What do you mean? You went all vengeance on that asshole. You broke his wrist!

That wasn't me, child.

"What?"

That was all you. She sounded proud.

Huh. I stared down at my feet. Maybe I'd grown a spine after all.

Lifting my head, my breath caught in my throat. Detective Conrad Sinclair lounged easily on the barstool by the window, right where I'd left him, devastatingly, jaw-droppingly handsome, somehow far more gorgeous than ever before. I watched him carefully, drinking him in, wondering idly what had changed to make him even more impossibly gorgeous than he had been only two minutes ago.

He was smiling at me. Watching me, and grinning from ear to ear.

THE END

THANK YOU

Thanks for reading! If you enjoyed this novel, please leave me a review and I'll love you forever. Reviews make a huge difference in helping with exposure, and I appreciate every single one of them.

If there was something you hated, or you spotted a typo, please email me at info@laurettahignett.com and let me know. I'm human, unfortunately, and so is my editor, but we do our best to get everything right (despite my habit of going back into a manuscript after the final proofread and adding a bunch of extra things...)

Dancing with the Vengeance Demon – Book two in the Foils and Fury series – will be available on 17 November 2022. Get it here!

Having just escaped the clutches of her manipulative and abusive husband, Sandy's finally settling into her new life in D.C. She's got the perfect job, perfect friends, and the perfect home. Oh, and a perfectly bloodthirsty vengeance demon sharing her body, but Sandy's doing an amazing job in keeping that little secret to herself.

But it's going to be a secret she'll struggle to keep.

A dark force is rising in Washington D.C. – a shadowy figure his followers call Lord Seth. Rogue vampires, evil magic-users and disenfranchised shifters are flocking to him, lured by his promises of power and justice, stoked by their violent misogyny. They call themselves the Blood Kings.

When her best friend's niece is discovered comatose, unable to be woken after a wild sorority party, Sandy is determined to figure out what happened to her. Another victim surfaces, then another, and the brutally hot Detective Conrad Sinclair reluctantly asks for her help to figure out what is happening to these girls, and why they can't be woken.

They're going undercover, hitting the party scene of Georgetown, to gather information and find out who is drugging these girls. Sinclair is a little nervous about putting Sandy in danger.

Sandy is nervous she'll eat someone's liver.

Can she keep Mavka a secret? Or will Sinclair find out, and feel honour-bound as the Enforcer to destroy her?

Dancing with the Vengeance Demon is Book Two in Foils and Fury, a fun, fast-paced urban fantasy series.

ALSO BY LAURETTA HIGNETT

Go back to the start with Imogen Gray series:

Immortal

Immortal Games

Immortal World

Immortal Life

Immortal Death

Then follow Sandy in the Foils and Fury series

Oops I Ate A Vengeance Demon

Dancing With The Vengeance Demon

Dating With The Vengeance Demon

Dying For My Vengeance Demon

Then go on with Prue's story with the Blood and Magic Series.

Bad Bones

Bare Bones

Broke Bones

Burned Bones

Bitter Bones

And then head to Chloe's series

Vicious Creatures

Fractured Gods

Ravenous Beasts

* * *

Fancy something different? Try this New Adult Paranormal Romance

Revelations Series

A cursed woman, destined to bring about the apocalypse.

The religious sect, determined to kill her.

The demon who wants to save her.

"It's Good Omens with a Twilight feel"

Book Cover by Mibl Art

First Edition 2022

Created with Vellum

Printed in Great Britain
by Amazon

61623087R00150